DANNY'S
MAIN

A CHARISTOWN NOVEL

THE **CHARISTOWN** SERIES

Lisa N. Paul
BESTSELLING AUTHOR

Copyright © 2015 by Lisa N. Paul
http://www.lisanpaul.com

Cover design by Regina Wamba of Mae I Design
Formatting by JT Formatting

First Edition: September 2015
Library of Congress Cataloging-in-Publication Data

Paul, Lisa N.
Super Dandy Publishing
Danny's Main (A Charistown Series Novel) – 1st ed
ISBN-13: 978-0-9892465-9-0

To you, the Believers,
Happily Ever After does exist when you find the person you
are meant to love and are *willing to fight for* every single day.

To you, the Achievers,
It is through your example that I have seen how brilliant love
can be when the newness wears off and the beauty beneath
shines through. Thank you for showing me that while Ever
After may not *always* mean days filled with happiness, they
will always be days filled with love.

L

CHAPTER ONE

Customer Service

Twenty-Eight Years Ago

SWEAT TRICKLED DOWN his spine faster than his army dress uniform could absorb it, but that didn't stop him from trudging into the small bar. He couldn't wait to peel off his uniform and stand beneath the punishing spray of the shower, but first he needed a drink. In fact, first, second, and third on his list were drinks, followed by a wash down and bed.

The anniversary of his brother's death always left Danny Marcus gutted, but over the past couple of years, numbness had crept in. It gripped him like a fist squeezing his soul, and no matter what he did to get it to release its hold, to instead feel the burning angst that used to whisper that vengeance was the only way to keep Jeff's memory from fading, the numbness continued to spread.

When Danny had enlisted and left for basic training just after graduating high school, he relished in the glory of retribution. *Payback*, he assured his grieving father on the day of Danny's mother's funeral. She had committed suicide two years after losing her oldest son, leaving her husband and two younger boys to grieve further.

"Payback won't bring Jeffrey back, son. It'll only take you further away."

His father's words had fallen on deaf, teenaged ears, but now, Danny was beginning to see the wisdom in his old man's advice. Being part of the 82nd Airborne Division certainly had helped to fuel Danny's adrenaline rush, but even the jumps were losing their spark. A restless soldier wasn't one needed in the air or on the ground patrolling the jungles of Korea—not that his performance was anything less than stellar—so when the opportunity had arisen for a transfer to Fort Meade in the third year of his four-year enlistment, Danny gladly took it.

He'd soon need to decide whether to re-up his commitment to the United States Army or move on to his original path, firefighting. However, that decision wouldn't be made that evening. Not when the emptiness threatened to consume him. Not when numbness spread through him from his fingers to his toes. Not when his brother's voice still whispered in his ear.

"Hey there, I'd offer you a beer, but it looks like you may need something a bit stronger."

"Huh?" That sweet sound certainly wasn't Jeff.

"I said you look like you could use a drink, Sergeant. What can I get for you?" The honeyed voice could have lulled him to much-needed sleep if not for the alarming beauty of the woman it came from.

"Shot of whiskey," he croaked, uncertain if he'd left his voice in his memories or at work. Either way, it escaped him the moment he saw the woman's crystal gray eyes. "A double, please."

The legs of his barstool scratched the scarred wooden floor as he planted himself on the seat and watched the young strawberry-blonde barkeep pour amber liquid into two small glasses.

"Here you go, Sergeant."

Hearing his rank still caught him off guard. Just like returning stateside, his promotion to sergeant was brand-new.

"Umm, Sergeant Marcus?"

"Sorry, you say something?" Christ, could he act like a bigger fucking tool? This chick couldn't be twenty if she was a day, and he was acting like a bumbling idiot. Even though her smile was warm and inviting, innocence personified, her eyes told stories of survival and heartache. Fuck, what could she know of heartache? He needed drinks, not conversation.

"I asked if you'd you like me to start a tab for you?"

"Yeah, sweetheart, keep the tab open and the drinks coming."

As if curtains were released from their ties, all of the openness in her expression vanished behind a veneer of a smile.

"Julie, are you giving that handsome sergeant a problem?" A bottled redhead bopped from one end of the bar to the other, stopping in front of Danny.

He hadn't needed his time overseas, in countless pubs, bars, and hotels, to know exactly what the older woman was. He didn't need her name tag, which read Bunny, to explain what she was looking for. Her tight clothes, Aqua Net-sprayed hair, shellacked face, and over-zealous smile told her whole story. She was a MiliSnag—a woman who did whatever she could to snag a military

3

man. From the looks of her, she'd snagged and bagged more than her fair share of men in uniform. He could practically see the DNA of the soldiers past lingering on the older woman's overexposed skin.

"Sorry, honey, she's still new here, friendly and all, but"—Bunny pushed herself up over the counter, the move accentuating her ample cleavage and wafting cheap perfume up his nose—"she doesn't know what men like you really need."

"Well, Bunny, being as you can clearly read me," he flirted, knowing her pour would be more generous if he was kind, "I bet you can tell the only things I need tonight are whisky, beer, and my thoughts." He leveled her with a smoldering glance that made women swoon. "You'll help me out, won't you?"

"Oh, sure. I love to serve a man who serves our country. I'll keep 'em coming, handsome, and I'll also keep an eye on you. Just call if you need me." Bunny batted her false lashes before pouring him another shot and a mug of beer. Her toothy smile tried for innocence in a way that would make her namesake happy but reminded Danny of a fox in soft rabbit fur instead.

No matter. He slammed back the warm amber liquid before reaching for the cold beer. Tonight was about remembering and then…once again, letting go.

UHHG, EACH SHIFT was the same damn story. Julie watched her manager throw herself at every uniformed male who walked through the door. Julie had only been employed at Chester's Pub a handful of months, but it was five months of long hours and, often times, back-breaking work. Double shifts tended to be that way—at least they were for Julie. After her first week, when Chester had kept a close eye on her, her boss kept irregular hours, popping in and out during the day. He always returned around closing time to cash out the drawer and close up the joint. Which left Bertha, a.k.a. Bunny, in charge of the staff. The woman could sell drinks almost as well as she sold herself, but a manager she was not.

Aside from Bunny and Julie, there were two female bartenders and two male bar-backs. Problem was, Bunny spent more time *hopping* on the bar-backs than helping out with the work. Therefore, aside from the revolting soundtrack of grunts and giggles, Julie was on her own to set up each day. Usually Bunny would assist a patron home—*customer service*, she called it—before the bar closed, leaving the remaining staff to cleanup. Chester didn't seem to care if Bunny was around as long as the bar was shut down correctly. A fine woman Ms. Bertha was. Julie swallowed the sour taste that seemed to follow thoughts of her manager.

Whatever, if she's what guys want... Julie shrugged, sparing one last look at the beautiful man at the end of the bar. Upon first glance, she wouldn't have guessed him to be like so many men she'd met before. There was something about him, something different. She couldn't put her finger on it, but she was obviously wrong if he was willing to flirt with Bunny. Julie had been wrong before. Hell, in the past year and a half, she'd been wrong more often than she'd been right. *Stay in the present, Julie. Work hard, make money, and move on.*

The evening passed in a flurry of pulled beers, poured shots, loud music playing from the jukebox, and the ruckus of men and women out to unwind. While a good portion of the customers were from Fort Meade, Chester's also brought in a bunch of civilians, both men and women.

Julie had been tending bar since she turned eighteen, but Chester's was the first establishment where the clientele were men and women who served the United States. That was *one* of the reasons she chose to work at the bar even if Bunny came with the position. After everything she'd been through, the thought of being around so much bravery, so much strength and courage, made it easier to get up each morning. She wasn't looking to "bed" a person in uniform, but if she could absorb some of their fortitude through osmosis… hell, she'd work her fingers to the bone just to be in their presence.

Around closing time, Bill, the cute new hire, set three cases of beer he'd just brought in from the storage room on the bar so he could restock the fridge. "Hey, Jul, have you seen Bunny? She said she'd give me a ride at the end of the shift..."

"Didn't she give you one before your shift started?" Julie deadpanned.

"Umm…" At least the guy had the decency to look chagrinned. Maybe he wasn't so bad. He shrugged, chest puffed out with male pride. "She wanted me. Who am I to say no, right?"

Wrong again, Julie. Wrong. Again.

"Well, slick, looks like that was the only ride you'll be getting from Bunny tonight, because she left about ten minutes ago to escort a customer home." She would have laughed at the baffled look on Bill's face had it not seemed so genuine. "Don't feel too bad. You may have had a chance if your shirt had stripes instead of letters."

"What?"

"Bunny prefers them in uniform, Bill. You haven't noticed?"

The young guy's glare conveyed more than words would have.

"Ahh, you did know, but you thought you'd be different." A pang of sympathy washed over her as she chose her words delicately. "I've only been here for a few of months, so feel free to disregard what I'm about to say, but some people are looking to fill glasses that are cracked. Doesn't matter how much they pour, theirs will always be half empty because they choose to keep a damaged cup instead of taking a chance with a brand-new one."

"Are you talking about Bunny?" he asked quietly, his brow lifted.

Julie stared at the guy, young just like her but obviously open to hearing what she was offering. "I don't know, Bill. Am I?"

Leaving him to stock the beer, Julie walked to the other end of the bar. Last call had been announced before Bunny's departure, so Julie was just squaring away tabs, calling cabs, and serving water to those in need. The sexy sergeant had remained planted on his stool for hours, leaving only to use the restroom. She'd watched him as he walked, telling herself it was to make certain he was tolerating his alcohol, but that was a lie. The truth was, she couldn't keep her eyes off of him no matter how hard she tried—not that she'd tried very hard.

He hadn't even noticed her prying eyes. In fact, he'd barely seemed to notice any of the many women vying for his attention. They would send him drinks, and he'd send them a crooked grin of gratitude. But each and every time a woman took the next step and approached him, Julie noticed the interaction swiftly ended with the woman nodding, smiling agreeably, and retreating to her friends. In the nearly two years that she'd been working in bars—first waitressing, then bartending—Julie had never seen such charming rejection.

"For a man who's been drinking most of the night, your tab is pretty light." Julie slid his bill across the bar with a smile.

"Thanks." The man accepted the slip of paper and raised his eyes to hers. Even though his hazel eyes were rimmed in red, his gaze was no less powerful, no less haunted.

She should have felt ashamed of the sexual awareness that spiked through her body at the sight of the clearly tortured man. Should have. But when he stood from the stool and dug his hand into his uniform pants and pulled out folded bills, Julie knew it was time to speak or forever hold her peace.

"How about if I pour you a glass of water and you sit here for a bit?" She wanted to kick herself for her overeager tone.

"You're a beautiful woman"—his eyes traveled her face yet, she could swear he didn't see her at all—"but I'm not looking for anything tonight. Truly sorry." His rough voice sent tingles up her spine, quickening her pulse and turning her insides to liquid.

She inhaled slowly, allowing her core temperature to cool. "So that's how you did it? I've been wondering." Julie swallowed, trying her best to keep the embarrassing smile from spreading over her lips. "Some real talent you've got there, ace." She wasn't sure what shocked her more: when he wrapped his large hand around her wrist to stay her movement or the way her body reacted to such a small touch. "Yes?"

"What's that supposed to mean?" His narrowed eyes penetrated hers as if begging for answers to more questions than the one he'd just asked.

Nibbling her top lip, she stared at the place where their skin connected. Heat climbed her neck and kissed her cheeks. *Cotton Candy.* That was what her father used to say, that she blushed pink like cotton candy and was just as sweet. The memory that hadn't crossed her mind in a long while was both a loving stroke and a sucker punch. Withdrawing her hand from the uniformed stranger's, she stepped back and swallowed again.

"What it meant, Sergeant, was as many women as I saw approach you this evening is as many as I saw you turn down. Yet they all left smiling, as if they hadn't been rejected. Now I understand why."

The man tilted his head, confusion warring with the sullenness he'd worn for hours.

"You make them feel regarded before letting them down easy." His brows pinched together as if he didn't quite grasp her meaning, so she tried to clarify. "It's hard on a woman's ego to be rejected. But the way you do it, well... you're good. Not a thing to hate about that. A regarded rejection almost feels like a stroke instead of a brush off." *Walk away, Jul, before you embarrass yourself further.*

"That how you feel? Rejected?"

Warmth once again raised the length of her neck. "Nope," she lied. "The only thing I was offering was a glass of water and a place to sit." Julie licked her dry lips and collected money from the customers looking to settle up.

Chester had shown up around last call and was likely holed up in his office, doing whatever it was he did back there, while Bill flirted with the woman who'd most likely be taking him home at closing time. A sprinkle of giggles fell from the mouth of Bill's new friend as she squeezed his flexed biceps. Oh yes, she'd be giving him a ride for sure.

"It's Julie, right?" the sexy sergeant asked, drawing her attention away from her coworker.

She nodded, sauntering back to him.

"One more shot of whisky…please?"

Most female bartenders would have probably given the guy anything he wanted, and by the hint of confidence in his request, he damn well knew it. But she wasn't most bartenders. Julie Bell was a rule follower, and she always had been. She'd watched him carefully during the evening, and while most wouldn't notice, his fine motor skills had definitely become impaired and his speech slightly slurred.

"I'm sorry, Sergeant, but last call was a while ago; I'm done serving for the night." She repeated his words from earlier. "Truly sorry."

A slow, easy smile tugged at his mouth, melting her from toes to shoulders in less than a second. It reached his eyes and made them sparkle. "A regarded rejection—very nice, Julie. You're right, I feel nothing but fondness toward you." The pair broke out in quiet laughter when he reached over the bar. "I'm Danny Marcus."

"Julie Bell. It's nice to meet you, Sergeant Marcus. But you're still not getting a shot of whisky."

He chuckled. "Just Danny, and that's fine. Truth be told, I may already be drunk."

God, the man's throaty laugh had her nipples drawing into sensitive peaks beneath her bra.

"If we're being honest, you've been drunk for a while." Julie grabbed a high ball and filled it with ice. "That's why I didn't want you to leave." She dropped her gaze and poured water into the glass.

The heat of Danny's touch once again startled her. "If we're being honest, Julie, then don't lie."

Inebriated or not, the man knew exactly what he was talking about, so she stood silently and waited for him to continue.

"I'm sure you're concerned for my safety, and for that, I'm grateful. But don't pretend you haven't spent tonight wondering what it would feel like to have me kiss you. And 'cause we're only doing truth here, my truth is I've been dying to taste your lips since the second I saw them."

Holy shit, it's possible I just had a mini orgasm from words alone. Julie shook her head, attempting to clear her thoughts before saying them. "You said you weren't interested in anything but your thoughts tonight." The reminder was as much for her as it was him. Julie snapped her jaw shut, the sound of teeth clacking startling her. With a small shake to her head, she attempted to clear her thoughts.

"Been holding memories close all day." His Adam's apple bobbed. "Without sounding like a cheesy loser, I'd appreciate the chance to hold you for a little while instead."

So much vulnerability, so much raw truth. She had a feeling he wasn't the kind of man to normally open up, nor would he appreciate the reminder of it when the sun rose.

Well, Mom and Dad, here goes my first act of rebellion. I hope it doesn't turn out as dumb as it sounds in my head. Her heart pounded as she placed a clean shot glass on the bar. His tentative smile built as his brows lifted in what could only be described as surprise when Danny watched her grab the bottle of whisky off the shelf.

"You're right, it does sound a wee bit cheesy, but you were right about something else too. "She poured half a shot and downed it neatly, sparing not a drop. "I want so badly to kiss you, I can almost taste it." The way his eyes lit up with excitement was comical. After pouring a generous amount of liquid into the glass, she inhaled deeply, slid the glass forward, and lifted her gaze to his. "But I'm not really a PDA kind of girl, and you're in no condition to drive. So how about you let me drive you back to the barracks, and you can pay me with a kiss good night?"

While it may have only lasted a second or two, the silence between them felt like an eternity. In that small window of time, Julie waffled between mortification and anger. She was no pure virgin looking for a prince, but she certainly didn't normally throw herself at strangers. If it wasn't for the dark look of desire shadowing his face, she'd have been rocking in the phone booth, wishing for a magical escape route. That said, from the way his nostrils flared and his gaze seemed to sear her skin, she knew her invitation was all but accepted. *Thank God.*

Danny downed the whiskey, left crisp bills on the bar top, and abruptly stood. "I'll be right back." He moved toward the restroom, his balance more impaired than it had been on his last trip.

Shit, maybe that last shot wasn't such a great idea. That's what I get for breaking the rules. "Hey, Bill, I'm gonna drive that guy home. You okay to help Chester close down?"

His incredulous look stung nearly as much as his words. "Going for the stripes now too, Jules? Huh, didn't peg you for that type."

"Wow, going for an asshole vibe, huh? Funny, I knew you were exactly that type." Julie clocked out, said goodnight to Chester, and met Danny by the door.

Bill's words replayed in her mind, but she wasn't attracted to Danny because of his uniform. In fact, she was attracted to him in spite of it. No matter how much respect she had for those who served their country, the last thing she wanted was to get involved with someone who willingly put their life in danger. *Stop it, Julie. This is just one night, one kiss.*

The short ride to the barracks was a quiet one, other than Danny giving directions to his living quarters. They seemed to be stuck in their own thoughts. With each passing minute, Julie wondered if the heavy flirting and promised kiss had more to do with the alcohol Sergeant Marcus had drunk than mutual desire. And by the time she'd pulled up in front of his place, she'd accepted, even found some sort of comfort in the fact that nothing further would happen between them. What the hell had she been thinking going home with him?

"Take a few aspirin and a glass of water before you go to sleep, Sergeant Marcus, and you shouldn't feel too horrible in the morning," Julie advised as she put her 1983 Datsun in park but left the engine idling.

Narrowed eyes met hers. "That wasn't the deal, Ms. Bell." Danny shifted in his seat, bringing his hand to the side of her face. The pad of his thumb gently brushed her jaw. "You lived up to your end; I'd like to live up to mine."

Giving her no time to reply, no time to refuse, Danny's lips were on hers. The air caught in her lungs and quickly released as he led the kiss like a dance. Soft and slow at first, he nibbled her lips as his other hand weaved through her hair, pulling her closer to him. His scent was whisky and mint and something uniquely him—primitive and masculine—and she couldn't help but sigh in appreciation. In that moment, he slipped his tongue between her parted lips while pulling her tighter, and their kiss deeper. The fine hairs on her arms stood at attention as their tongues glided together and their breaths tangled. She felt bereft when he pulled away. Need pulsed through her veins, and desire burned at her core.

"Come inside with me, Julie." His tone was a gentle command, but his eyes begged.

She didn't want to over think the situation; she only wanted to feel. "Okay, Danny." She turned off the ignition, dropped the keys in her purse, and followed him into his living quarters.

The sparse open space held a worn couch, a small dinette set, and multiple boxes in various sizes—clearly an indicator of a move, but in or out, she had no idea.

"Are you coming or going?" she asked, gesturing to the open creates.

"Just moved in. I've only managed to unpack the kitchen and the bathroom," he slurred. "The necessities. Been like a goddamn scavenger hunt for the past three days." He looked at the chaos and sighed, saying more to himself than to her, "I'll finish unpacking this weekend. "He ambled into the small kitchen and opened the cupboard to the left of the sink. "Want something to drink?"

She wasn't sure if she spoke her decline or just shook her head, but Danny left the glass in the cupboard, closed the door, and stalked over to her. "You're so fucking beautiful."

Not at all smooth or poetic, but sexy as sin, and Julie swooned before his hands made purchase on her skin. Their lips crashed as his tongue surged into her mouth in a hungry kiss. A ripple of excitement shimmied down her torso when she was pulled tight against his body. His large hand cupped the base of her skull, twirling her long silken ponytail around his knuckles, and to her surprise, he yanked on the tresses just hard enough to cause a bite of pain. That bite bloomed into pleasure that she'd never before experienced.

"Ahh, Danny—"

"Shh," he whispered into her neck. "Let me make you feel good. Watching you move behind that bar all night… got me so hard but wondering what you look like when you come, what you'd taste like," He grinded his hard length into her, "That's the shit that keeps us going when we're fighting for our fucking lives."

Every dirty word that left his mouth stoked the small flame his kiss had ignited within her, spreading warmth through her veins. She'd never had a guy, no matter how intimately she'd known him, speak so frankly about sex,

15

and in one short evening, this man had managed to unwrap desires she hadn't been aware of.

Breathless, she stared as Danny's deft fingers slowly unfastened the buttons on his dress uniform. His white tank top barely registered before it was swiped over his head and tossed to the floor. Julie swallowed. Twice. Even the cocky grin that stared back at her couldn't detract from the ridiculously sexy man before her. Tanned skin covered rippled muscles on a frame that seemed even more devastating with his shirt off. She smoothed her tongue over suddenly dry lips as she consumed him with her eyes. Hell, just seeing the man was like getting a glimpse of the ice cream truck in the dog days of summer—she'd do just about anything to get a lick of the sweet confections being offered.

Stone still, he watched, as if getting pleasure from her appraisal. She stepped toward him and her hand lifted of its own accord, aching to touch the warm flesh of his right bicep, where the American flag was boldly inked.

"My first tattoo," he grunted as she lightly traced the red, white, and blue art.

She nodded, although his gaze stared straight ahead and his body tense, a perfect position of attention. Without breaking contact, she slowly walked around his frame, stopping behind his broad back. A massive pair of wings stretched from shoulder to shoulder over his beautiful smooth skin. There looked to be some sort of parachute in the middle of the wings, the number eighty-two etched boldly through the strings.

He answered her unasked question. "My jump wings. I'm in the 82nd Airborne Division."

Reverently, she ran her palm over the entire tattoo and sent up a silent prayer of thanks to him and all of the men and women who so boldly served their country every day. Then she continued her perusal to the front of his body.

At first glance, her eyes landed on the dog tags that rested in the valley of his thick, defined chest. But as she reached for them, she noticed the tattoo neatly printed on his left pec, directly over his heart. Her stomach dropped as panic sliced through her gut. July sixteenth. Today was July sixteenth. What the hell? With trembling fingers, she caressed the ink, then lifted her gaze to his. She saw his pain.

"My brother."

Julie swallowed back her gasp and lowered her head so he wouldn't see the tears that threatened to fall. No matter the meaning behind the date, Danny's expression made it obvious that July sixteenth was a permanent heartbreak. "She understood that all too well. Without thinking of the consequences, Julie leaned forward and pressed her lips to him, to his *brother,* giving all she had to the beautiful broken man before her.

As if her gentle kiss shattered the façade holding him together, his vulnerability showed, leaving raw desire in his gaze. He pulled her roughly, almost violently, to him, and his lips crushed hers. Hunger the likes she'd never felt before burned in her belly, demanding satisfaction, begging for more. Spirals of ecstasy shot straight to her core when Danny's tongue went from tracing her lips to plunging between them. Julie mewed as she pressed her body against his, needing more contact, more skin, more…more.

"Lift your arms, honey," he insisted, hands already at her waist. The thought of not taking things further barely crossed her mind as she followed his command and watched her tank top hit the floor. "So goddamn sexy." Glassy, red-rimmed, hazel eyes stared at her pink-cotton-clad breasts as if he'd won the lottery. He licked his lips before shifting his eyes to hers. "I wanna see what's under that bra, but the deal was a kiss. Know we've already crossed that line, but I won't move further unless you're onboard."

Oh my God. Was she on board? Should it matter that the man was drunk and may not remember her name in the morning? Maybe, but she didn't just want to take her clothes off for the man—she wanted to burn them. Instead of giving that answer, she reached behind her back and unhooked the pink cotton. The way his eyes widened as the straps slid down her shoulders would be permanently burned into her brain. Yes, being taken home by Sergeant Marcus had been a great decision after all.

"Fuck." The word was a prayer of thanks and a seductive sigh of gratitude from what sounded like a beholden man.

When his gaze returned to hers, she saw the carnal desire of a famished wolf with the whisper of a conscience on his shoulder. In a movement too fast for her mind to process, Danny had her in his arms, then lying on her back beneath him on the sofa.

"Danny…"

"You want me to stop?" There wasn't any anger in his question, just concern.

"No, I don't."

"Then don't stop me. Can tell *you* need to feel this. *I* need to make you feel it. At any time it feels wrong, tell me no, and I'll stop. My honor, Julie…my word."

By the look on his face, his honor meant so much, but his word meant everything. So she replied the only way her heart would allow. "Don't stop, Danny."

He didn't.

When Julie left his place a couple of hours later, her body hummed in a way she'd never thought possible, muting any nagging voices that chastised her Bunny-like behavior. With memories like those, did she really need a repeat performance? *Sure, Julie, make sure to tell yourself that if you never see him again.* Shaking off that ridiculous notion, she slipped behind the wheel of her car and headed home. Of course she'd see him again, probably that day. There was no way he didn't feel the connection she did. Right?

CHAPTER TWO

Lysol and Vagisil

DANNY COVERED HIS eyes to stop the sun from scorching his retinas through his closed lids. "The fuck?"

He sat up on the couch and immediately regretted the decision to move. Not only did he not remember passing out on the sofa the previous night, he couldn't remember how the hell he'd gotten home. Never smart drinking on a Monday—left him feeling like shit for the rest of the week. Dropping his feet to the ground, he spotted a glass of water and two pain killers on the kitchen table. Like a freight train, memories of a sexy as shit strawberry-blonde pummeled into his brain.

"Julie Bell." Even the sound of her name got his dick hard. Flashes of her firm body, soft skin, and lush tits invaded his mind. The way she writhed beneath him when her climax hit, his tongue lapping up her sweet cream. Christ, he could still taste her, feel her. And then… nothing. The memories fucking ended. "What in the mother hell?"

He swallowed the aspirin and gulped down the water, trying to recall the details after he'd rocked her world. She straddled him, and he knew by the hungry look in her eyes exactly whose world would be rocking next...but then it was blank. Had she blown him? Had they fucked? The empty spots were unacceptable but would have to stay blank for a while longer, because he needed to get to work.

His new position was interesting. There was something exhilarating about being a squad leader and training other men in the field maneuvers they needed to know to perform properly in battle. But while he got better acquainted with his coworkers and procedures, the hours seemed to drip by. He wanted to get his ass over to Chester's so he could finally fill in the holes from his time with Julie. Her soft touches and addictive kisses haunted all day, and while one and done was his usual MO, he wasn't so quick to toss away the quick-witted beauty. After all, if he didn't remember the *one*... how could he be *done*?

Only one patron sat at the bar when Danny walked into Chester's during his lunch break. The older man had a mug of beer in one hand and a cigarette in the other as he watched the Orioles at bat. Danny scanned the rest of the establishment, noting the only other people around were the redheaded MiliSnag and a beefy-looking guy who Danny hadn't seen the night before. They had exited the restroom together, each wearing a satisfied smirk.

"Thanks for the lesson, Bunny." Beefy snorted, zipping up his fly. "I won't forget where to stash the plunger again."

The woman winked and wiped her mouth in what Danny assumed she thought was a sexy gesture. "See that you don't. I'd hate to have to keep reminding you, Earl." She winked as she fluffed her hair. "Oh!" Her eyes widened the minute they landed on Danny, and she fluttered her lashes. "Sergeant Marcus, it's so nice to see you again."

He would have laughed at the instant change in her demeanor, from slut to subdued, had the whole scene not made him want to puke. He was no Boy Scout, but a woman wiping another man's cum from her lips while openly flirting with him turned his stomach. His eyes dropped to her nametag before he forced a polite greeting. "Bunny."

"Aww, you remembered," she cooed. "How sweet."

"Your name's on your shirt, ma'am." There was no fucking way he'd let her get the wrong impression from him.

"Umhmm." Her grin was all teeth and no charm.

"Listen, I'm looking for Julie. She here?" Seven words. That was all it took for her sugar to turn to vinegar.

"Earl, go get the glasses from the kitchen. Now. No, she doesn't come in for a few hours still. Lazy little girl took the morning off." She must have sensed she'd hit a nerve, because her backpedaling came on strong. "Just kidding with ya. She works a lot of doubles, so I suggested she take it easy this morning. I like to look after my little ones. They're like my family, ya know?"

Beefy came in from the back room with a case of glasses and laid them on the bar. He not-so-subtly pinched the redhead's ass and walked back through the kitchen.

Danny grunted in disgust. "Yeah, family. Sure. Can you please tell Julie I came by? And give her this." He scribbled his phone number on a cocktail napkin, folded it in half, and reluctantly gave it to Bunny.

"Sure, Sergeant. You can count on me." Bunny smiled before pushing through the door to the kitchen.

"She treats the customers like family too." The older gentleman snorted before sipping his beer. "If you know what I mean."

Danny chuckled as he left the bar. Yeah, he understood the guy loud and clear.

THE BAR WAS packed with wall-to-wall people, as seemed to be the norm for Saturday nights at Chester's. From July through August, Saturday nights were "all staff mandatory." Even the cool air blasting from the air conditioner did nothing to cut the stifling humidity of the mid-July heat. With the tables and chairs on the outside deck filled with thirsty customers, the four bartenders took turns providing waitress service to the deck patrons in order to keep the foot traffic from overrunning the bar. Even Chester hung around on Saturday nights in case drunken tempers led to drunken conflicts. The whole scene would have been chaos had it not been run so incredibly smoothly.

Julie needed the loud music, the demanding people, and flirty men in order to keep her mind off of the fact that a certain Sergeant Marcus had never bothered to contact her after their one interlude five nights before. Sure, she'd slipped out before the sun came up, but awkward morning-after conversations weren't something she'd had practice in, and starting them with a man who could easily shred her confidence wasn't something she'd been looking to do. Christ, the things he'd done to her body... just thinking about them made her panties wet, which quickly led to frustration over the fact that he'd so easily moved on, giving her not even a second thought.

Could've been worse, she repeated to herself as she poured another round of tequila shots for the enlisted men who were looking not only to blow off steam but find ladies who were as enthusiastic about the prospect of *blowing* as well.

"Hey, pretty lady, how 'bout you pour one of those for yourself?"

Stopping mid-pour, Julie looked at the private first class and offered her sweetest smile. "Aww, aren't you sweet. I appreciate the offer, but I don't drink while I'm working." The guy's disbelieving look made her continue explaining. "Can't serve all of you men quickly enough if I'm tipsy, can I?" She punctuated her statement with a flirty wink, rung up the round, and placed his generous tip in the bucket behind the bar.

She'd learned while bartending back in high school that a small amount of sugar always brought in the highest tips, but too much sweetness brought the largest amount of trouble. As if proving her point, Bunny leaned over the bar, breasts smashed against the sticky wood, so a man could lick salt from her neck and reach into her cavernous cleavage for a tiny slice of lemon. Her hyena-like giggles drew attention from both drunken men and irritated women. All of that for what? The clink of fifty cents that the pock-marked, yellowed-skinned ancient man dropped on the bar before strolling out the door into the thick night air. Yeah, Bunny's sugar was more like fly paper. Ick.

"Sugar, can we get two pitchers of beer and four wine coolers? Any flavor will do." The deep, melodic voice didn't quite match the average height, medium-build man who stood before her. His sandy-blond hair was pulled away from his face and tied into a low ponytail, and his eyes, the most intriguing shade of turquoise, held promises of laughter with a hint of something darker deep inside. While his handsome face promised light, his attire was various shades of black, from his Metallica T-shirt to his faded, ripped black jeans. "Do I have something funky between my teeth?"

Julie flushed. "Oh, I'm so sorry, I didn't mean to stare. Your voice…well, your eyes…shit. I'm sorry, I must sound like a freak."

"No, you're not the first person to react that way." The man seemed almost embarrassed by the attention he received. "I'm Alex Lawson, the lead singer for Lawson Road. My band and I are just here for some quiet drinks on the down low. Think we can do that?"

Lawson Road. Holy shit. She loved them. No wonder his voice sounded so familiar. They were just starting out, not quite huge but no longer small, and she was serving them drinks at Chester's. Then his words settled in, and she understood that he was asking her not to blow their cover.

"Alex, your secret is safe with me. But here's a bit of advice."

The attractive man leaned across the bar, nearly within touching distance. His scent infiltrated her nose, his turquoise eyes penetrating…

"Your advice?" he prompted.

"Right, my advice—you may want to keep yourself, your band mates, and your girlfriend away from the older redhead over there. She's like a shark, that one. If she smells blood in the water, she'll attack, and you all are like

25

the damn Red Cross blood bank. She'll alert the media, try to seduce you, and cry when you run screaming, all within ten minutes."

"We'll keep a tab open and only order from you tonight." Alex chuckled, grabbing the tray of drinks she'd prepared while they spoke. "Thanks for the heads-up, sweet thing. I speak for all of us when I say we do appreciate it."

An hour later, Julie had just finished her deck shift and was grateful to be inside Chester's once again. She hadn't thought anything could be more revolting than Bunny behind the bar until she'd spent an hour with Bunny on the deck. For Christ's sake, between the way that woman gyrated on men's laps and the amount of fingers that traveled up the inner thighs of her Daisy Dukes, if they were better friends, Julie would have gifted her a can of Lysol disinfectant spray and a tube of Vagisil at the end of their shift. STDs were created in the panties of Bertha "Bunny" Tryshon.

The worst part about Bunny's actions was men assumed Julie had the same loose...morals. That was often when Chester's presence was appreciated. While Julie wasn't certain that Chester didn't partake in Bunny's well, she could tell that he respected Julie's desire not to make herself part of the menu. In fact, he almost threw up invisible walls around Julie. As soon as he saw any sort of questionable behavior toward Julie or any of the other bartenders, he "handled" the situation outside of the bar quickly and, most of the time, quietly.

Julie stopped at Alex Lawson's table on her way inside. "Hey, guys, I'm just about to head back behind the bar, but since the crowd seems to have thinned out a bit, I figured I stop by and ask if you wanted me to get another couple of pitchers and wine coolers ready for you?"

"Perfect timing, sugar." The provocative tone of Alex's voice coupled with his flirtatious ocean eyes made it painfully clear how the man was gaining legions of fans all over the country.

While Julie could appreciate his beauty, her gaze darted to the attractive woman sitting to his left. She was the band's bass guitarist and, rumor had it, Alex's long-time girlfriend. Julie was not nor would she ever be a man poacher, but it was clear that the bassist didn't know that. So when her palm not-so-subtly moved up Alex's thigh and pressed against his groin at the same time she whispered something in his ear, punctuating it with what appeared to be quite a nibble, Julie felt her neck flush crimson.

"Umm, okay, I'll just go and fill your order." Unable to rip her eyes from the seduction transpiring at the table, Julie backed away in an attempt to leave before creating an even bigger scene.

Alex snickered, his hand covering his girlfriend's and moving it in a suggestive motion. "Ethan, you mind following Julie to the bar and grabbing our drinks? Jerry and Vicky are gonna save our seats while I take Tara outside for a couple a minutes."

Ethan smirked. "Just make sure to wipe the backseat down when you're finished." Ethan pressed his hand on the small of Julie's back. "Come on, let's go get those drinks. A and T will be thirsty as hell when they come back."

Julie lifted the hinged wooden arm at the side of the bar and slid behind it, keeping it lifted for the other bartender leaving for the deck. "Same as before, right?" Julie smiled sheepishly, trying to get the beguiling image of Alex and Tara out of her head.

"They're quite the pair, aren't they?"

"Oh my God." Giggles pealed from her throat. "So it wasn't just me? They were... that was..." Julie fumbled for words as she filled the pitchers. She wasn't a prude—clearly she had no problems with flirting or, hell, with going home with a random man—but Alex and Tara were so public with their affections, so illicit with their behavior. While Julie felt embarrassed by some of the actions, some of it turned her on.

"Trust me," Ethan said, leaning over the counter and bringing his body within inches of hers, "it isn't just you. If you think that's hot, you should see them argue." He fanned himself. "It'd singe your eyebrows off."

The belly laugh that left her lips startled even Julie, but not as much as the voice that came from her right.

"Ahh, now I understand. Looks like I'm not the only jumper between the two of us, huh?" Danny stood at attention, but gone were the uniform and blank stare. In their stead was a spectacularly gorgeous man in a brown T-shirt and jeans, sporting the look of a jilted lover—flared nostrils, pinched brows, a curled upper lip, and all.

"Danny?" Her heart leaped at his presence before her breath hitched at his response. Was he insulting her? The one-night thing worked both ways.

"Clearly you don't waste any time between beds, now do you?"

Had his words not come from what seemed like a place of hurt and had Julie not been at her place of employment, her response would have been far less quiet and far less civil.

"Here's your drink order, Ethan." She knew her forced smile wouldn't fool a blind man, let alone the nice guy who seemed extremely interested in stepping in to protect her in that moment, but she pasted it on to save them the discomfort and embarrassment. "I'm just going to deal with Sergeant Marcus here."

"Do you need my help?" Ethan asked.

When fire grew in Danny's hazel eyes, Julie knew that he may be angry, but there was no way in hell she needed protection from the man. "No, I'm perfectly fine."

Ethan nodded and walked back to his table.

"What in the hell, Danny? You don't get to come in here after nearly a week of silence and—"

"A week of silence, my ass. I came here the very next fucking day. Woke up with a pounding head, an empty apartment, and no memory of how the night had ended." He rubbed the back of his neck. "I wanted to see you, damn it. Ask you what the fuck happened between us." His head snapped to the far right side of the bar, and he snarled, "I left my goddamn number with that worn-out redhead before I left."

"You came here… to find me?"

His hazel eyes blazed so hot they singed her skin. "Uh, yeah. But clearly you've moved on. So…forget it." His broad shoulders were tight, his face stony as he turned to leave, and Julie knew she'd never see him again.

In a voice loud enough for him to hear but quiet enough not to cause a scene, Julie called, "Danny, I'm serving drinks, that is all you saw. As for you stopping by this week, no one told me. I didn't know."

Julie's mind was spinning. He *had* come. He'd tried to contact her and left a way for her to reach him. She was going to kill Bunny—unless he got there first.

"You." Danny's growl carried over the voices as he made his way toward Bunny.

Julie watched, entertained as Bunny's eyes went from soft and flirty with the thought that a male was looking for her, to round with awareness when she realized just who it was and what she'd done.

As the place quieted, Chester made his way in from the deck. His eyes landed on Julie. "Things okay?"

"Yep." Julie grinned. "Nothing Bunny can't handle, sir."

Chester flicked his gaze over to an angry but reined in Danny and a typically drama-filled Bunny before turning his back. "Yell if you need me," he called over his shoulder.

"Sergeant Marcus, what a pleasure—"

"Do *not* pull that syrupy shit with me." Danny's chest expanded and depressed, his demeanor every bit that of a well-trained leader. "Did I or did I not come in here five days ago looking for Julie Bell?"

Bunny tucked a stiff chunk of hair behind her ear. "Well, hmm, I can't exactly remember what day it was that your fine ass graced my eyes." She bit her lip and looked at Julie before looking back at Danny. Oh yeah, guilt covered her face as clearly as the mascara on her lashes.

The muscles in Danny's jaw clenched, leaving Julie to wonder just how much pressure it could take before the bones shattered. "Okay, ma'am, do you remember when I handed you my phone number and asked that you to give it to Julie?"

"Hmm." Bunny tapped her bright pink fingernail on her matching pink lip.

Unfortunately for her, Earl came out from the kitchen with cases of beer and grinned when he saw Danny. "Hey, man, good to see you again."

As if she could physically see the tension leaving Danny's body, Julie exhaled the breath that had been held prisoner in her chest.

"It's Earl, right?" Danny asked the bar back. When the guy nodded, Danny's brow lifted. "You remember seeing me earlier this week?"

"Uhh, is this some sort of a test? Yeah, dude, I remember seeing you. I just said hi, didn't I?"

And there went Danny's jaw, tight as a spring. "Yes, Earl, you did, thank you. Do you remember why I came by?"

"He can't answer your questions, Sergeant," Bunny interjected. "Look at him, poor boy obviously doesn't know anything, and we are clearly busy here."

"He was here looking for Julie," Earl grunted over Bunny's shrill voice. "And you didn't seem to think I was such a lil' boy when you were on your knees, purring like a cat, with my dick down your throat." He clenched his fists tightly, then released one to wave his hand in the air. "You didn't seem so convinced I was useless when you were begging to have it shoved up your ass. I was pretty fuckin' great then, wasn't I?" Earl's chest heaved as he looked around the silent bar, then from Danny to Julie. He scuffed the toe of his boot on the floor before speaking softly. "I'm sorry. I should have told her you came callin'.

Obviously I'm not as smart as I thought." He threw an aggravated look in Bunny's direction before he slid out from behind the bar and headed to the deck.

The room remained quiet as stares darted from Bunny to Julie and back. If not for Bon Jovi's apropos "You Give Love a Bad Name" blaring from the juke box, Julie might have exploded into flames of embarrassment. Leave it to JBJ to save the night.

"Next round is on the house," Chester boomed, coming from who knew where to join the women behind the bar.

The crowd erupted in appreciative delight.

Had Julie not been standing as close to him as she was, she wouldn't have heard him grumble, "Two choices, Bertha: finish the shift and get paid for the night, or walk now and don't. Either way, your time here is over."

"What?" Bunny's eyes grew wide as her jaw fell open. *Hmm, no wonder the men appreciated her.* "Screw you, Chester!"

"Been there, darlin', and it ain't worth losing customers. Previous offer's officially off the table. You needed to make a scene, I can make one too. Leave my bar now."

"Well, I don't need this shithole place," she huffed, attempting to fluff her Aqua Net-hardened hair while shimmying past the bartenders frantically filling orders.

Something in Julie snapped. After everything she'd lost, everything she'd survived, she had finally found some semblance of happiness at Chester's Bar. And while she had no clue as to what would happen between her and Danny, she couldn't just let that woman get away with what she'd said…with what she'd done.

"Hey, Bunny," Julie called, stopping the irate woman in her tracks.

"What the hell do you want, you little bitch?"

Julie reached into the bucket behind the counter and pulled out two quarters. Summoning her sweetest smile, she dropped the coins into Bunny's hand. "I figured you'd want these, you know, since you worked so hard for them. There're a bit…sticky, but they're all yours." With her parting shot, Julie turned her attention back to the customers, doing her best to ignore the applause her action received.

ROOTED TO THE ground, Danny watched Julie work, her movements just as fluid as the drinks she poured. When his buddies had suggested they go out for beer after a long day of softball between 1st and 2nd platoons, followed by them helping him unpack his shit and settle into his new living quarters, he could hardly refuse. When they decided on Chester's Bar, he could have come up with at least three different options, but his suggestions would have led to questions, and the questions would have led to razzing, which was the last thing he felt like dealing with. However, he wanted to avoid seeing Julie after she'd so blatantly blown him off, so he'd suggested they sit on the deck and his friends agreed.

Each time a server had approached them, Danny found himself caught between wanting to see the shiny strawberry hair and wanting to purposely ignore her. Finally, he inquired about Julie's whereabouts. His every instinct screamed for him to find her, confront her, then walk away as easily as she had. What he hadn't planned on was how her smile made his pulse race or the way her tank top showed just the perfect hint of cleavage to make his cock twitch in his jeans. What he never would have guessed was how the pale pink hue of her cheeks aimed at another man would release a possessive feeling that he'd never felt before. *Mine*.

Logic told him she was no more his than he was hers, but logic wasn't making his feet move toward her. Logic wasn't propelling air through his lungs. Logic had no place in his mind when he'd nearly ruined everything with speculation and accusation. Thank fuck the woman understood Caveman, because clearly logic had left the building. It took every ounce of military training and composure Danny had not to throttle the smaller man receiving Julie's delight, but Danny knew she saw past his thin mask of civility. She saw what must have looked like confusion or, embarrassingly enough, desperation, and she nicely dismissed the other dude, who made her smile before a bigger scene was made.

Danny had left his phone number and they never connected, fine—maybe she wasn't interested, though fuck, that stung—but at least she had enough respect to make the rejection a private affair. However, once again, the sun-kissed strawberry-blonde shocked the shit out of him by throwing out venom instead of bullshit. The second she accused him of giving her the brush-off, the hands on the clock stopped moving, making time stand still. *What the ever-loving fuck does that mean?* He could have dealt with being disposed of—okay, clearly he hadn't handled that well—but seeing confusion and disappointment on her face? Hell no.

Could he have been a bit smoother with the redheaded trouble-maker? Probably. But the chick hadn't just messed with him, she'd messed with *his* girl. His girl? No, that was wrong. Yet everything about it felt right, from his thoughts straight down to the tip of his cock.

Shit, he needed to talk with Julie, and he wasn't leaving until they did. Sparing another quick glance around the crowded bar, he walked out to the deck, laid enough bills on the table to cover the drinks and a generous tip, and informed his buddies that he'd find his own way home. Their catcalls and whistles faded as he stalked to a recently vacated stool in front of a sweaty, sexy Julie Bell.

A grin spread across Julie's lush mouth as she untied her apron and sauntered to his side at two in the morning. "I see you decided to stick around."

Unable to pull his stare from her lips, Danny shrugged. "Said I would."

Chester's had closed its doors an hour earlier, sending the staff into frenzied clean-up mode. When Julie had explained the lengthy process to Danny, he simply crossed his arms and said he'd wait. Her arched brow told him she didn't believe him, but she didn't need to. Danny was a man of his word, another lesson drilled into him by his father. *Rich or poor, son*, he'd say, *the only thing of value that you ever truly have is your word—live and die by it.* And Danny did.

After cleanup, Chester summoned the staff into his office for an impromptu meeting. It was quick, only about ten minutes by Danny's count, but when the door opened and the staff ambled out, an energized buzz floated around them. They dispersed into the night, leaving only Danny, Julie, and Chester in the quiet bar.

"Sergeant," Chester's thick voice called.

"Yes, sir?"

"Sorry about what happened with Bertha. While it'd be easy to place all of the blame on the woman, no good man should ever have let that happen. Her actions were revolting, but I let them continue in my establishment for far too long. My fault." The guy actually looked ashamed. "Julie there"—Chester nodded in her direction—"is a smart girl. In the short time I've personally known her, I've seen her work damn hard. She's trustworthy and loyal, qualities that sure as shit ain't easy to come by. Whole lot more than the pretty exterior men seem so keen to focus on. Although from where I stand, looks like I don't need to sell her to you." In two long strides, Chester closed the distance between them. The affection in the older man's eyes was replaced with a hard glare. "You, on the other hand, have somethin' to prove."

His words were a gut punch, no doubt. The thing was, Danny had already seen past Julie's surface. She'd already ensnared him with her wit and gentle charm. Wasn't that why he'd come looking for her…twice?

The bar owner continued, "Respect, Sergeant. That's all I'm saying. You respect her, and you and I will be just fine."

Danny inclined his head. "Of course, sir."

Chester nodded, first to Danny, then to Julie. "Take tomorrow off, girl. You haven't had one of those since you started."

Julie's body stiffened. "Chester, I'm perfectly fine. I'll—"

"That's an order, Ms. Bell." Chester scoffed over his shoulder before heading into his office. The click of the door effectively ended the discussion.

"So much for respect...I was supposed to work a double tomorrow," Julie huffed as they walked out the door into the humid night air and strolled toward the well-lit parking lot behind Chester's. She looked at Danny, and a glimmer sparked in her gray eyes as if his presence had somehow sunk in. "How did you get here tonight, Sergeant Marcus?"

"Buddies."

Julie looked around the empty street. "And those buddies just left you behind?"

Danny's brow lifted. "They'd never 'just leave' me anywhere. I told them I'd be fine, and they knew I would be."

"So are you...fine?"

Between the husky tone of her question and the way she bit her bottom lip, Danny's heart punched his chest. Looping his arm around her waist, he pulled her toward him and lowered his lips into her hair. The scent was reminiscent of its shade, strawberry and honey, sweet and sweat, feminine and strong, just like the woman in his arms.

"I am now," he murmured and dropped another kiss on the crown of her head.

Slowly, Julie backed away from his embrace. The inches between them, while few, felt far and wide. Though she was the one who'd created the separation, the longing on her face hinted that maybe the distance was a defense and not a rejection. "Pretty sure of yourself, huh, Sergeant?"

He heard the tease in her question, but there was no hiding the uncertainty in her pretty gray eyes. "Ms. Bell, when it comes to you, the only thing I'm sure of is how much I missed you this week." He reached for her hand and interlaced their fingers while extending his other arm to her chin and tilting her head back until their eyes met. "I want you. I won't bullshit about that. Hell, I still have no clue if I've already had you, and it's screwing with my goddamn head. But I promise—I give you my word—I only want to talk to you. Get to know you better. And I had no intentions of walking away from you tonight until we made that happen." He felt his lips begin to lift as his eyes traveled from her curious eyes to her parted lips.

Skepticism was written all over her raised brows. "Are you drunk?"

"Not in the slightest."

"Okay. How about this time, we go to my place? And just so you know, the only screwing that happened between us is what's going on in your head."

Her admission stunned him, but that was followed immediately by relief. While there was no way to change the past, knowing their first time together wouldn't be when he was a drunken fool filled him with an inexplicable sense of joy.

"Wait." The backs of his knuckles inched slowly down the soft skin of her jaw. "I remember going down on you." The image of her face as she flew apart under his ministrations was branded into his eyelids. Her sweet moans and tangy taste were the only reminders he'd need-ed as he stroked himself off in the shower both morning and night. "If memory serves me right, you were quite eager to reward me for the mind-blowing orgasm I gave you."

Julie swatted his arm. "I'll give you that—it was pretty freaking mind blowing. And I was prepared to do some *blowing* of my own, but some super sergeant I know passed out before I got his pants unbuttoned. And regardless of the fact that I went home with a virtual stranger, there was no way in hell I was performing any sort of lewd acts on an unconscious man." She tightened the hair in her ponytail holder and bee-lined to her car.

"Umm, Jul? Just for future reference, you know, since we're no longer strangers and all…" Danny quickened his pace to meet her at the driver's side door of the Datsun. "Feel free to perform any lewd acts you want on me while I'm sleeping or unconscious. I promise…I'll love them."

The drive was pleasant but not as talkative as he'd hoped. Danny found himself chuckling as Julie sang, albeit slightly off key, to Prince, Bon Jovi, and Robert Palmer. She didn't live far from Chester's Bar, only about fifteen minutes or so, but the short distance may as well have led them to an entirely different state. They'd gone from the flat dry land where the barracks and bar resided to the plush grassy neighborhoods where driveways were filled with station wagons and yards with swing sets. When she pulled her red Datsun into the driveway of a modest but beautiful two-story home, questions began to overload Danny's brain.

"Jul, do you live here alone?"

"Y-yes." There was no masking the hesitation in her answer.

"Is this your home?"

Julie shifted the car into park and faced him, the engine still running. "I brought you here to *my* house. *My* home. And I know you'd like to talk, get to know me, but not just yet. Not right now." Her eyes moved to the house before coming back to his. "I have nothing to hide and everything to hold on to."

Her audible swallow nearly gutted him. What the hell had happened to the beautiful woman who'd already stolen his attention and unknowingly laid claim to his thoughts? "Julie—"

"Maybe it would be better if we went back to your place after all. No harm, no foul." Her upper lip slid between her teeth for a beat as she wiped imaginary dust from the center console. "Because as much as I want you, I'm not sure I'm ready to do *this here*." Her steely gaze darted to the single-family home at the top of the driveway before coming back to his. "This"—she pointed between them—"is supposed to be fun. That"—she nodded at the house—"is the real me. Let's go back to your place."

Emotions whipped through Danny like a hurricane, from sympathy for the unknown pain the woman next to him had faced, to anger for the hurts she'd dealt with, to lust for the sexy woman who brought out every protective instinct he never knew he had. *Again with the caveman shit. I'm screwed.* "Turn off the car, woman. Let's go inside and take it slow."

She blushed. "Oh, you misunderstood. I…umm, I totally want to have sex with you. I have an orgasm to repay, and since you're sober tonight, I'm betting you have a few things you could show me? I just hoped to save the talking until after playtime, okay?"

"Fuck." He gritted his teeth. "Yeah, honey, I think I can agree to that, but—and I can't believe I'm about to say this—the 'get to know you' portion of the evening will not be forgotten, no matter how hot our fire burns. Get it?"

With a curt nod, she pulled the keys out of the ignition.

"Words, Julie, I need words."

Once again she turned and faced him. "I promise I'll let you into my mind as soon as you've satisfied my body."

"Fuck me."

CHAPTER THREE

I Wasn't The One Who Needed Help

SHE ENTERED THE well-lit, quiet house the same way she did each night. The only difference was the large hand resting on the small of her back. The heat from his touch penetrated her sweat-dampened tank top, making goose bumps blanket her skin.

"You cold?"

She let the question go unanswered, knowing damn well the cocky sergeant knew her physical response had nothing to do with the ambient temperature and everything to do with the slow boil his touch seemed to generate.

"This is some place you've got here."

His statement was filled with questions. How could it not be? They hadn't shared their ages, and even though she sometimes felt decades older than her almost twenty years, she certainly didn't look it.

"Thank you." Unready to hit the hard topics just yet, she needed to shift his focus. "Would you like something to drink, maybe an iced tea or lemonade?"

Mission accomplished. Danny's mouth ticked up. "Love some iced tea, please."

She beckoned Danny as she strode into the kitchen. She pulled two mason jars from the cabinet and the pitcher of iced tea from the refrigerator, all while feeling the weight of his stare on her every move.

"I hope you don't mind it sweet." She gestured to the pitcher.

"Drink it sweet, drink it tart"—his gaze dropped to her lips—"cool, hot…just want it on my tongue, Jules."

Julie blinked twice, then swallowed loudly. For a woman who poured drinks for a living, never had the task been so difficult. It was obvious when Danny saw his words had the desired impact because he chuckled. The sound was warm syrup over hotcakes—smooth, liquid, delicious, and setting her ablaze.

Facing each other, they stood at the kitchen counter. While he seemed to marvel over the glass pitcher in her hand, thoughts of him sifted through her mind. He was the hottest man she'd ever seen and the only one she'd brought home since her parents had left. What it was about him she didn't know, but something was screaming that she should trust him. She wanted nothing more than to listen to that voice.

Rolling up on her toes, Julie pressed a kiss on Danny's cheek, then turned her back, leaving him in the kitchen with his half-filled glass in hand.

"I need a shower," she called over her shoulder. "I'm a sweaty mess." The knot in her stomach tightened as parts of her wished she could disappear from the brazen behavior. Other parts bloomed, coming free from restraints she'd never realized she wore. "Invitation's open."

"Goddamn," he muttered as the sound of glass clunked in the stainless sink and the facet turned on.

She waited a second while he must have been cleaning their glasses. When the water turned off and his heavy footsteps thumped around the linoleum, she hurried up the stairs. Julie covered her mouth to mute her giggle as she bounced into the bathroom. She was in trouble when it came to Danny Marcus. Her heart wasn't beating double time because he had rinsed their drinking glasses and possibly put them away, as if he'd already found comfort amongst her things. She hadn't welcomed a man into her adult life, let alone her home. Therefore, the ease they seemed to find with one another had her insides twisted and melting all at once.

Hot spray pounded on Julie's tired muscles. Four consecutive twelve-hour shifts had definitely done a number on her feet, not that she'd ever admit it to anyone. Hell, she'd been ready to work another double the following day had Chester not forced her to take the time off.

She poured a generous amount of Gee Your Hair Smells Terrific shampoo onto her palm and massaged it into her long locks. Thoughts of Danny walking around her home, amongst her things, unnerved and thrilled her all at once. While his presence was large, it wasn't intimidating, even on the car ride back to her house earlier. The air snapped with his mere being, but not once had she felt suffocated by his existence.

"That invitation still open?" A rough voice asked through the glass shower door.

The question startled Julie, although she recovered quite nicely. "Only if you're willing to scrub my back." She stepped under the spray to rinse the shampoo from her long tresses as the door slid open, bringing cool air to her hot skin.

"You asking if I mind touching your naked skin?" His seductive tone felt like steam hugging every inch of her form.

Slowly she opened her eyes. His muscular body filled the shower stall as desire showed all over his face.

"Fucking gorgeous." His tongue slicked over his bottom lip. "Every single inch of you is perfection beyond dreams."

Funny, she thought, as she took in his nakedness for the first time. "I think I know exactly how you feel."

Wetness that had absolutely nothing to do with the shower pooled between her thighs as a heavy throb pulsed deep in her core. They hadn't even touched, and already her body responded to his like iron to a magnet. Need pushed her closer, wanting to connect with the one thing meant to truly hold her tight. Him.

Beads of water splashed against his chest before rolling over each defined ab. Despite the moisture surrounding them, Julie's mouth went desert dry as she stared wantonly at the length that rapidly thickened between his legs. She wanted him. All of him. On her skin, beneath her touch, inside her. Her hunger seemed just as desperate as his desire.

"You keep staring at me like that, honey, and we won't make it out of this shower. Hell, we won't manage to get clean."

Ogling him from toe-to-top once more, she shrugged. "I'm not sure I have a problem with that."

Uncertain which was louder, the beating of her heart or the pounding shower, Julie's breath caught in her lungs as Danny's chest inched closer. Flesh brushed flesh and her eyelids closed as naughty thoughts pummeled her mind. *Click. Squeeze. Snap.*

Her eyes snapped open. "What are you doing?

Once again, he reached past her to replace the conditioner bottle on the shelf behind her. Soft hazel eyes met hers, his long lashes clumped into spikes from the water. "When's the last time someone took care of you?" Without waiting for a response, he continued, "Turn around."

Kisses from heaven. There was no other way to describe how his strong fingers felt massaging her skull. When her hair was rinsed, he made good on his promise to scrub her back, and she made good on her desire to stay dirty.

"What are *you* doing?" Danny asked in a guttural moan when Julie wrapped her small hand around his shaft and lowered herself to her knees.

"Taking care of you."

Giving oral sex had never been one of her favorite things to do—in fact, receiving it hadn't been at the top of her list either—but the blissful delight Danny had brought her that night on his sofa, the way his absence had burned, and the complete joy that had consumed her when she learned that their night together had been more than a drunken mistake made Julie want to give more to the man staring down at her than to anyone she'd ever known. Eyes locked on his, she swiped her thumb over the thick head of his erection, then repeated the motion with her tongue. Danny widened his stance, his stare not leaving hers. A second lick turned into a third until Julie wrapped her lips around him, sucking him into the warm depths of her mouth.

Danny groaned as his lids slid closed. "So good. So fucking good."

His encouragement was her incentive as she wrapped one hand around his hard shaft and fed him into her greedy mouth. Each time her tongue touched a spot under the head of his dick, he'd gasp his pleasure. He threaded his fingers through her wet hair, gripping the locks even though he seemed to restrain his movements.

"Lick me, baby, suck my cock. Fuck… oh, God…"

His pleasure became her aphrodisiac as her clit pulsed, begging for relief. The hand that wasn't working him slid to her needy place, and as she licked and sucked with enthusiasm she never thought possible, her fingers rubbed small circles on the sensitive nerves at her core. An unchecked moan slid from her mouth as Danny's dick hit the back of her throat.

"Fuck me"—his gaze cloaked her—"you touching yourself, honey? Sucking me off turning you on?"

She nodded, her eyes heavy with arousal. Her mouth full of him, words weren't an option.

"Fuck." The word was drawn out in an erotic sigh. "Do not come, Julie. Leave you for me. Understood?"

Understanding filled her over-stimulated brain as she pulled away, letting him drop from her mouth but not from her hand. The water at her back was losing heat, but she refused to have this thing between them based on anything but truth. "Then you do something for me."

"Go on."

"Don't hold back. I can tell you are…don't. If I'm not doing it the way you like, tell me. But otherwise, do not hold back."

Danny closed his eyes, and she hoped she hadn't read him wrong. "Open your mouth, Julie, and suck me down. You don't want me to come in your mouth, I'll give you warning. You stay on me, you swallow what I give."

Arousal slid from her core as his words tingled every part of her body. She leaned forward and took him in again, starting with her tongue and working her way down. As Danny's body started to shake, he wrapped her hair around his fist and pumped, fucking her mouth and calling her name.

"Gonna come, honey," he warned as his thrusts slowed in order to give her a second to detach.

There was no way she was leaving him unfinished. She wanted everything he had, everything he offered. So instead of peeling her lips from his shaft, she took him deeper and hummed.

"Jesus Christ," he grunted.

He thrust in and out of her mouth until warm liquid burst on her tongue and down her throat. Delicious it was not, but it was Danny's. Therefore, she would take it any time he wanted to give it to her.

"Holy shit, Jules," he rasped. "That was…holy fucking shit."

The water was turned off, and she was lifted into his arms and carried out of the shower, out of the bathroom, and onto the bed. "Danny, we're soaking wet."

"Ummhmm." He disappeared back into the bathroom and returned with the bath towels she'd left on the counter. Two fluffy towels—yes, she'd been hopeful.

Once the cotton was wrapped around him, hugging low on his defined hips, he strolled over to the bed. Up on her elbows, she watched him sit beside her and move the soft towel up and down her body.

"Curious," he muttered, the cloth on her shoulder. "I think I'm drying you off, but goose bumps keep covering your skin. Can you explain that one?" His flirty tone had her every nerve alert and ready to be touched by him. "Wonder what would happen if I dry you here…"

His gaze moved to the wet skin of her chest, and her breath labored in her lungs. He dabbed the soft cotton over her sensitive peaks. A sigh left her lips like a song as fire burned inside her belly.

"Hmmm," Danny said, "doesn't seem like your body wants to be dry, honey." A devilish grin sent her pulse racing and her insides thrumming. "Guess I'll just need to keep you wet."

Without a second's delay, his tongue darted out in sweeping circles over her pointed nipple while his hands explored her body. Calloused palms ran over her skin, setting off sparks that turned to blazes. She was burning beneath him and had no desire to put out the flames.

"Oh God, oh…God…"

His teeth grazed her nipple, then the other, inflicting pain, something she'd never known to ask for. Then the moist heat of his tongue lapped the sting and, like a balm, only pleasure remained.

"So good, Danny," she panted.

Following his hands, his lips traveled slowly, inch by inch, over her ribs, her belly, the ticklish spot at her hips, and when his fingers entered her tight channel, she squeezed her eyes closed and mewled at the indescribable feeling. *Holy shit, how does he know how to do that?* His wrist turned, and the pads of his fingers made contact with

LISA N. PAUL

her g-spot—or as she referred to it, her "me-spot," because she'd been the only person who could find it. Lost in the knowledge that he had found her hidden treasure, she nearly shot off the bed when Danny's warm tongue slicked between her fold and across her clit.

"Your mind stays with me."

"Oh, believe me, it's only with you."

"Mmm, so sweet, Julie. Your pussy's damn sweet."

Thick fingers plunged in and out, fucking her brilliantly as he lapped at her clit. He brought her higher, her body tighter, as release coiled in her gut, waiting for just the right moment, the right touch to go off.

"Give it to me," he rasped, her juices glistening on his lips. His fingers stilled inside her before he lightly tapped her g-spot. "I wanna watch you come."

The tapping turned to pressure on the special spot—no thrusting, no movement, just pressure as he sucked on her clit—and the foreign sensation set her off like nothing she'd ever experienced, nothing she'd ever heard of, nothing she'd ever forget.She lost all sense of time and self. It stole her breath and left her wondering how she had ever settled for less. Amazing.

Tremors rippled through her body in small waves of bliss as Danny's mouth moved from her core to her hips. Ever so slowly, he traveled up her body, putting out the fires he'd stoked on the way down. Boneless and sated, Julie reached for his silken hair, running her fingers through the still-damp strands. Her breaths slowed as her muscles, sore from work and relaxed from the scrumptious orgasm, melted into the mattress. Her lids became heavier with each gentle lick and sensual suck. And then…she was gone.

HE KNEW THE minute he lost her, yet he couldn't stop himself from finishing the tour he'd started. Every inch of her skin was silk, each measured breath she took was precious. *What the ever-loving fuck, Marcus? Precious breaths?* He looked at his hard cock. *Nope, haven't grown a pussy...yet.* Sure, Julie Bell had fallen asleep on him—*how's that for payback?* The devil on his shoulder teased—but Christ, the woman had rocked his world in the shower. Truth be told, she'd been shaking his foundation since the day they'd met.

Danny's eyes raked over the naked form sleeping next to him. From her long strawberry-blonde hair, to the faint dusting of freckles that kissed the bridge of her nose, to the plump kissable lips that had been wrapped around his cock like a goddamn dream, down to the most perfect set of tits he'd ever had his hands on, the woman could have been created specifically for him. And that was based solely on the superficial. But there was more. She was more. Sex or not, he intended to get inside Julie's mind, because she was already burrowing her way into his heart.

———•———•———•———

"MY PARENTS WERE amazing people." Julie's tight words hung in the dark room.

Danny was a light sleeper—something he'd learned in the army—so as soon as he realized that she was speaking *to* him and not in her sleep, he rubbed his eyes with one hand while pushing himself up to a sitting position with the other. He could make out the outline of Julie's body, the white blankets tucked beneath her arms, but he couldn't see her face, her eyes, or her mouth. A purposeful act, he assumed.

"They loved me like crazy, and they loved each other even more. I grew up knowing what it felt like to be surrounded by happiness," she said. "Life wasn't always perfect. We had our fair share of heartaches, and my parents dealt with issues that they thought I knew nothing about. But even when things were tough, they were…God, they were strong."

Danny reached out. He wanted to touch her, wanted to offer an anchor for the pain he knew was sure to come.

"No." The sheets rustled as she moved farther from him. "You can't touch me. Not yet. I only got through what I did because I had no one else to lean on."

He heard her swallow, and the pit of his stomach felt as though it filled with lead. He reluctantly placed his clenched fist on his lap and listened.

"Because I was an only child and we didn't have extended family on either side, they never traveled unless we went together. The one time they did leave me with a family friend, I was four and I got a horrible ear infection and ended up in the emergency room. Needless to say, after that, we were a package deal traveling the country." Her giggle sounded like it held years of good memories. "I turned eighteen in late fall of my senior year of high school, and we joked that my parents could finally travel without me because I was officially an adult. However, they still had an arm's length of reasons why they couldn't leave. They didn't want to miss seeing me off to prom, they wanted to be around in case I stressed out during finals, and of course, they had to see me walk for graduation."

Danny's desire to comfort Julie was bordering on obsessive, but he reminded himself that her needs were important at the moment, not his own. So his fists stayed clamped in the sheets and his mind stayed focused on her story.

"I assured them that if they went in the spring, they would be back for all of the milestones they wanted to see and they'd be well-rested and ready to keep me calm and focused. That seemed to be the incentive that finally pushed them forward and led them to booking a two-week dream trip to Mexico.

"Their preparation became a running joke at the dinner table over the weeks leading up to their departure. It wasn't the packing or their itinerary that kept them busy, but their concerns for *my* meals and *my* laundry in their absence. The whole thing was silly because they'd taught me to do those things years before, claiming it was a parent's job to raise independent children. But my dad begged me to suck it up and allow my mom to worry about me. He said it would make her feel better about leaving, so I did as he asked and nodded a lot and smiled each night until we all broke out into laughter." Julie took a deep breath. "The morning they left, Mom handed me pages of instructions, including numbers to the electric company, the gas company, old friends of my father's from his time in the Marines, the family dentist just in case I somehow managed to lose a tooth—all bases were covered if there was an emergency and I didn't know what to do." Brittleness infused Julie's voice. "She hugged me as if she'd never hugged me before and she never would again, and they left for their Mexican paradise."

Quickly, Danny scrolled through his memories for what events had happened in the past couple of years, and within seconds, Mexico City blazed like a red flashing sign. "Shit, Jules, they were in Mexico City, weren't they?" He wheezed as if the air had been knocked from his chest. The 1985 Mexico City earthquake was so huge, so completely devastating, it came with a foreshock in May 1985. The main event happened on September 19, 1985, and it had two major aftershocks, one on September 20, 1985 and the second seven months later on April 30, 1986. The magnitude of the final aftershock was 7.0, even though the event occurred more than two hundred twenty miles away. It caused major damage to Mexico City, and many more lives were lost.

The mattress trembled beneath him as her soft sobs filled the otherwise quiet room. His heart ached and his gut churned as he thought about the two devoted parents who'd reluctantly left their child but did so in the most strategic way in order to be back in time to witness the life events they'd coveted so deeply. In the end, they'd missed them all.

"All of that preparation," she croaked, "all of those instructions, and none of them helped me during the emergency. Because I wasn't the one who needed help. They were."

He stared in her direction, silently begging his vision to sharpen in the darkness. Ultimately, he remained impaired to anything more than the muted image of her body twisted around itself.

She continued, urgency lacing her tone as her sentences came out in rushed huffs. "They were supposed to arrive home on May first. I waited for them. I knew they weren't coming, but I waited anyway. I quickly learned how parents felt when they stayed up at night, waiting for their children to arrive home after missing curfew. That...that feeling of anger that gets swallowed up by prayers, prayers to any god who will listen, to please deliver your loved ones home safely. You promise you'll bank the anger and just give hugs if only you see your loves again." She hiccupped. "They didn't come, and my anger swelled. After five days, when I got confirmation that amongst the tour of one hundred people my parents had been with that day, only three had survived and my parents weren't in that tiny, lucky group, I had no prayers left. None.

"I went numb, completely anesthetized, but I needed to keep myself together and finish school—not for me but for them. Prom didn't happen—there was no way I could have stomached that without Mom and Dad by my side— and I didn't walk in the graduation procession, but I did graduate with honors. Finals were cake. I'd been granted immunity from taking them due to the tragedy I'd suffered, and since my grades were fantastic, not sitting for the exams wouldn't have lowered my GPA too drastically, but I chose to take them. I *needed* to focus on my studies. I had to concentrate on the tests that were marked in green on my calendar, and I couldn't let myself look past those dates because my whole life had changed. My plans for after graduation were gone, and after those circled green dates, I had...nothing."

Dizzy with information overload, Danny sat up, pulled in deep breaths, and tried to process how someone so grounded, so light-hearted, so sweet could have possibly gone through that brand of hell. He'd seen a shit-ton of bad in his years—he'd walked through fire and nursed the blistered skin left in its wake—but he had his father, his brother, and his squad to support him. Julie had…no one. NO ONE.

The silence fell heavy around them. With no more than her shallow breaths and soft sniffles, Danny was left with more questions than answers. However, he only had one pressing thing he had to know in that moment. "Julie, how? How in the hell have you made it this far?" His gut churned. She'd been the one to open up the book of her life, and he needed to turn a couple of pages. Just a few. "This house, it's the home you grew up in, right?"

"Yes."

Carefully, he continued. "You said you had no family?" He rubbed at his jaw, grateful for the darkness, that she couldn't see the tears stinging his eyes.

"No, my parents were a bit older when they got married, so I was their only child, and their parents were deceased."

Danny swallowed the lump in his throat. "Did you have anyone?"

The mattress beneath him shifted just before the room lit with the soft glow from a side table lamp. It was a move he hadn't seen coming and one that surprised the hell out of him. After being stuck in the dark as she described her nightmare, the light made him feel uneasy, disoriented, as if the present was the dream and the darkness the reality. With her legs still pulled tightly to her chest, Julie draped the arm she used to turn on the lamp back around her calves and tilted her head. Paths had been made down the flawless skin of her cheeks, ones she clearly hadn't bothered to wipe away. While her gray eyes were bloodshot and rimmed in red, they were no longer filled with the tears of a victim, but with the strength of a survivor.

"I didn't have family, no." She pulled her top lip between her teeth and released it. "But I wasn't completely alone. My mom"—she snorted—"with all of her obsessive list-making, had put together a pretty impressive list of friends that she and my dad kept in touch with over the years. Some I knew, most I didn't, but they all knew about me. While I was rolling my eyes, shaking my head, and making fun of my mom, she was contacting their friends and mailing them copies of their vacation itinerary and information about me. They must have thought she was crazy. But within hours of finding out about my parents, I had people at my door, offering help and support. My parents"—she brought her eyes to his—"they left for something amazing and beautiful, something they were supposed to enjoy. It was supposed to be selfish and carefree, but even in doing something for themselves, they made sure I was completely protected and surrounded by as much love as they could give me."

Danny watched Julie swallow, her body still pulled tight, a protective barrier of sorts to keep her safe. His fingers knotted together and clenched to keep from reaching for her when she had clearly expressed her need for physical solitude.

"It took me quite a while to realize it, but even with them gone, I've never been completely alone."

How could that be? He felt lonely for her. "I just"—he shook his head—"I can't imagine how you got through all of that pain and still shine with so much brightness. Not to sound like a wuss, but you radiate with it."

A small grin lifted the side of Julie's mouth. "I think that's the reason why I flipped on the lamp. I couldn't tell you my story face to face. It's still too fresh, too painful. But I need you to remember the woman you've seen, the woman you've kissed, the one that had you jealous"—he raised an amused brow, and she smiled—"yes, jealous when another man had her attention. I'm *still* that woman. You wanted to get to know me, but my past isn't a slow over-dinner-and-drinks kind of story. It's a trial-by-fire sorta tale."

"Not that it affects the outcome, but how have other men reacted?"

Julie's eyes narrowed. "No other man has ever had the opportunity to react."

Indescribable amounts of something akin to possessiveness and pride washed through him as he stared at what had to be the strongest woman he'd ever met. His own mother hadn't had the will to live, even though she had two children and a husband who loved her beyond reason, and this young woman stood like a tree in a hurricane, bending with the winds, moving with the rains but never breaking under the pressure.

"Sorry, I lied." Danny's gravelly voice cut through the quiet. "Your answer did change the outcome." Julie's wide eyes and slacked jaw would have been funny under other circumstances, but her insecurity was unwarranted. "I need you to believe me when I say I'm honored you shared that with me. And you're right, honey, the light was essential. It didn't wipe away your past, but it sure as hell cleared up any notion that I may have had regarding pity. I don't pity you, Julie Bell. I admire you. You're a soldier, a beautiful one…a strong one. Thanks for letting me in."

"Danny… it's all you." She paused, a shaky breath escaping her lips. "Now will you hold me, please?" Had her husky tone and penetrating gaze not been his undoing, her words would have.

"Oh," he exhaled, letting go of the crumpled sheets at his sides, "you have no idea how long I've been waiting to hear you say that."

As he encircled her with his arms, emotions warred through him: sadness and anger for the beautiful woman who'd been forced to walk through hell on her own; pride and confidence that she'd not just walked the distance but done it with grace and integrity; arousal beyond all belief that someone so magnificent wanted him enough to share her story and bare her soul. And he wanted it from her. All of it, every single piece, but most of all, he wanted to *give* back. Show her that there were no catches, no fine print, nothing that would make her regret trusting him.

He wiped the wetness from her cheeks with the pads of his thumbs, then brought them to his lips. Tasting her sadness sent physical pain through the left side of his chest, and he knew that he never wanted her to cry those tears again. "Come here, Jules." He pulled her close and lowered them to the mattress, face to face, skin to skin. "We barely know each other—" She attempted to interrupt until he placed a finger on her soft lips. "Yet I've never known someone more. Thanks for trusting me with you, honey. Won't let you down."

"I want you, Danny." Her gray eyes consumed him. "All of you."

"You got me, Julie. Christ, you totally got me." There wasn't *much* he'd rather do than sink deep into her pussy, claiming her as his own, but there was one thing. "When I take you, you're mine. Our pasts will always be with us, baby. Can't make them disappear. Don't want to. That said, when I slide into you the first time, I want your mind on us. Only us. Not the tears that came before, not the pain, the battle, the survival—just you and me. Understand?"

Her wide eyes stared at him as her shallow breaths filled the air. She'd heard him, but did she want the same thing? Just another reason to hold off for a little bit longer. It fucking killed him, but he wanted to build something between them. Something real. If she wasn't into it, there was no reason to start. He accepted her silent nod as a temporary answer, wrapped her tightly against his body, and waited for sleep to claim her. When her breathing evened out, he joined.

CHAPTER FOUR

Are You Crazy?

SUNLIGHT POURED THROUGH the window, pooling her bed in warmth she hadn't felt in… Christ, she couldn't remember the last time. Well, she could remember, but she never let her mind travel back to those days. While she hadn't had a lot of rest, due to the man snuggled up beside her and his insatiable need to give her pleasure, the sleep she'd had was deep, restful, and fortifying.

She'd had sex with men before her parents' death, but she'd never spent the night with any of them, being that she was in high school. The couple of times she'd tried to lose herself in sex after the earthquake had been a colossal waste of time, ending in fake orgasms and walks of shame.

There in her bed, in that moment, Julie's body still hummed from the climaxes that Danny had coaxed out of her. She was sated even though they hadn't had intercourse, and wrapped in his arms, she felt incredibly safe. *Safe. How the hell can I feel safe with this man? I barely know him.* Then she chastised her inner voice. *You barely know him? You spilled your fucking guts to him last night, you silly tart. He probably kept you steeped in orgasmic bliss just to shut you up.*

"Your whole body just tensed," Danny spoke, his voice thick with sleep. "Whatever it is that just crossed your mind, it isn't true."

With her back pressed to his front, he couldn't see her face, nor could he see the slight grin his words caused. "How do you know what I'm thinking isn't true? Maybe I'm remembering how great it felt to have your mouth on me last night."

"Honey, the way your muscles tightened and your breathing hitched, there's no way you were thinking 'bout coming." He pressed his groin against her. His hardened length teased the crack between her ass cheeks, instantly fusing her body to his. "See what I mean? No tension comes with thoughts of what I can do with your body. Which leads me back to my original statement—whatever bullshit you allowed your mind to spin about last night, about me, or about my deep-rooted desire to get the hell out of this house ASAP, it's all crap. You let me in, Julie, and I'm fucking cozy as hell."

Goose bumps broke her skin as his big palm ran from her wrist to her shoulder just before sliding to her breast.

"Now that I've had a look into your world and had a taste of who you are, I'm not leaving unless you toss my ass out. End of story. You got it?"

Julie's throat thickened as his words touched parts of her his hands never would. Still facing the wall, she nodded her understanding.

"Words, honey, I need your words. Look me in the eyes and tell me you understand what I just told you."

Rolling onto her back, Julie swallowed hard and stared into the bottomless hazel depths that seemed to consume her. "You're not leaving unless I toss your ass out."

Danny's grin warmed her, so she continued. "Which sucks for you, because I intend to keep you for a long, long time." When his grin morphed into a full-watt smile, gratitude to Chester for the impromptu day off flooded her brain. A sexy man, a large bed, and no place to be sounded like the makings of a perfect day.

AS THE DAYS passed, Julie continued to work hard, but she spent less time taking on double shifts and more time behind the scenes with Chester, learning how to order liquor and glassware. Working non-bartending hours got her out of the bar at a better hour, giving her and Danny more time together. They had dinner together after Danny got done with work each night, and due to their mutual love of ice cream, they began their ice cream tour of Baltimore. Each time they went out, they would go to a new ice cream shop and rate the ice cream on a scale they had made up. Julie quickly realized that no matter where they went, no matter how many flavors were offered, regardless of the toppings provided, her spicy lover only ever chose plain vanilla ice cream.

"Honey, there's no reason to dress up perfection," he'd say each time Julie would giggle at his unoriginal order. But that seemed to be Danny to a tee. The man knew what he liked, and he made no apologies for it.

On the nights that Julie did tend bar, he waited until close and escorted her home.

Then there was the making out. Damn. The man blew her mind every time he touched her, every way he touched her. Even though he didn't spend every night at her house, when he did, very little sleeping was involved. Yet they still hadn't had sex. They knew each other's bodies, knew which buttons to push and which to lick, but he'd yet to make love to her or fuck her or any other euphemism for sex. After the sweet but still clear rejection he'd given her the last time she'd all but begged for sex, she wasn't willing to try again.

"It's open," Julie shouted when the doorbell chimed. She had rented a movie, and Danny was coming over with pizza and beer.

"Hey." He dropped the pie on the coffee table and slid the beer in the fridge, grabbed her waist, and pulled her close.

As always, his minty flavor invaded her senses, and her body melded to his. She relished the way his perpetual scruff prickled her cheek and his heat radiated through their clothes. Her moan spoke of delight, which he clearly understood if the way he grinded his hips into hers was any indication.

"Woman," he growled, "been over two weeks since that first night in your bed."

Julie stared at him. The night was crystal-clear in her memory, as she'd thought about it dozens of times, but his mention of it startled her. "What about it?"

"Been waiting patiently for you to come to me." Calloused fingertips stroked the curves of her bare shoulders. "Watching you fly apart with my hand and my mouth is a damned dream, but I want you, honey. I wanna watch as I slide into your sweet pussy. I need to feel you pulse around my cock. Been waiting for you to be ready, baby, and I'll continue to wait"—his eyes were molten as he licked his lips—"but you have any idea how much longer that'll be?"

"Are you insane? I *did* come to you, on that first night in my bed." She snorted with exasperation. "You rejected me. Did you honestly think I was going to try a second time? Let me answer that for you—no way!" Chest heaving, lip caught between her teeth, Julie's eyes roamed the sexy man facing her with shock on his face. She only saw that face for two seconds before she was hefted over Danny's shoulder, carried up the stairs into her bedroom, and deposited onto the bed.

"Look at me." His command left no room for misunderstanding, so she did as she was told. Danny's knees hit the carpet as his eyes met hers. "Think there was a misunderstanding between us, and for that, I'm sorry. That night…" His lids slid closed as he inhaled. "You gave me your past, your pain, and without you knowing it, you snagged a piece of me. The piece that wants to protect you, the piece that dares anyone or thing to try to hurt you again." He opened his eyes. "Wasn't giving you a regarded rejection, honey. I was giving you the chance to decide if you wanted all in with me. I screwed up, I'm sorry."

He'd been giving her the chance to walk away? "Danny…again, I need to ask," she semi-repeated her earlier question, "are you crazy? We've spent nearly every free minute together for two weeks. I've done things with you, sexually"—her cheeks warmed—"that not only have I never done before, but I've never even imagined. I'm here. I'm in. I was beginning to think you didn't want me in that way." The admission felt sour leaving her mouth, but it was true all the same. A sigh left her throat when he placed her hand over his hard length.

"Didn't think I wanted you? Really? Can barely breathe with wanting you. I work with a bunch of men, training them for combat, and a memory of your naked tits comes to mind and that's what happens to me." His eyes shifted to where her hand gripped him. "Coming to you each night...fuck, gets me through each damn day."

His burning eyes held her captive as he pulled his shirt over his head and dropped it to the floor. Like Pavlov's dog, her body instantly responded to seeing all that rippled muscle and satiny skin.

"So sexy when your eyes get wide and you lick your lips." He grinned. "Feels like you wanna eat me." Danny unsnapped his jeans, and the sound of the zipper echoed in the quiet room. "But I'm the wolf tonight, Little Red."

Swift moves left Julie naked and flat on her back with nothing more than a Danny Marcus blanket to keep her warm. Perfect.

SHE'S BEEN WAITING for me. Danny looked at the beautifully naked woman beneath him. *Never again.*

Gray eyes penetrated him as their bare skin touched. Trust, understanding, commitment. She was *in*. In his heart, he'd known it the whole time, but his damn head had needed to hear it. Now that he had, he was never letting her go.

"So beautiful," he whispered before he leaned in and took her lips. Claimed them.

Her lids slid shut and her mouth opened on a sigh, allowing his tongue to enter and slide against hers. He deepened the kiss and swallowed her moan as his hand slid from her cheek to her breast. Kneading the flesh, he plucked her nipple, loving how she responded to his every touch.

"Can't get enough of your tits. Can spend days sucking them, touching them, watching you squirm." His attention moved to the other breast, and her body arched as she fed herself into his mouth. "Greedy." He chuckled but didn't leave her hanging.

With his mouth on her chest, Julie sifted her nails through his hair and across his shoulder blades. Her touch, as always, lit him up, sending electricity thrumming through his veins, straight to his cock.

"More, Danny."

Her words may have sounded sweet, but they were no less of a command than any he'd dish out. So he gave more. His hand looped around her wrists, keeping them restrained above her head, while his other hand dragged down her slim torso, between her thighs, and into her wetness. She gasped, and he grinned.

"Drenched, honey."

"You make me feel so good," she admitted with an unfocused stare. "I need my hands. I want to touch you too."

"Can't happen, baby, not this time." He slid one finger, then two into her core, applying perfect pressure to her clit with his thumb. An erotic as fuck moan tore from her throat, hardening his dick further. Nope, there was no way she could touch him, not if he wanted to last. "You're so close, I can feel it. Your pussy is squeezing my fingers. It wants this." He rotated his wrist, lifting his finger to her special spot, and rubbed.

"Oh... yes... that feels...oh." Her body trembled as her pelvis arched, reaching...reaching for release that he'd gladly give.

"Give it to me," he hoarsely demanded into her neck as his thumb stroked the sensitive bundle of nerves between her legs.

And she did. The way her body trembled around him was breathtaking, made him feel like a king. Now he wanted to feel like her man.

"Gonna take you, Julie," he promised. "I'm gonna make you mine."

"I've been yours," she croaked. Julie wrapped her legs around him as he moved to grab a condom from his jeans. "What are you doing?"

"Protection, honey."

"I'm on the pill." Julie's eyes were clear suddenly, the haze from her orgasm gone, and she seemed damn ready to make a decision that affected her life.

"You sure?"

"Nothing between us means nothing between us."

Holy shit, he'd never fucked bareback. His parents and older brother had drilled that lesson in hard. But he wasn't just fucking Julie, was he?

"Nothing between us," he confirmed as he claimed her mouth once again. When his cock was at her entrance and the wetness grazed the tip, Danny lost his breath. "Fuuuck."

He entered her slowly, inch by inch, reveling in her warmth, loving the way she squeezed him. He claimed her gently, as if she were porcelain, holding back in order to keep her safe.

"Damn it, Danny, more!" Julie arched her back, thrust her hips to his, and grinded against him, looking for everything he was holding back.

Her actions snapped him out of the bareback-bliss he'd been trapped in and dumped him exactly where he'd spent his entire sexual career—on *top*. "Sorry, honey, it's just...your cunt feels so fucking good. Gotta give a man a break when you take him to heaven for the first time. But you want more? I'll give you more."

He felt her blush right in his balls as he pulled nearly the whole way out, then slammed back in.

"Ahhh, God."

"How's that for *more,* baby?" He repeated the move and got the same response.

"Don't. Ever. Stop." Julie panted each time their bodies were flush together.

Hot and wet, soft and sweet—*home*. Danny had had plenty of sex, but never once had he found home. Just as that thought tiptoed through his mind, Julie's pussy squeezed him. Her climax was building.

"Danny, oh, it's never felt like this...before."

She closed her eyes so quickly, he assumed she hadn't meant to vocalize that thought.

"No, baby, it hasn't. But this"—he sank deep into her warmth—"is us. Always gonna be."

He lowered his weight onto her, thrusting in and out until her pussy coated him in her warm release, then he finally let go. The climax that had been building from the second he'd felt her bare—the one that had traveled from the base of his spine to his balls, that had twisted up every nerve in his body into a sphere of energy—released from him into her, taking with it a part of him he was sure he'd never get back. He was certain he'd never want it back. That part was Julie's. He was Julie's.

CHAPTER FIVE

Thank God For That

"I SPOKE WITH my brother today."

"How is Neal?"

Julie adored Danny's *baby* brother, although at twenty years old and standing six foot three, he wasn't such a baby anymore. They'd met at Thanksgiving a few months earlier when Danny took Julie down to North Carolina to spend the holiday with his family. She fell for both Marcus men almost instantly. Mr. Marcus—Allan, as he demanded she call him—was practically a carbon copy of Danny, just older and a bit more refined. In the man's eyes was loss but not defeat, and throughout the long weekend, he shared fatherly wisdom that Julie had forgotten she'd missed getting from her own dad.

Neal was a different story altogether. Young, spirited, and carefree, he was quick with inappropriate jokes. He'd had Julie laughing from their introduction to their hug good-bye. The only time his serious side showed was when his engine company was called out on an emergency. A huge fire had broken out in a small town nearby and the station needed more hands on deck, so Neal left in a hurry. He came home twelve hours later, the glimmer snuffed from his eyes and the spark erased from his tongue. The next morning, however, he was back to himself, as if the day before had never happened. Both Allan and Danny took Neal's change of mood in stride, so after giving him a hug, Julie had stepped back that day and followed Danny's lead in giving the younger guy his space.

Back in their home, Danny poured her a glass of wine. "He's great. He's Neal, you know? Anyway, talked to a few of his buddies in Baltimore, and they said they'd keep me posted on any positions that become available in the local stations." Every time Danny spoke of his future, his eyes lit up like the fires he intended to battle.

Soon after they had started dating, Danny explained that he had no intentions of re-uping once his four-year contract with the army was complete. To say his admission made her happy would have been an understatement. When he mapped out his plan to follow in his father's footsteps and become a firefighter like Allan and Neal, some of her excitement was extinguished. Fires were dangerous, but she kept her anxieties to herself. After ten months of dating—ten overwhelmingly happy, incredibly intense, sexy, mind-blowing months of dating—the thought of him running *into* burning buildings instead of *from* them scared the shit out of her.

"What's the matter, honey?"

"What?" Julie stared up into the gaze that claimed her heart more and more each day.

"You're biting your upper lip, baby." Danny's roughened thumb stroked across her lip, releasing it from its imprisonment. "Bottom lip means you're wanting; top means you're worrying. Talk to me."

This is it. You need to tell him; no more dancing around the issue. In all the time they had spent together—at Chester's while she worked, at her house on the nights they stayed together, the trip to meet his family, the hours of talking and making love until the sun came up, fucking when gentle just wasn't enough for either of them, the possessiveness he emitted as he watched her tending bar, the jealousy she felt when women tried to flirt with him and she could do nothing but serve drinks and smile—in all that time spent loving *on* one another, they had never professed it *to* one another.

The lack of words hadn't been an issue, not even a thought really, as they were affectionate and vocal about their pleasure in each other. She'd say she loved his touch, his laugh, his eyes. He returned with he loved her smile, her lips, her heart, and her sweet pussy, but never had they crossed that final threshold. He was hers, and she his. They were young, but she believed in him, in them. She knew in her heart that he would never hurt her. Yet each time the image of him surrounded by flames crossed her mind, she got breathless, panicked, and petrified. The idea of losing him was more frightening than any of the losses she'd dealt with before. Emotions built up in her chest like champagne bubbles, trying to reach the surface without care as to which got there first.

"I'm yours, Danny, and I love you," she blurted. "I'll support you and your decisions, but I've got to be honest, the thought of you fighting fires scares the shit out of me. The thought of losing you…I won't let myself go there."

Danny's chest expanded. His eyes softened the way they did when he made slow, sweet love to her, the way they did when she wrapped her arms around his neck and

73

pulled him down so she could kiss him, the way they did the first time she'd made him blueberry pancakes after learning from his father that blueberry was his favorite. It was his *love* look, and she did, in fact, love it.

"You love me, huh?" His long, muscled arms circled around her waist, securing her in a hug, a feeling she longed for when they were apart. "Well, thank God for that, honey, because I've been in love with you since the morning I woke up hung over with nothing but a fuzzy memory, a glass of water, and a couple of aspirin."

What? Astonished by his admission, she stood silently for a beat.

"Don't look so surprised, Jules. You've known that you love me if not just as long, then close enough," he murmured into the top of her head. "I learned back in the beginning of our relationship that if I had doubts, I'd ask you instead of assuming. No doubts here. Just didn't wanna rush you, sweetheart, make you admit something you weren't ready for. That being said, I was only giving you until July to come to terms with it. It was killing me not to tell you every fuckin' day how much you owned me."

"J-July?" Julie stammered.

"Yeah, honey, July. You couldn't get those words that I've seen floating around in your eyes out of your mouth by our one-year anniversary, I was going in after them."

An unrestrained laugh burst from Julie's chest. "Danny, oh my God, baby, I wasn't holding back." The sharp glare he gave her made her adjust the statement. "Okay, I wasn't holding back intentionally. Clearly I love you, you said yourself you knew it. Guess what? I knew you felt the same about me. I just... I was scared to admit it, okay?"

Out loud, her reasons sounded a bit juvenile, but after what she had been through, juvenile worked for her.

"Talk to me, honey," Danny repeated.

"I've lost the only people I ever loved. Admitting, even to myself, how I felt about you scared me. Deep down I knew my feelings, hell, on the surface I knew them, but I couldn't voice them without feeling selfish."

"Selfish?" He cocked his head. "In what way?"

"I guess I was scared if I admitted my feelings, something would happen to you. And you, Danny Marcus, are the most amazing man I've ever met. The world deserves to have you in it." The feel of his rough hand on her cheek was enough to get the butterflies flapping in her belly.

"I'm certainly not complaining, baby, but what changed your mind?"

She inhaled deeply before letting the breath out slowly. "In a couple of months, you'll be discharged from the army and start the Fire Training Academy. You're going to be a firefighter."

The process was a lengthy one though. The application process took almost twelve months, then he'd go through twenty-one weeks of training. Afterward, he needed to find a job. Hopefully his brother's friend would pull through on that part.

Sighing, Julie closed her eyes, reached for the strength deep within her, and finished her thought. "You're going to fight fires, Danny. It's fucking dangerous. I can't lose you. I won't. So if you're going to do this, you'll damn well do it knowing I love you with my whole heart."

INCREDIBLE. THAT WAS the only word he could use to describe the feeling surging through his body. Hmm, maybe invincible, indestructible, and head-over-fucking-ass in love. Yeah, those would work too.

"Honey?" He reluctantly placed a few inches between their bodies while keeping her hands firmly grasped in his own. "I know how much you love me. I feel it every single day, deep down in the marrow of my bones. I feel it because you own me." He moved one hand to her chin and tilted her head back so he could look directly into her gray stare. "You…own…me. You're part of the reason I'm on the path I've chosen. If I'm not fighting to make our world safer for you, the least I can do is watch over our little section of it."

"But—"

"No, babe, listen, I know you're scared. Firefighters, like soldiers, risk their lives every time they go into the field." He slid his hand up her cheek and through her silken hair until he cupped her head. "But my father was a fighter, and Neal is too. The protective gear that's issued is state-of-the-art stuff, honey. Plus, why do you think the training is so intensive? It's gonna be fine. I'm gonna be fine. Promise." The small hairs on the back of his neck prickled when he uttered that last part. Danny didn't make promises he couldn't keep, another lesson his father had drilled into him as a child, but Julie needed reassurance, and Danny believed in himself enough to make the statement.

"Don't make promises you can't keep," she muttered before wrapping her arms tightly around him.

Smart woman, Julie was. The only response he gave was a tighter hug and a silent prayer that he'd never make a liar of himself.

CHAPTER SIX

Now You've Got Her

"SCARED OR LIBERATED?" Chester asked as he slid an icy mug of beer in front of Danny.

"What's that?" Danny barely heard the question because his eyes were glued to Julie's firm, Daisy Duke-covered ass as she made her way from behind the bar to the storage room. The woman's body could tempt a priest, and he was no saint.

Chester's deep chuckle pulled Danny's mind straight out of the gutter. "I asked if you were scared or liberated? Every soldier feels at least one of those things at the end of their service, son. So which is it?"

The question wasn't one he'd given any conscious thought to, but it had definitely swirled around in his chest over the past few weeks.

"Peace," Danny finally replied.

He'd joined the army as a boy on a revenge mission. He'd wanted to avenge his brother's death, his mother's demise, and his family's pain. He had dragons to slay and monsters to kill. What he got instead was a sense of unity, the strength of knowledge, and an understanding of his brother that he'd have never gotten had he not committed himself to the armed forces. Jeff had died believing in his country, fighting for his people, and honoring his oath. After four years, Danny was leaving the army as a grown man with his demons slain and his heart no longer numb. That last part had to do with the strawberry-blonde beauty that had invaded his life and colored it in a way he'd never noticed was missing.

"Peace," the bar owner repeated. "I like that."

Chester had become not just a mentor but a friend to Danny over the past year. When he learned that Chester had been one of Julie's father's friends, one of the people who'd kept tabs on Julie after her parents perished in Mexico City, Danny had felt a sense of gratitude to him. But when Julie explained just how the man had helped, that gratitude turned into unwavering loyalty.

"How did you end up at Chester's?" Danny had asked over coffee and cinnamon rolls one morning.

The faraway look Julie sometimes wore when the past caught up with her flashed across her face, but instead of being paired with tear-filled eyes, it came with a smile. "Ahh, Chester. Apparently he came to the funeral." She shrugged. "Honestly, I don't remember most of that day. When we spoke after the fact, he explained that he didn't approach me—something about too many people suffocating me with *their* need to feel good about themselves." She and Danny laughed, knowing Chester would absolutely say something like that. "About a year after my parent's deaths, I heard from Chester for the first time."

"Wait." Danny's head snapped to attention. "What the fuck? He left you alone for nearly a goddamn year? What kind of an irresponsible son-of-a—"

79

"Danny." Julie placed her hand on his arm, and the simple contact lowered his blood pressure instantly. "I said it was the first I'd heard from him, not the first he'd checked on me. Remember what I told you the first night we got together? I was never really alone. Apparently Chester and my dad knew each other from boot camp and infantry training. They went separate ways after that, but they remained close. Chester stayed in the marines for many years after my dad got out, and apparently, Chester has people."

"People?"

"Yeah, people. I didn't ask many questions, but according to him, during one of our first conversations, his people had been keeping an eye on me. When the 'well-wishers' and the 'sympathy parade' got back to their real lives, he knew I'd need him. So he waited. Said he was a little surprised that it took as long as it did, but then again, he knew how amazing my parents were."

"Okay..." Danny stretched out the word, not sure where the story was leading.

"One night, after I got home from work—I'd been waitressing seven days a week at a joint where they let me bartend two shifts out of twelve for extra cash and experience—I had a message on the answering machine from one Chester Murray. He explained who he was, how he knew me, and that he expected me—expected me—at his bar the following day or he'd send his people to collect me. That was all left in a sixty second message."

Danny chuckled. "What'd you do?"

"What do you mean? You've heard his voice. I asked some people I worked with about his place to make sure it wasn't too seedy, and I went to his bar the next day. Sure as shit didn't want a man that sounded like that sending anyone to my house."

Danny laughed. His woman was smart and had no idea how funny she was. Beautiful was something. Funny was something. Smart, funny, and beautiful was practically unheard of. "What happened when you got there?"

Julie's eyes had danced with the memory. "I was dead on my feet when I walked into Chester's Bar. That was back when I was pulling as many double shifts as I could in order to keep my mind occupied and my body out of this house."

Danny thought back to when they had met and her schedule was jam-packed with hours. He remembered thinking she must have needed money, before he learned about her family. Then he realized she needed the hours, not the cash.

"Anyway, I shuffled up to the bar and had my very first encounter with infamous Bunny." They simultaneously rolled their eyes. "From the scathing look she gave me the moment I asked to speak with Chester, you would have thought I'd shoved a picture of her, sans makeup and hairspray, in her face and threatened to release it to the media. She claimed he wasn't there and that I'd wasted my trip. Thankfully his office door was open and when he heard me leaving my name, he came out to introduce himself, or I would have never come back. Bunny was a raving, territorial bitch. I mean, Chester's great and all, but the man is old enough to be my dad. Eww!" She shivered. "I'm not that kind of girl."

Julie explained how she'd turned down the job Chester offered her, but the old guy refused to give up on her. After a handful of offers over a handful of months, he wore her down and got her working under his roof. Respect for the guy who never gave up on a *brother's* kid was something Danny would never forget.

Chester spoke, bringing Danny's mind from out of the past. "The question, and it's somethin' you don't need to answer as much as you just need to think on, is if you found your peace and you found your woman, then why are you running from one thrill-seeking mission to the next?"

The cool liquid turned to ice as it hit the back of Danny's throat, frosting a path straight down to his stomach. "What the hell are you talking about? Firefighting runs in my blood." Danny grunted. "It's a goddamn honor."

Pressing open palms against the bar top, Chester leaned forward, towering over the scarred pine. "I recommend you *think* on it, Marcus." Chester's next words came out slowly, and Danny couldn't tell if Chester was speaking slowly on purpose or if it just seemed that way because of the truth he saw in the man's eyes. "You made it through the army, boy. Four years of trainin', fightin', and prayin' that you'd make it out differently than Jeff. And here you sit, drinkin' a beer on the night of your discharge. Four motherfuckin' years, Danny.

"You think that was hard?" he continued. "You think signing up for a war and leavin' your family was difficult? Tryin' to keep your mind focused in order to get your brothers to safety…you did that daily, no?" Chester placed two shot glasses on the bar, filled each with tequila, and slid one in Danny's direction before nodding at Julie, who was tending to customers on the deck outside. "Now you got her. Her love, her pain, her loss, her happiness…all that is with you on every single call you get. Firefighters are amazing, boy. It takes heart, soul, and skill. You have that. You gave that. Four years you gave that. You sure you still wanna give it? Knowing what you have to lose…knowing what she could lose?"

Nausea churned in Danny's gut. What the hell? This was his plan, their plan. He had always planned to be a firefighter like his father. The army had been off course, not this. "Chester, you're wrong, man—"

The older guy raised a hand. "I don't need answers tonight. In fact, I don't need answers ever. It's just a question I've been thinkin' about. Do what makes you happy, and take care of our girl."

CHAPTER SEVEN

Took Tommy Jones

"SERIOUSLY, THAT WAS the best Christmas I've had in years," Julie said through a yawn. She unfolded her cramped legs, stretching yet again in the passenger seat of Danny's Ford Ranger. The sleep she'd just woken from faded away as memories from the past few days replayed in her mind like the holiday music Danny's father had insisted play throughout the house.

"You say that every year." Danny grinned, his hand rubbing her upper thigh and sending tingles to her core.

"And I mean it every year." She giggled.

They'd left North Carolina at the crack of dawn, and six hours later, they were almost home to a slush-covered Baltimore. After four years of marriage, the heat between them still snuffed out even the coldest temperatures.

"I love that you love spending time with my dad and Neal, honey." Danny squeezed her thigh, his eyes never leaving the road.

Julie gripped his hand. "Danny, they're *my* family too, and they have been for quite some time now. Being with them..." She sighed.

How could she put into words what Danny had given her when he gave her his last name? It sounded cliché, but she hadn't just gotten a husband—she'd gotten a father, a brother, and an extended family of sorts. She got holidays back, something she'd thought gone forever. She got fatherly phone calls when she was feeling ill. She got a brotherly teasing when the situation arose, something she'd never known she was missing. While she'd never had the opportunity to meet Danny's older brother, Jeff, or his mother, Renee, she still felt their love when she was in the Marcus home and she felt their loss while with the Marcus men.

"Being with them," she continued, "brings me more comfort and happiness than you'll ever know. Thank you for sharing them with me." Even with his hand under hers, she was powerless to stop him as his palm inched up her jean-clad thigh to the seam between her legs.

"Everything I have is yours, honey," he muttered as his middle finger pressed against the denim. "Everything you have is mine. We made those vows. We honor them." His voice was rough as his left hand white-knuckled the steering wheel. "Unbutton your pants, baby. Gimme what's mine. We'll be home in no time. Neither of us is getting out of this fucking car until the windows are steamed and we both come… at least once."

By the time he threw the truck in park, Julie was coming down from her first climax.

"Mmm, you could teach a course on one-handed-orgasm-giving while driving," she said.

"Sure the DMV wouldn't look too kindly upon that, babe." Danny smiled, unclicking his seatbelt.

Julie's eyes settled on the bulge in her husband's jeans. The man was sex personified. Just his heated looks got her wet and ready.

"That lower lip has always been your tell, Jules... want. Question is, how do I want you to take me? In that sexy mouth of yours or in that tight pussy?"

Either one was perfect to her. She found pleasure in giving him his.

The driver's seat slid back. "Fuck me, baby. Now."

Excitement traveled through her blood as she moved from her seat to his. Her jeans had already been unbuttoned and pulled halfway down her hips. She just needed to slide them off one leg and move her panties to the side. He felt so heavy in her hand, so thick, she almost wished he'd chosen a blow job—until she lined him up to her entrance and sank down. Then she thanked her lucky stars he'd wanted to fuck.

"Oh oh, God, Danny. You feel so..."

"Ride me, honey, ride my cock." He grunted, thrusting his pelvis into hers.

His hands felt amazing on her skin. His tight grip on her ass would no doubt leave marks, marks that they'd admire when they made love later that night. He pulsed into her, and she tightened around him, her release within her grasp.

"Can feel you, baby, so close. Tight little cunt is squeezing me. Fuck, Julie, fuck..."

His thumb swiped at her clit, and bliss hit, stealing her breath and pounding her heart. His orgasm reignited hers as he held her tighter until his tremors stopped.

"You were right," she teased, lightly touching her lips to his. "The windows are steamed up and we both came."

Chuckling, Danny nuzzled her nose. "You, more than once."

———————————

LAUGHING, SHE UNLOCKED their front door while he carried their luggage over the threshold. "I could have carried a bag or two, you know."

"First of all"—Danny dropped the overstuffed duffle bags and roll-away suitcase on the tiled entrance floor—"my woman doesn't carry heavy shit; you know this. Second"—he waved at the collection of luggage—"the fact that we even had this much crap for a four-day trip is in-fuckin-sane, honey."

Julie stared at Danny. His jeans were unsnapped, shirt unbuttoned, hair screaming that he'd just gotten fucked in the front seat of his truck. The man was so sexy it was sinful, and it was natural. "Not all of us can wake up in the morning and look like that." She pointed at him.

"What do you mean?" A slow smirk creased his mouth, the smirk that said he knew exactly what she was talking about but wanted to hear her say it.

Danny wasn't stupid or blind; he knew he what he looked like, but he wasn't arrogant about it. As he'd said in the past, "Being attractive is good and all, but having the woman I'm in love with look at me with such carnal desire, like she could pull out a spoon, drag it across my flesh, and taste only hot sex and sweet promise, is better than a hundred women vying for my attention."

With answers like that, how could she ever deny the man anything?

Shaking her head, she pressed her lips together, trying and failing to keep her smile hidden. "I mean, you're the most beautiful man I've ever seen. Seriously, you're gorgeous, sexy…" Danny's grin widened, so Julie decided to rein his ego in a bit. "Hell, you're pretty, sweetheart. You'd make a beautiful girl." When Danny's brows snapped together, Julie saw his intensions and dropped her purse. But even as she backed away from what was sure to be relentless tickle torture, she continued to tease, "So pretty with your long lashes and big hazel eyes. I'd call you Danielle if you were a girl."

"Run, Julie," Danny warned.

Julie screeched and complied, running through the hallway and up the stairs. She didn't get more than a foot into their bedroom before she was lifted off the floor and tossed onto the bed.

"Hope you don't have to pee, honey," Danny warned as his fingers met her bare skin and the tickling began. Peals of laughter danced between them as they rolled around the mattress. "What's the matter, baby? This girl too strong for you?"

After minutes of playing and Julie struggling to keep her bladder from giving up, the phone rang. "D-Danny. Danny, the phone," she stammered between rounds of hiccups and giggles. "The phone's ringing."

"Oh no, you started this. You think I'm gonna let the phone finish it? Tell me I'm the supreme master, and I'll stop."

"Never." She attempted to roll to her side as the answering machine clicked on.

"You've reached the Marcus's. We're probably avoiding you, so leave a message and we'll call you later," the outgoing message recited.

"Danny, Julie, are you there?" Danny's father's voice was wrong. The sound of terror in it was so present, it felt tangible. "Please, if you're there—"

Danny lunged for the phone and yanked it off of its cradle. "Dad?" His voice echoed, the answering machine playing both his voice and his father's.

"Daniel, oh, God, Daniel…oh my God."

"Dad, what's wrong? We just left you this morning …literally just got home."

A knot formed in Julie's stomach, one she hadn't felt in over six years, but one she recognized immediately. On her knees, she crawled to Danny's side, resting one hand on his back as the other twisted in the bed sheet.

"Neal…it's Neal," Allan said.

They'd said good-bye to Neal the night before because he'd had to report for his shift at the station. Forty-eight hours on, one-hundred-twenty off was the rotation Neal was on for the month. Danny's schedule had an extra twenty-four hours off built into the rotation, making the trip to North Carolina convenient. So they'd said their "see-ya-laters," and off Neal went. Apparently a two-alarm fire broke out in the early morning. Faulty Christmas lights, old batteries in the smoke detectors—the age-old recipe for disaster. Julie saw the stories on the news every year, and every year her heart broke for the families who'd lost everything on Christmas. Every year she prayed for the firefighters, including her husband, who got called out on the holiday, wishing them a safe return home.

"WHAT ABOUT NEAL?" Danny's flat tone was colder than the temperature outside.

"They got the kids out." Allan sounded detached, matter-of-fact. "All four of them. They got the mom and the new puppy to safety…but when he went back in for the father…" Allan's voice cracked.

"What the fuck?"

Danny knew his brother like the back of his hand. He knew Neal had probably been one of the first into the burning house and searching for life. Where some of his coworkers' excelled at caring for the rescued, Neal's gift was searching out victims. His brother was thorough, and if the knowledge that Neal could have missed someone sliced through Danny, he could only imagine what it must have done to his brother. Blood rushed through his ears, muting the sound of his father's voice, words he needed to hear but prayed would stop.

"Who'd he take with him?" Firefighters never entered a burning building alone. The answer would tell Danny if Neal had known how bad the situation was before reentering the building.

"Took Tommy Jones with him."

Tears burned Danny's eyes as his hands balled into fists. His brother had known. Tommy was one of the best in the battalion; he'd been Neal's mentor. Neal knew if anything went wrong, Tommy would be there to get the victim to safety.

"Why'd they let him go back in? He's just a kid," Danny screamed.

"He's one of the best, Daniel. Don't you dare take that away from him. Besides, it was two houses, son, all hands on. Neal and Tommy went in with backup on the ground working their balls off to put out the flames." Allan's voice trembled. "Got into a Mayday situation."

Danny gulped air, trying to swallow around the lump in his esophagus. "How?"

"Tommy and the victim were already out, on the first rung of the ladder…second story. Floor gave out under Neal. Fucking floor gave out, Danny. He never had a chance; my boy never had a chance."

Warmth seeped from Danny's closed eyes as the phone dropped from his hand. His baby brother, his comic relief, his closest friend…gone.

"Dad?" Julie's voice was thick with emotion, but Danny still couldn't open his eyes. "I'm so sorry… just so, so sorry. We-We're heading back down. Okay?"

"Jules," his father croaked, "I don't know how this happened. Two of my boys…gone. Please drive carefully. I love you both. Take care of my son, please."

"We love you too." She sniffled. "Be there by tonight."

The sharp tone indicated that the answering machine had stopped recording. It also reminded Danny that the entire conversation had been taped, therefore there would be no way to convince himself that it didn't really happen. Julie kneeled before him, her palms on either side of his face. He knew her hands were always soft and cool, but he couldn't feel her touch. He saw her lips moving but couldn't hear her voice. He was numb, cold, dazed.

"…Then I'll get you and we'll leave, okay?"

He nodded, not knowing what he'd agreed to and not caring as long as he could stay in the darkness that had taken hold the moment his father told him his brother was gone.

"Be careful, sweetheart. Sit tight."

If seconds ticked by, then they could have been minutes. If they were minutes, they could have been hours. Time didn't exist in the black where his mind had traveled. The scales no longer balanced between life and death with his mother and both brothers in heaven and he and his father in hell. How could he make sense of a life where those who saved others perished so young, their existence fading before their lives ever truly began? What made him so fucking special that he still stood when both of his brothers had fallen? He fought in war. He fought in fire. Why? Why?

"Danny, sweetheart? We're here, baby." Julie's warmth penetrated his skin. "We're back at your dad's."

Back in North Carolina? How in the hell? "How... when?"

"We just got here. I got us packed with fresh clothing, made sure you were re-buttoned, then walked you to the truck. Once the house was locked up, I drove us here. That's how." Her eyes were bloodshot and filled with tears, but her tone was strong and fearless. "As you like to say, 'We took vows, baby,' for better or worse. This is *worse*, this is indescribable, but I'm here with you, Danny. I'm not gonna let you down, and I'll never let you go. It's gonna be horrible, but we'll get through this together.

His mind spun with awe, with shock, with pain, but also with the inability to form words. He squeezed her hand, brought it to his lips, and gave it a simple kiss. That was all he had left to offer in that moment, so he gave it to her.

"Come on, your dad's probably waiting on us. Although judging by the car in the drive, I can see he isn't alone."

The late-model Mercedes belonged to Anita, his father's girlfriend. Allan had formally introduced her to Danny and Julie just a few days prior, but they had spoken over the phone over the past few months. Anita was the first woman Danny's dad had gotten serious with since Danny's mother died, and Danny was happy his father had moved on with such a kind woman. Seeing her car in the drive made him feel lighter. He couldn't stand the thought of his dad being alone, not even for a minute.

With Julie's cool fingers laced through his, they entered his childhood home. How could it be that they had left the house only that morning? After loading their car and having coffee and waffles with his dad, Allan had given them tight embraces and made them promise to call the minute they arrived in Baltimore. He said he'd miss seeing their faces, and Danny joked that Anita was probably waiting around the block for them to leave so she could come over and spend the day *making merry* since Allan insisted the woman didn't spend the night while the *kids* were under his roof.

Smiles. Laughter. Warmth. Things that had stayed in Danny's mind during the long ride home. But as he walked through the same doors they'd exited no more than fifteen hours prior, the place felt smothered in a dank chill. Shards of broken glass glittered on the tile floor, crunching with each step he and Julie took, announcing their presence without any need for words. The bookcases that Danny,

Neal, and their father built just months after Jeff's death and his mother's suicide—"much needed father-son time" his dad had called it—were lying face down and splintered. The dry wall where the cases used to stand held fist-sized holes with streaks of crimson.

"Dad?" Danny croaked, having never witnessed a breakdown of such violence.

When word had come of Jeff's death, his father drank, cried, and mourned. He explained to Danny and Neal that a real man felt his feelings, dealt with them, and continued to live. When his mother took her life, Allan grieved for his first love and helped his sons mourn the loss of their mother and deal with the fact that she had chosen to leave them. But this…Danny wasn't certain how much more loss his father could take. How much more loss he himself could bear.

"Son. Oh, God, son…you're here."

Wrapped in his father's loving arms, Danny knew he had reserves of strength left. He just needed to tap into them. For his dad, he could do it. Julie squeezed Danny's hand, and he realized they were still connected. Just as she'd promised, she hadn't let go. She nodded before releasing his hand.

Embracing his father, Danny whispered, "I'm here, Dad. We're gonna get through this and continue to live. Cause that's what real men do, yeah?"

"HE WAS ALREADY dead," Danny snarled at Tommy Jones, the firefighter who had gone back into the townhouse to rescue the last victim the night Neal died.

Julie reached out, attempting to calm Danny, but he brushed her away and jumped out of the chair he'd been sitting in. Tommy had called the Marcus house earlier that morning and requested a visit with Allan and Danny. It had been two days since the fire, two days since they arrived home in Baltimore, made love in the Ranger, and chased each other around their house until her sides hurt from laughter. It felt like months, but it was two damn days.

The funeral was planned for the following afternoon—no viewing, just a service followed by the burial. In the meantime, Julie and Anita took turns fielding calls and turning away visitors at Allan's and Danny's requests. The men had insisted that the day of the funeral would be a circus and they didn't need to "entertain the monkeys" until then. But Tommy's request to visit was honored since he was the last one to see Neal alive. So there they sat— Allan, Anita, Danny, Tommy and Julie—around the kitchen table, full but untouched coffee cups, loaded but unspoken questions.

"Yeah," Tommy confirmed, "the victim was already dead when we got to him."

"Explain," Allan, a retired fire chief from the very station where Tommy and Neal worked, demanded.

"Apparently the husband and wife had been sleeping in different bedrooms. He was a drinker, situation wasn't pleasant, divorce was in the cards, but they hadn't yet told the kids." Tommy shook his head. "Fire broke out when everyone was sleeping. Mother woke to the smell of smoke and started screaming. She thought she woke everyone. A neighbor must have called 9-1-1, thank the Lord, 'cause by the time she got up, the entire back of the first floor was consumed in flames.

"We got there, got in, and Neal grabbed two of the kids right out of their beds. They couldn't get out of their rooms—fire was right outside their fucking door. The mom was stuck in another bedroom with the two other kids. Got them out. The kids started talking about the puppy who was stuck in the crate in the front of the house. Two guys went in and got the dog...in and out fast, no worries. That's when the wife screamed for her husband." Tommy's eyes drifted between Danny and Allan. "You know Neal would go back in."

Allan nodded woodenly.

"He'd been on the second floor, seen the devastation there," Tommy said. "The minute he screamed he was going in, I followed. According to the wife, the spare bedroom was in the back of the house."

"Where the fire started," Danny stated the obvious.

"Yeah," Tommy nodded, swallowing hard. Julie could see the man was reliving each minute as he spoke.

"We got in quick enough, or so we thought. The victim was lying on the bed, unresponsive." Tommy looked at both men. "You know how it is—we didn't even try to wake him. I just threw him over my shoulder and headed back to the window. The floor was so fucking hot, it was beginning to buckle and smoke was pluming through the vents. We thought we had time, Neal and I. I hurried. I just needed another step or two, and he could have gotten out. I was on the second rung when I heard it...I felt it... the whole damn house shook. The fucking floor caved in.

"The mayday call was executed flawlessly, but the fall was too bad, the fire too out of control." Tommy rubbed his hands over his face. "Thing of it is, the father must of had a heart attack and died before the fire ever started. The family's already received the preliminary autopsy results. There was no smoke in his lungs, but he did suffer from a massive cardiac event."

"So what you're telling me is"—Danny paced, his hands clenched into tight fists—"my brother died trying to save a fucking dead man?"

Julie gasped as Danny's fist went through the wall, retracted, and punctured the drywall a second time.

Allan rose slowly, rounded the table, and stopped in front of his remaining child. "No, son, what Tommy is telling us is Neal died doing what he lived to do. We're firefighters. We protect those who need us when their lives are in the balance. Those little children didn't know their daddy had died. They only knew he was stuck in their house and couldn't get out. Neal got him out, son. Dead or alive, that man was rescued."

AS PREDICTED, NEAL'S funeral was well attended. Okay, well attended may have been a grand understatement. Hundreds of people came to pay their respects to the fallen hero, the former high school quarterback, the town heartthrob, the soldier's brother, the fire chief's son, and the all-around amazing man Neal Marcus had been. The eulogies were both heartbreaking and warming as people sobbed and giggled over the stories shared. When Danny spoke of his baby brother, Julie found it almost painful to breathe. It wasn't until Allan wrapped his strong arm around her and pulled her in tight that she exhaled for what seemed to be the first time in days.

"He's gonna be all right," Allan whispered.

"But will you?" Julie countered.

Her father-in-law drew in a deep breath and let his eyes close for a second before he stared at the podium where his son stood. "A parent never gets over losing a child. Ever. And I've lost two. I won't be the same man I was—I can't be—but it's my job as a parent to continue on. To love Danny, to love you, and to be grateful for the time I have left on this earth. Memories are for the living, and I wouldn't trade one minute of my time with my boys. So yeah, darling, I'll be sad, but I'll be okay."

"I love you, Allan," Julie murmured. "Thank you for giving me Danny and for making me feel like one of yours."

"You are mine, sweetie."

If she never saw another casket lowered into the ground, it would be too soon. Everyone left the cemetery and headed back to the Marcus home, but Danny needed more time. So she stood by the newly buried plot, wrapped her arms around her stoic husband, and let her thoughts wander. Other than the eulogy, he hadn't spoken much since his outburst the day before, and she didn't want to push him. She didn't fear Danny and knew he'd never lift a finger in anger, but she knew grief. She knew each person lived it differently. If he needed silence, she'd offer her support quietly.

"I don't mean to interrupt, but…I'm interruptin'."

The familiar voice blanketed Julie, and an audible sigh escaped her lips as she turned to see the man standing behind them.

CHAPTER EIGHT

Ended Up Being Your Ladder

DANNY'S HEAD JERKED up from the fresh dirt the second that deep voice hit his ears. Pivoting, he faced his friend, a man who had come to mean so much over the years, even though they didn't see nearly enough of each other since Danny and Julie had moved to Baltimore several years before.

"Chester... what? How did you know?"

The older man shook his head. His sorrow-filled eyes moved from Danny's face to the cemetery ground. "Your woman does a good job of keepin' me informed, boy. Always has."

Danny's gaze moved to Julie in time to see a small lift on the side of her mouth.

"How do think I always know the latest gossip from Chester's Bar? It certainly isn't from the few times a year we see him." Julie wrapped her arms around the man who'd been her salvation before Danny was ever in the picture, and squeezed. "The old guy loves to chat on the phone." Julie smiled upon releasing Chester. "Who knew?"

"Shh, that's supposed to be a secret," Chester said gruffly before turning his gaze back to Danny.

"You drove all the way down here from Laurel?" Danny asked, unable to hide the surprise he felt.

"Boy, I'd fly around the damn world if you guys needed me. Damn shame you don't know that yet."

Tears stung Danny's eyes as Chester pulled him in for a quick hug. The rich smell of Chester's leather coat permeated Danny's senses, reminding him of the first year Danny and Julie had spent in Laurel together.

"Are you done standing out here?" Chester asked.

Danny looked at Julie, who shrugged. Her unwavering support and understanding had been noticed and appreciated, even if he hadn't yet expressed it.

"Yeah, we're done," Danny said.

"You wanna go straight back to your dad's place, or you wanna go for a drink somewhere?"

Danny looked from Chester, to Julie, and back to Chester. It hadn't occurred to Danny not to go home, but now that the option had been presented, the thought of spending more time in that house felt just as confining as his brother's coffin had looked. "I'd love a drink, man. Jules, what do you say?"

Her small smile felt like sun he hadn't seen in months. "I say let's go for drinks, but we need to call your dad first. I don't want him to worry."

"Ahh, I got one of those mobile phone things in my truck," Chester gloated. "Feel all James Bond-ish. Call your pop, and we'll catch up. You look like you could use a talkin' to, and you know I can only give advice in my office."

"Your office?" Julie's brows arched.

"Yeah, Julie girl, my office…you know, my bar. But since we're a long ways from there, any bar will do. Just need a couple a drinks, and our boy won't know the difference."

The heavy laugh that left Danny's chest felt foreign, but something told him that a few hours with Julie and Chester was just what he needed to feel more like himself. At Chester's car, Danny called his dad and explained the situation. His father sounded a bit relieved and even told him to take his time.

"Follow us," Danny told Chester after he hung up. "There's a bar a few miles from here in the hotel."

Safely tucked in the Ranger with the engine idling and the heat blowing, Danny looked at his wife. "Honey, you called Chester."

The statement sounded simple, but he was so incredibly touched by her actions. Over the past few days—he'd lost count of how many—he'd been a wasteland, a void. And while Julie was grieving with him, sharing in his pain and feeling her own loss, she'd still managed to pack his suit before they'd left Baltimore, organize the funeral, keep him fed, and contact someone who was extremely important to them both.

"Yes, Danny, I did. He's family."

Danny let the word roll around in his head. He'd been lucky to have his own family, but with his mother and both of his brothers gone and a wife he loved more than life, the word *family* was taking on new shapes…new boundaries.

As if she could read his thoughts, her cool palm cupped his chin, keeping their eyes connected. "Family doesn't always have to come with blood. It only has to come with love." She leaned forward and pressed her lips to his.

For the first time since receiving his father's phone call, he felt her kiss. Christ, it felt good. More, he needed more.

Honk! A horn blared behind them. Chester's Jeep rolled up to their side, and he motioned for Danny to slide down his window. "Boy, not that I mind seein' you love on your woman, but I'd appreciate it more with my ass on a stool and a drink in my hand. So drive."

"IS IT POSSIBLE to still be hung-over?" Danny asked after swallowing two pain relievers and a large gulp of water.

"Anything's possible with the way you and Chester drank the other night." Julie rubbed his thigh with her right hand while keeping her left on the steering wheel.

It had been two days since Neal's funeral, and while the pain was razor sharp, Danny preferred it to the numbness he'd suffered before he laid his brother to rest. He welcomed the agony over the paralysis he'd felt in the years that followed Jeff's death. He could deal with hurting because it would lessen over time. He'd been through it, as had his wife. It was she who'd pulled him through to the other side the first time. He had been stuck in a revolving door of mourning, unable to get out of the cycle, and she somehow jammed the motor long enough for him to leave safely. She saved him then, and she saved him now.

When they'd gotten to the bar after the funeral, Chester opened a tab, ordered tequila shots and a couple pitchers of beer, and told the waitress to "keep the drinks coming till the *pretty boy* either passes out or pukes." While most of the conversation from that night had been coming back in dribs and drabs over the past forty-eight hours (due to the puking *and* passing out), there was one part Danny remembered quite clearly. It was something Chester had told Danny the night Danny got discharged from the army, something that had floated around in his subconscious for years but came to the surface only while sitting face-to-face with his old friend after placing his baby brother in the ground. Julie had gone to the hotel's front desk to book a room for Chester, seeing as the man had matched Danny drink for drink, shot for shot.

"Hey man," Danny slurred, "you remember what you said to me on my last night in uniform?" Danny remembered, even through his drunken vision, how incredibly sober Chester had looked in that moment.

"Yeah, boy, I do. Why?"

Danny nodded. "You asked why I was running from one thrill mission straight to another if I'd found my woman and my peace." Danny rubbed his eyes, trying to wipe away the alcohol-induced cloudy vision. "I was always supposed to be a fire fighter, Chester. It's in the Marcus blood, like loyalty, but when Jeff died, that loyalty split. I needed to fight for him, avenge him, become who he was so he was never forgotten. But after four years, I hadn't brought him back and I hadn't become him. I only lost parts of me. So I figured it was time to go back to my original plan, be the Marcus man I always dreamed I'd be. 'Cept I met her... my Julie. You told me that every time I took a call, I'd take her with me, but it's more than that, man. She's in every breath I take. Not sure it's fucking normal, so I've tried to ignore it. Tried to shove it down. But once again, feel like I'm doing a job tailored for someone else. Then Neal's accident…he lost his life. Lost his goddamn life. Hell, I'm thinking I need to stop tempting fate."

"What are you saying, Dan?" Chester's brow arched as he filled their glasses with beer.

"I'm saying I know I can walk outside and get hit by a bus tomorrow. Can have a weird accident and die. But I'd rather take those chances than continue doing a job that feels more like a familial obligation than a labor of love. Not when I'm putting her happiness on the line every single day."

It may have been the ridiculous amount of tequila running through Danny's blood, but he swore Chester's eyes softened. "Congratulations, son. Now you've found your peace."

The rest of the night disappeared down the toilet and into a black haze. According to Julie, the waitress had more than earned the generous tip she received. Chester phoned in his good-bye from his mobile early the next morning while on his way home to Laurel.

Now Julie was driving them home, and Danny watched her command his truck. Without alcohol fogging up his brain, he knew it was the right time to discuss their future. "I'm gonna quit the station, Jules."

Surprise worked its way over his wife's face. "Babe…" Julie sighed as she flipped on the turn signal and pulled over to the side of the quiet road. "Sweetie"—her clear gray eyes searched his—"this isn't a decision you should be making right now."

"It's not," Danny admitted. "You know I haven't been in love with my job since…well, almost the start. I told you I'd be okay. I promised you the gear was state of the art, and it is. But Neal still died. Can you honestly tell me that you won't panic every single time I go to work now, knowing there's a chance I won't come home?"

Julie cocked her head, utter confusion on her face as well as in her tone. "Dan, are you kidding me? I get sick to my stomach every time you leave for work. I vomited for the first few months after you left our house."

What the hell? How had he never known? Why had she never told him? "Julie, you never told me any of that. Why?"

"Because it wasn't your cross to bear. You run into burning buildings, and your goal is to get in and get out as fast as humanly possible while saving lives and containing the fire. The very last thing you need is having my fears on your back. So I do what all of the other spouses do—I cry with fear when you leave and with joy when you come home."

Chest tight with guilt over the blissful ignorance he'd hidden behind for years, Danny quickly unlatched his seatbelt, threw open the passenger door, and got out of the Ranger. As he stalked around to the driver's side of his truck, his future flashed before his eyes, and while he'd known it from the first time they'd met, it was never more clear than in that moment. All of the running he'd done, all of the danger he'd faced, all of the time he'd given—none of it filled his heart more than the woman who shared his life and his last name. She was the thrill he'd been seeking, and she'd been his for five years. Things were about to change.

Danny threw open the driver's side door and growled, "Get out of the car."

JULIE'S HEAD TIPPED back as her eyes met his. When she had offered to drive home from North Carolina in order to give Danny some much needed rest, he'd reluctantly accepted. His body had shut down within minutes of hitting the road. For two hours, the sound of his soft breathing brought her comfort as the miles ticked away. But awake, with raw determination blazing from his eyes, two things struck Julie. The first, it would take a lot more than a couple hours of sleep to remove the dark circles and soul-shredding grief from Danny's beautiful face. The second, it didn't matter how many flames her husband had fought; the fire burning in his eyes now had been missing for years. Shame *on you for being so blind*.

"Get...out...of...the...car. Now."

Her heart beat faster with his command. She found something about the way his voice deepened and his eyes darkened sexy as hell. Her body always seemed to follow before her mind had time to catch up. Hopping out of the Ranger, she closed the door, then grabbed his hand and followed him to the other side of the truck, away from the open road. As sparse as the traffic might have been, her husband never took chances with *her* safety.

"Seems like we got ourselves into a bit of a situation, honey. Seeing as I believe I'm the one who started the mess, I'm gonna be the first one to pull out the mop and start cleaning. But you can bet your sweet ass you'll be following me."

"All right, Mr. Clean, let's hear what's got you so whipped up." She smiled as she stood with her hands tucked into her winter coat pockets and her back pressed against the Ranger.

"Mr. Clean? Really? Come on, Jules, look at my hair. Hell, I have hair." Danny chuckled. "Don't look a thing like that guy."

Relief had overtaken her the second he stated his intent to leave firefighting behind. She would never have asked nor suggested he give up the career he believed ran in his veins, but he didn't seem to relish the job the way Allan and Neal did. She felt as if he was going to work halfhearted each shift. One didn't fight fires halfheartedly. Therefore, each call he went on ramped up her anxiety even further.

The humor was gone from his eyes, replaced with something akin to regret. "Seriously, honey, I fucked up. You told me back when we were dating that you were uncomfortable with my career path, and while I heard you speaking, I didn't listen to your words. I thought I knew it all. Had my shit planned out and found an amazing woman to be my life partner—"

His words gutted her. He hadn't fucked up. He was following a path he thought was his. His brother's death was devastating, but she didn't want it to make him question his every life choice. Sure, she lived in constant fear, but her parents had always told her that the person who loved her would never try to change her. She loved her husband. "Danny—"

"No, baby, hear me out, please." She nodded, and he continued. "You know where I went wrong? I didn't treat you like a partner. A lover, yes. A best friend, sure. But my life partner? No, honey, I screwed up on that part, and the mess began. I knew almost from the start that we were gonna spend forever together. I knew what you'd gone through and the loss you'd suffered. We should have discussed my path. It should have been ours."

Each word he spoke was balm to a piece of her soul, a piece that he'd unknowingly bruised years before, and was still tender to the touch.

With one hand on the truck's roof, Danny leaned in closer. "I apologize. I'm sorry that I led you instead of walking beside you. Seeing that look on your face, knowing the fear you had almost every day for four years, makes me sick. Men and women are out there every damn day doing it, just like Neal. Heroes, each of 'em. But it's not me. It never was, and I put you through that for no reason."

Tears welled within her eyes and gratitude swept through her as years of tension slowly unfurled from her limbs. "Danny...I...I want to kiss you. I also want to throttle you."

And it was true—she was dizzy with conflicting emotions. She'd grown up admiring how her parents supported one another. They didn't always agree, they weren't always successful in their ventures, but they always backed each other. Looking back on the past four years, she wasn't certain how she'd survived it, but she had.

"I'll accept kisses and throttles, but, my love, this is where your hands get muddy."

LISA N. PAUL

She knew. In that second, it all became crystal clear. But she let him spell it out because she deserved to hear it.

"Honey, you are not, have never been, and—if I can help it—will never be a quiet woman. You speak your mind, and you do it in a way that isn't rude, condescending, or cruel. It's truth how you see it and usually it's truth—period."

He wasn't wrong. That was who she was, how her parents had raised her, and how she'd had to be during the year and a half she was on her own. It was who she still was, except when it came to Danny's job.

"I didn't listen back then, Jules, but you stopped talking. Don't do that, babe. I'm a man—stubborn as hell, isn't that what you say?"

Julie stifled a giggle.

"One day we're gonna have kids, and if those little guys are anything like me"—he waggled his brows— "you're gonna be talking all the damn time."

The mention of future children sent warmth tingling through her body. They'd talked about having a large family when they first got married, and over the past year, they'd been actively trying without success. But both believed it would happen when the time was right.

"We could just as easily have a bunch of little girls, babe." Julie snorted, throwing out the one thing that shook her husband to the core every single time. "Then it'll be you doing all of the talking when they have you wrapped around their little fingers."

Placing his muscled arms against the Ranger, one on each side of her head, amusement danced in Danny's hazel eyes. "Only talking I'll be doing is with the punks that try to date my daughters. But I won't need words for that. My Louisville Slugger will work just fine."

"Danny…" Julie sighed, flattening her palms against his sculpted chest. "I'm sorry too. I think I was so busy trying to support your decision, trying to be okay with it, that I forgot to challenge it. I forgot to be your partner and ended up being your ladder instead." The lines between his brows told her he needed more of an explanation. "My fear of losing you in the beginning was debilitating. The last thing I wanted to do was push you further away by holding on too tight. I felt like you would have resented me if I expressed any disapproval about your career path. I was wrong." Saying the words made them hit harder inside her chest. "You needed me to push a little. To question your choices when I saw they weren't making you happy. And if we argued, then we would have worked things out the way married couples do…with lots of make-up sex. Trust me, Danny, I've learned my lesson. And I won't forget it." Even with the cold air whipping around them, the heat from his body warmed her from the outside in, melting the frost that had formed even before Allan's life-altering phone call.

His lips touched hers gently at first, a tentative greeting after a long absence. Then his tongue breached her mouth, his hands gripped her head, and the kiss went from sweet to seductive, tender to ravenous in a blink. Julie felt her insides melt into a puddle right there on the side of a quiet road somewhere between North Carolina and Maryland.

"Fuck," Danny murmured, his soft breath sending tingles up her spine, "I want you so bad, honey."

Feeling weightless in his arms, her legs wrapped around his waist, and he pressed her against the cool metal of the Ranger.

"Feels like we've been straight to hell and back, Julie." He nipped her earlobe while grinding his hardened groin to her sensitive one. "Now the only place I wanna be is in your heaven."

Oh my God, his words, they undo me every single time. Her hips undulated against his. The groan that came from deep in his body vibrated through his chest, making her smile, but not as much as the car that sped past, honking.

"Fuck," he repeated, although his meaning was significantly different than the first time. His eyes slid shut before he slowly placed her feet on the pavement. "Lost my goddamn mind. Jesus, Julie, I'm not sure I would've stopped had we gone much further."

Her heart thrummed with excitement. Danny's desire was contagious. If she didn't already crave him all of the time, his hunger for her would be her downfall. "I'd like to believe I would have stopped you." He lifted a single brow, and she laughed. "Fine, maybe I wouldn't have stopped you because I would have loved to have you inside me, but I know there's no way you'd lay me down on the cold, dirty asphalt to fuck me."

"Shit, honey." Danny grabbed her hand and pressed it against his hard shaft. "You know you make my cock hard when you talk dirty."

"Mmm, you are hard." She stroked him twice through his jeans before pulling her hand away. "It took me how long to make out with you in public?" She shook her head as a smile stretched across her face. "No way am I going to have sex with you where others can see. Nope."

Danny's gaze grew dark. The muscle in his jaw ticked as he tilted her head back, once again bringing them eye to eye. "Julie, eyes."

She hadn't heard that tone more than a few times, but she'd named it his don't-fuck-with-me voice. When he used it, he was dead serious.

"Look at me, baby," he said. "I think you're the most beautiful woman in the world. Men stare at you and wish you were theirs. You are not; you're mine. You chose me, and that makes me one lucky motherfucker. Will I kiss you in public? Touch you in public? Fuck yeah, I will. That's *me* claiming *you*. However, *you* chose *me*. Your sex is a gift you give to me. Only me. That's something I cherish, and I don't share things I cherish, Julie. I worship them."

His molten gaze turned her muscles into mush as her knees slowly gave out. Danny wrapped his arm around her waist in a steadying hold, opened the passenger door, and lifted her into the seat.

Before closing the door, he said, "Honey, I'll make it my mission to let any man know just how damn lucky I'm getting, but they'll never see anything more than we're both willing to show. Got it?"

She blinked twice, then nodded.

"Words, honey. I need words."

"I understand," she answered softly, unable to form anymore syllables.

A devilish grin split Danny's face as he nodded and closed the car door. As if being contained alone in the small space could sever the sexual tension that tethered the two of them, Julie breathed deeply and exhaled slowly.

She had mere seconds to pull herself together. *"You're mine, "he'd said. "Your sex is a gift... you chose me." My God, he feels the same way about me as I do about him.* Knowing that she was loved just as hard as she loved was a heady feeling. While Julie had always known that Danny was in love with her, on that day, at the side of the road, after four years of marriage, and at the end of a God-awful week, she learned her husband wasn't just in love with her. She owned his soul, the same way he owned hers.

"You okay, baby?" Danny asked as he climbed into the driver's seat, a sexy smirk still firmly in place.

Was she okay? Her nipples were drawn into sensitive pebbles that sent goose bumps down her legs each time she twisted in her seat. Her panties were wet with arousal from both his delicious friction and his dirty words, and her heart was pumping overtime from the knowledge of how deep his love went. She was a beautiful disaster about to come undone, and she wouldn't fray unless she took him with her.

She licked her lips. "Yeah, I'm better than okay." She smiled as a plan formed in her mind.

Once Danny pulled back onto the road, Julie popped in a mix tape she'd made not too many weeks before. Madonna singing about being "Crazy For You" filled the car. She had the order of the music memorized, and Julie's hand found purchase on her husband's knee, slowly teasing up until it made contact with the thick bulge between his thighs.

"You starting something you intend to finish?"

"Yep." She popped the *p* at the end of the word before popping the button on his jeans and releasing his erection from his underwear.

"Nice." Danny sighed with a shit-eating grin.

When the bass line of George Michael's "I Want Your Sex" pounded through the speakers, Julie took Danny deep in her throat.

"Fuck me," Danny roared as he grabbed the steering wheel with both hands.

CHAPTER NINE

Wanderlusty

AFTER RETURNING HOME from North Carolina, Danny tendered his resignation to the station. They offered him counseling, offered him more time to grieve, but Danny had already left the position before he entered the station. In the end, the captain and other firefighters said their good-byes and wished him well. Danny walked out of the firehouse without a weight on his shoulders or a plan for the future. Not his brightest idea, but one he and his wife had come up with together.

He entered the café where he and Julie had planned to meet after he left the station.

"How'd it go?" Julie asked, already sitting at a small table with his coffee waiting.

He shrugged, approached the table, and kissed his wife's soft cheek. "Actually, it was easier than I thought it would be." Straddling the empty seat she'd saved for him, he quickly recounted what had happened at the station, and how the captain suggested grief counseling. When the Captain said, "If you truly love the job, Marcus, you can't just walk away," it hit him yet again how little love for it he actually had.

A proverbial light bulb glowed above his head as a plan began to take shape. "Jules, you and I never went on a honeymoon because I started at the academy immediately." Another thing, looking back, that he could kick himself for. *What's that saying? Hindsight is 20/20.*

"I know." She winked and picked up her mug to sip what he knew was decaf with too much creamer and too much sweetener.

They had gotten married in a simple service at the Baltimore County Courthouse, attended by no more than his father, Neal, and Chester, followed by lunch at a nearby restaurant. Even though the occasion hadn't been marked with frills and cake, it had been the most important day of his life.

He'd never forget the sheer bliss, followed almost immediately by complete anguish, on her face when he went down on bended knee before her.

"There's nothing I want more than to marry you, Danny Marcus." She'd touched her throat as her eyes filled and great big tears rolled down her cheeks.

"Honey, if you're so happy, why are you so sad?" Rock-hard fear gripped his gut.

"I'm gonna marry you"—the tears continued to flow—"and my parents won't be there to walk me down the aisle. My mom won't help me pick out a dress, my dad won't get the father/daughter dance we always planned…"

He had never heard Julie sob the way she had that night. Other than when she first opened up to him, she only spoke of somber but positive reflections of her parents. He knew she grieved and he saw her cry, but he'd never seen her in such raw pain.

"What can I do, baby?" he had asked as he knelt on both knees with her small hands wrapped tightly in his.

She turned her head, breaking their eye contact. He thought in that moment that she knew what she needed from him but was too afraid to ask. He rose to his feet, swept her up in his arms, and carried her to the sofa, where he sat down with her planted on his lap.

"Julie, I wanna spend every day for the rest of my life with you. There's something you need, something that will take away the sadness that's tearing you up right now; tell me, honey, and I'll give it to you."

Nodding, Julie's gray stare met his. "I do want to marry you, but…" The *but* nearly killed him until she completed her thought. "But I can't go through with a wedding. I can't do it without them. I know you'll try to convince me that it's every girl's dream or that I'll regret it later. It was my fantasy once too, but now the thought is a nightmare. I have enough of those to last a lifetime."

Relief, then heartache. That's what he felt, but it wasn't what he said. "Honey, you wanna marry me?"

"Yes," she answered with confidence.

"It kills me you don't get to have your fantasy wedding and your daddy/daughter dance. I hate seeing your heart breaking when I know how happy you are with us, but I'm not gonna convince you that you'll regret anything, baby. I'm gonna marry you, and if at any time in our lives you wanna have that big dream wedding, just let me know, and we'll do it." He used his thumbs to wipe away her tears. "You're taking my name. A man has never been so lucky." He touched his lips to hers. "Whatever you want, as long as it's in my power to give you, it's yours. Forever."

She'd smiled brightly on their wedding day. A real smile, one that declared true happiness. The only thing that had stood in the way of their union was work. Danny was set to start training, a twenty-one week program, and Neal and Julie had needed to request time off from their jobs for the wedding. Within two months of Danny sliding the engagement ring on Julie's finger, the wedding band followed. There was no time for a honeymoon, but she didn't complain.

"Where did you go just now, sweetheart?"

Julie's question popped his memory bubble, dropping Danny back to the coffee shop. "I was thinking about the day we got married, how beautiful you looked."

Julie's eyes got soft the way they always did when they discussed that day. Blessed and bittersweet, she called it.

"We slipped right into married life and never looked back."

"Are you complaining?" she teased. "'Cause it's too late to return me, and I wouldn't go quietly."

Danny's laugh filled the quiet café. "No, babe, no one else in the world I want. However, I'd love to be able to finally take you on that honeymoon."

Julie subtly covered her mouth, but Danny saw the happiness radiating from the tiny lines that appeared on the outsides of her eyes.

"I know you've always had a serious case of wanderlust with no outlet," he said. "My dad gave us all of that money when we got married. I'm thinking we could take some of it and plan a two-week vacation to the destination of your choice. Other than a couple of sick days, you haven't taken any time off since you started managing

O'Brian's. I'm sure you can get the time off...if you want."

HE WASN'T WRONG. Julie had started as a waitress at O'Brian's Ale House the week after she left Chester's Bar. In fact, Chester Murray had gotten her the job. With Danny attending the Fire Training Academy in Baltimore and hoping for a job in a station in Baltimore County, Chester's was a hike and a half. Chester and Sheila O'Brian were friends, which meant Julie got hired sight unseen. After six months, Sheila was grooming Julie for a management position. O'Brian's was work, but it was also fun, and it was her safe place when Danny worked days at a time. Sheila's brother was a firefighter, and her husband was a volunteer firefighter, so she knew the ropes and showed Julie how to keep her shit tight when Danny was on duty.

Sheila would be more than happy to give Julie two weeks off because she'd already "okayed" four weeks of leave.

"Jules, do you want to go away for a couple of weeks?" Danny asked.

"Yes and no, Danny," Julie answered in a sing-song voice, pleased when she saw confusion on his gorgeous face. "I absolutely want to take our long-awaited and well-deserved honeymoon, but I don't think two weeks is enough."

"Wha—"

Julie lifted a finger to her lips. "Shhh…" Danny's pinched brows and dropped jaw made her laugh. "Sheila and I had a long chat last night after my shift. We think that O'Brian's will be fine without me for at least four weeks." She stood and stalked over to his chair to plant herself on his lap. "Effective as of today, you're unemployed, so how about it? Wanna take a month and get wanderlusty with me?"

"Fuck me," he growled, making her core pulse and her panties wet.

"I plan to do that in several different countries," she purred.

"Let's get out of here, woman," Danny commanded quietly.

"You lead, I'll follow."

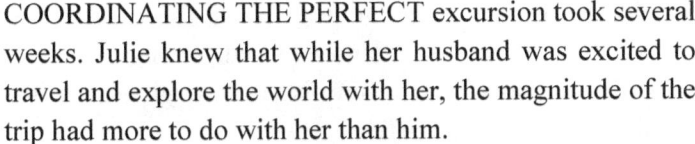

COORDINATING THE PERFECT excursion took several weeks. Julie knew that while her husband was excited to travel and explore the world with her, the magnitude of the trip had more to do with her than him.

Traveling with her parents had been her post-high-school-graduation plan. They'd planned three months of explorations before she settled into the "real world," as her dad had referred to it. At the end of her freshman year in high school, they mapped out a journey that would have taken them through Asia, and they tweaked it throughout the fall of her senior year. While the trip was meant to be her parents' graduation gift to her, the expense was astronomical. Julie wanted to pitch in as much as possible, so she worked any job she could find, from babysitting to serving ice cream at the local Friendly's. As the vacation expanded, she stopped serving ice cream and got a job at a local restaurant. The minute she was old enough to serve alcohol, she started working in a pub. After all, with alcohol came bigger tips, and each tip was money set aside for their dream vacation.

Her dream ended the day her nightmare began, and world discovery became a memory that was both wistful and cruel. When she and Danny got married and they realized there would be no time for a honeymoon, her disappointment was less sharp and quick to fade.

But when Neal died, paralyzing fear struck Julie in ways that far surpassed what she'd felt after she lost her mom and dad. She had mourned and struggled after the earthquake that consumed her parents, but part of her knew that she would be okay, that she'd move forward, and while life would be painful, it would continue. When the news about Neal hit, all Julie saw was Danny. Danny running into a burning building. Danny succumbing to flames or to damage the flames caused. Danny no longer in her life, in her world. Terror clawed through her gut like nothing she'd ever felt before.

So when her husband told her that he no longer wanted to be a firefighter, she could almost envision the orange flames being suffocated for the last time, hear the sizzle as the oxygen left the fire and the embers turned to ash. They were safe, free. Alive. And there was nothing she wanted more than to celebrate their existence by experiencing all life had to offer. Starting with the globe.

IF BEAMING SMILES, frequent Post-It notes, and a never-ending supply of destination pamphlets didn't clue Danny in to how happy his wife was, her expressions of joy would have done it. He thought he'd seen her happy, blissful, even thrilled in their years together, but this school-girl side of Julie was brand-new, and he loved it.

"Eeep, I can't believe we're finally going," Julie squealed, her round eyes glued to the window facing the plane at Baltimore-Washington International Airport.

"The world is ours, honey," Danny promised as he stood behind her with his arms wrapped around her shoulders. He planted a kiss on the top of her silken strawberry-blonde hair.

And for the four weeks that followed, it was.

The Changing of the Guard at Buckingham Palace was something he'd seen on television, but that wasn't nearly as cool as seeing it in person. Snuggling in the high-speed train to Paris felt luxurious—even a bit naughty when he draped a blanket over them and made Julie come quietly so as not to disturb the other travelers.

Once in Paris, they did all of the "touristy" things—the Eiffel Tower, the Louvre, Arc de Triomphe. But what the other tourists didn't get that he did was the look of fascination and awe that blanketed his wife's face and softened her eyes.

He fell in love with Julie day after day on that trip, without exception.

TRAVELING TO SPAIN was a dream. What was she thinking—the whole damn trip was a dream. But there was something special about Barcelona. The city still sparkled with its post-Olympic shine.

As they traveled from place to beautiful place, taking in sights and turning them into memories, something clicked in Julie's mind. The old saying "everything happens for a reason" played on a loop in her mind as the trip wound down, and she realized that while her original plans with her parents would have been an unbelievable dream come true, she couldn't imagine sharing her first world traveling experience with anyone but Danny.

"How's this for the grand finale?" Danny whistled, taking in the magnificent sight around them.

Julie had planned the whole trip, but Danny had requested she let the last four nights be his special surprise. She couldn't turn down the determined look in his eyes, so she, with a bit of hesitation, handed her husband the reins and asked no questions. Looking around the island paradise, she realized that had been a wise decision.

Bora Bora was heaven on earth. The small South Pacific island northwest of Tahiti was surrounded by turquoise water and coral reefs. Never had she seen something more exquisite, and never could her dreams have imagined such beauty.

"Danny, oh my God, this...this is beyond words."

"This is what I *should* have given you when you accepted my last name." He cupped her cheek, lifting her eyes to his. "Stunning."

In that moment, she wondered if her husband was still talking about Bora Bora.

For four days and four nights, they worshipped the sun, snorkeled in the lagoon, hiked, and made love. They stayed in a bungalow perched on stilts above the lagoon, making the lapping sounds of water part of their sound-track each night.

"I can't get enough of you," he rumbled, his hands stroking the sensitive flesh between her thighs.

"You've had me three times today, sweetheart." Though she certainly wasn't complaining. She could spend full days devouring her man, and that was exactly what she'd intended to do on their last day in paradise. Mission accomplished. Warm water splashed around them as the jets from the hot tub massaged her skin.

"Fucked you, baby. Over and over again." As always, his naughty words had her body tingling before his fingers penetrated her. "Wanna make love to you this time, savor you, yeah?"

Emotion made her throat so thick, her words got caught.

Danny didn't need them. "Bottom lip, honey…"

With that, he shut down the jets, scooped her up, and exited the tub. With lagoon water lapping in the back-ground and a warm breeze blowing through the open room, her husband gave her the most poignant memory of their whole trip.

CHAPTER TEN

Hint Number Three

THE BEDROOM WAS still dark when Julie's eyes popped open. A slight wave of nausea rolled through her, reminding her of the lulling waters she and Danny had seen in Bora Bora. The feeling was becoming more familiar with each passing day. Six weeks had passed since they returned home from what had been the most enchanting time of her life. In each day, she and Danny found a sense of peace that neither had realized was missing before their trip.

When her tummy clenched again, she slid out of bed, mindful not to wake her husband. There was no reason to get him excited if the test was once again negative. She tiptoed to the bathroom. Once the door was shut and the light on, Julie pulled out the home pregnancy test kit she had purchased several days before. Her period was late—two weeks late, to be exact—but over the past few months, her previously regular cycle had become more sporadic. The doctor had informed her that nerves could mess with her menstrual cycle, and since she had been nervous about their trip, she didn't jump the gun when her period was late…again. Two weeks late, however, was something to be concerned with.

Her hands fumbled as she opened the box and pulled out the articles inside. She'd purchased a different brand of home pregnancy test, foolishly hoping the new test would give different results, positive ones. Butterflies replaced the nausea as she read the instructions. *Oh, God, I want this. Please let me be pregnant.*

As soon as the stick was dipped in the "first morning urine" resting on the vanity, Julie sat on the closed toilet lid and waited. *Three minutes*, she thought as she stared at her watch, *may as well be three hours.*

"Jul?" The bathroom door creaked open, and there stood Danny, sexy from sleep but awake enough to look concerned. His presence infused the small bathroom with security and comfort that instantly settled Julie's nerves. His eyes searched her face before they landed on the countertop. "Woman?"

"I…I didn't want to wake…" She shrugged as heat moved from her neck up to her cheeks.

"Baby," Danny tsked, shaking his head, "you leave my arms, I feel it. You don't return, you bet your sweet ass I'm awake."

She dropped her gaze as her cheeks rose, the smile too hard to fight. She should have known he'd wake up without her by his side. The man kept her tucked close as they slept; she often felt as though he protected her even in sleep, and she loved it. Since marrying Danny, her nightmares were all but gone, and she owed that to the feeling of safety and love that he provided.

"Danny, umm, I think I might be pregnant." She looked at her watch. "We'll know in about thirty more seconds."

Puffing out his beautifully naked chest, an expression of confidence formed on a very alert Danny. "Julie, honey, you should've just told me you were doing this. I could've saved you the time. You're preggo, babe."

How was it possible for him to look so serious even with his lush lips curved into a shit-eating smile? That was what crossed Julie's mind. What crossed her lips was, "Stop it, you have no idea what you're talking about."

"The fuck I don't." His brows arched as if to punctuate his statement. He lowered himself before her, his knees resting on the blue, fluffy bath mat, his large hands on her bare thighs. "It's my job to know your body."

Goose bumps rose on her heated flesh as his hands slid down her legs and rested on her knees. Slowly he parted her legs, exposing her most intimate parts. There was something so sexy, so naughty, and so primal about him when he just watched her, staring at her nakedness, as an expression of his desire for her. She'd lost her inhibitions with him years back, but Christ, she got so seduced by his hunger.

His gaze shot back up to hers. "Your pussy is mine, is it not?"

Her heart thundered as she whispered the answer. "It is."

"Been licking it, eating it, savoring it for years now." His nostrils flared, and his voice lowered. "I'd know *my* pussy if we'd been separated a decade and I was blindfolded the first time I tasted it again."

A delicious shiver surged through her, pulling her naked nipples into tights buds and sending a rush of wetness to her exposed core.

An appreciative growl vibrated in Danny's chest. "This is *my* pussy, and as sweet as it is, over the past month or so, it's been changing."

Julie's body tensed as she tried to pull her knees together.

"No way, honey." Danny's eyes lit up like candles. "Said there was a change, never said it was bad." He moved his hand to her center. With his eyes never leaving hers, he dipped one thick finger into her warmth. "So wet, always so wet and responsive. And lately, a bit more swollen." He plunged a second finger in, turning his wrist and immediately finding her sweet spot.

"Ah, Danny, that feels so good...too good." Her body was wound tight. He hadn't even touched her clit, and she felt tremors of an orgasm in the pit of her belly.

"Yeah." He bent down and dropped kisses on her upper thigh. "Hint number two, beautiful, you've been more sensitive lately." His finger swiped her g-spot again, massaging with perfect pressure as her breaths became shallow and uneven.

"Oh, God," she pled, "you can't possibly imagine..." She couldn't finish the sentence. She had no words.

"Oh, honey, I can imagine," Danny groaned.

Julie whimpered as his face disappeared between her legs. The minute his talented tongue entered her while he caressed her clit with his thumb, she unraveled. Thrusting herself onto his face, Julie rode his tongue like a pole dancer out to make rent. Her pulse raced as tremors shook her legs. Her climax consumed her, stripping her of air and rational thought. When it passed, every muscle in her body was shaking like gelatin and her mind was practically blank.

"Hint number three"—Danny grinned as he wiped his mouth, then licked her juices from his hand—"you taste sweeter than you ever have. I can't get enough of you, baby. I think about it constantly."

Her breath and wits were finally coming back to her. "Danny"—she shook her head—"none of those things can possibly be signs..."

She watched in fear as her husband picked up the test stick. An enormous smile broke over his face. "Told you you didn't need that test. We're gonna have a baby, honey."

Tears filled her eyes as the news sank in. "I'm... we're...oh my God! Danny!"

Instantly she was lifted into his muscled arms and carried back into their bedroom.

"It's too damn early to call anyone, but Dad and Anita will be here later for the Memorial Day barbeque. Why don't we celebrate just the two of us?" He waggled his brows, making it as clear as the line on the test just what kind of celebrating he was up for, and she wanted nothing less.

They were finally starting their family. Life was amazing.

CHAPTER ELEVEN

Always You

RAYS OF SUNLIGHT stretched through the bedroom blinds, painting stripes of gold on Julie's skin. Danny lay on his side, his head cupped in his hand, and watched her chest rise and fall with each soft breath. *She's having my baby.* His throat tightened as thoughts of the little person forming in his wife's stomach filled his mind. He'd had a feeling she was pregnant for the past couple of weeks, but if his parents and older brother had taught him anything, it was never, ever ask a woman, no matter who she was, if she's pregnant.

"How was I supposed to know she was just fat?" Jeff had asked their mom as she placed an icepack over his shiner.

She'd flicked his ear. "You never ask a woman when she's due, ever. In fact, the only time you inquire about a lady's baby is when she's actually holding it, fool." She flicked him a second time and left the kitchen, giggling.

So no, he hadn't said anything to Julie, but he hadn't been lying when he told her how he knew. He licked his lips, her flavor burned into his senses. There had been other signs as well. He'd noticed she was falling asleep as soon as her head hit the pillow, and while he could find creative ways to wake her, the dark circles under her eyes made him want to hold her close while she slept. Her pus-sy wasn't the only thing changing. Her sweet tits were get-ting bigger and firmer each day. His dick twitched as he stared at the pretty pink nipples that peeked out of Julie's blanket-covered form.

She'd given him everything he'd ever needed and was about to give him everything he could ever want.

———————◆———————

"WHAT'S THIS?" ALLAN asked, holding a tiny green gift bag.

Danny snaked out his arm, grabbed Julie, and pulled her against his chest. "Just open it, Dad."

Excitement clicked from Danny to Julie like a New-ton's cradle as they waited for Allan to remove the newly purchased item from the small bag.

"A plush Dalmatian?"

As his father tried to make sense of the stuffed toy, Anita shrieked. "Oh… oh… you're… oh, Allan, they're pregnant!"

She embraced Julie, murmuring words of elation, while Danny waited for the news to hit his father. Allan's eyes widened as he stared at the black-and-white dog.

Danny smiled. "Every firefighter needs a mascot, right?"

"Oh, Daniel." Allan's eyes welled with tears, making Danny's follow suit. "Come here, son." Allan opened his arms, and Danny walked into them. "I'm so happy for you and Julie. So much joy and love you and your brothers have given me. Enough to fill every single day of my life, even the horrible ones, with beauty. I wish that for you, Daniel. Congratulations, son."

"Thanks, Dad," Danny said around the lump in his throat. "I can only hope to be half the father you've been."

The news was shared again a few hours later when Chester arrived. The bag he received contained a pair of shot glasses that Julie had found at the local gift shop when she and Danny went out first thing that morning, and they read, *"Lil Shooter."* Upon pulling the glassware out of the small bag, Chester's face held the same blank look Allan's had.

Julie beamed. "It might be a while, but we figure there's no one better than Uncle Chester to teach our kid the dos and don'ts of drinking." She placed her hand on her flat stomach and shrugged. "Think you can keep those for him or her?"

A smile split Chester's face barely a second before he swung Julie into his arms. "Julie girl, anything and everything for you. Your parents would be so proud." He looked from Julie to Danny. "Thanks for including me in your life. I'm honored. You need me, I'm here."

"WHAT ON EARTH would make you think I'd miss today's appointment?" Incredulity laced Danny's voice. "Honey, have I missed any of *our* prenatal visits yet?"

"No." Julie shrugged, guilt blooming in her belly for having thought, not to mention vocalized, her concern about Danny being unable to make the ultrasound appointment.

He had started a new job, bartending at a popular club in the heart of Baltimore, when they returned from their vacation. The money was great, but the hours were long and the management strict. They didn't take kindly to staff being late for any reason. Since the only appointment Julie could get with the ultrasound technician was in the late afternoon, she'd prepared herself to see their baby for the first time...alone. She'd been fidgeting in the chair, sucking back water and praying they would call her back before her bladder exploded, when Danny strutted into the obstetrician's office. All thoughts of bladder blowout vanished when his hazel eyes met hers.

He leaned over her chair and pressed his lips to hers. Mint and pine filled her senses.

"You're my reason, Jules." He gave her another soft kiss. "Always, you."

Julie sighed. His actions always spoke just as clearly as his words, and his words were the best. As it did whenever it heard Danny's voice, the baby kicked, making its presence known.

"The bean feels neglected, sweetheart," Julie teased, rubbing her baby bump before placing Danny's hand directly over the spot where their future soccer player was practicing.

There was nothing better in the world than Danny's face when he felt their baby move. The first time he'd felt it, with misty eyes and a thickened voice, he uttered, "Magic, honey. You've given me magic." Each time since, he'd smile as if it was the greatest thing to ever happen and he was the only man to experience such a miracle. She grew more in love with her man as she watched him fall in love with their unborn child.

"Mr. and Mrs. Marcus, we're ready for you."

The nurse's words pulled them out of their bubble and into the here and now. It was time to make certain their baby was developing properly with ten fingers and ten toes. They were also hoping to learn if they would be painting the nursery pink or blue.

THE TECHNICIAN HANDED Julie a towel and closed the door behind her, leaving a speechless, slack-jawed, glassy-eyed couple in the cramped room.

"We're having a daughter," Danny whispered, his hands trembling as he used the towel to wipe the gel from Julie's belly.

She nodded, words still caught in her throat. Their baby—their daughter—looked perfect. She measured exactly where she should for twenty weeks and three days.

"A little girl," Danny said, his eyes almost as round as Julie's stomach. He pulled her into a tight embrace, and she felt the rapid beat of his heart.

It was one thing to hear the technician utter those words, but for them to come from her husband… "Oh my God." Tears flowed freely down her cheeks. "A healthy baby girl. Danny! We saw our sweet baby." Putting a few inches between them, she looked at his handsome face. The inner light she saw radiating from him mirrored her own feelings to a tee.

"Come here, honey, I need you in my arms."

"And there's no place I'd rather be, but"—she hesitated, a pronounced bounce in her stance—"if I don't use the restroom first, you're going need to change your pants before you head into work." She smiled over her shoulder and saw Danny throw his head back as laughter erupted from his chest.

THE WEEKS FLEW by as she and Danny worked long hours and, in their free time, prepared their lives and their home for the arrival of their little girl. The walls in the third bedroom turned pale pink, and Danny spent hours flexing an artistic talent Julie barely knew he had. The day he unveiled his finished mural of a castle nestled in the clouds on the nursery wall, he told Julie, "The perfect fairytale for my princess."

Beautiful furniture was ordered and set to be delivered four weeks before her January seventh due date. Each time Julie walked out of Macy's department store, she found herself with another tiny, new onesie in the prettiest shade of pink.

"It called to me," she'd say to Danny as he shook his head and smiled.

"There aren't enough days in the year for all the clothes you've bought for her already."

Yet she'd catch him gently fingering the soft cotton wares as she'd pass the nursery on her way to their bedroom.

And their lovemaking...*holy hotness*, she thought as she undressed and stepped into the shower one afternoon in mid-October. Sex was an area that they had always excelled in, but it had become indescribable. Between the pregnancy hormones amping up her desire, which she'd read was normal, and Danny's insatiable appetite going from possessive to downright dominating, which she attributed to his primal need to protect his unborn child, their days began and ended with mind-blowing orgasms. She was not complaining.

The friends Julie had made through work over the four years she'd been at O'Brian's, both coworkers and regular customers, weighed in daily with regards to Julie's pregnancy. And as all pregnant women could attest to, the minute the baby belly popped, so did the advice from every well-intentioned person. She'd been warned about how husbands tended to stay away from their wives sexually during pregnancy and if Danny still "participated" in sex—yes, "participated" was the word that had been used—then Julie shouldn't be upset if he treated her like a fragile doll and left her to "take matters into her own hands."

"Pun completely intended, darling," the women of the Sweet-Heart Club, who reserved the twelve-top table for the first Monday of each month, squawked before sharing their labor and delivery nightmares.

Julie wasn't their waitress, but they often requested management to assist even the most capable servers, and Julie was management.

Little did the Sweet-Hearts know that Danny treated her in no such way. During the first prenatal visit, her husband had flat-out asked exactly what was and wasn't okay sexually for her and the baby. While Julie had felt herself flush in embarrassment at the time, she thanked her lucky stars every time the man rocked her world.

"You've been in there a while, honey," Danny called from outside the shower stall. "I wanna fuck you, so you coming out or am I coming in?"

Nope, no fragile dolls in the Marcus house.

She turned off the taps, her lip tucked between her teeth as moisture pooled between her thighs. "I'm coming." She startled when the stall door slid open.

"Get out of the shower, babe"—his eyes raked over her body—"and you will be."

AFTER FOUR GLORIOUS orgasms—three of them hers—the pair showered again, that time together, and dressed for work.

"You and Sheila started looking for your replacement?" Danny asked before sliding the toothbrush into his mouth.

Julie finished applying her lipstick, rubbed her lips together, then looked at Danny's reflection in the vanity mirror. "We've discussed it." She hesitated while rolling the lipstick tube between her clammy hands.

Danny rinsed off his brush, put it in the holder, and crossed his arms. "Spill it, Jules. What aren't you saying?"

Sometimes she wondered if it was to her benefit or detriment that the man knew her as well as he did.

"I can't wait to have this baby." She rubbed her palm over the ever-expanding bump that chose that moment to move, as if she knew her mommy was talking about her. "And I know we decided that I would stop working and stay home with her, but a piece of me wants to continue to work." Without waiting for Danny's response, she quickly added, "Part time, of course. I just really enjoy being a part of O'Brian's. I've worked since I was fifteen years old, and while I know that our daughter will fill my heart and my time, I can't imagine leaving the work force completely."

When her parents had died, everything they owned was left to Julie, including two very large life insurance policies. Before Danny and Julie got married, they decided to sell her childhood home and start over fresh in a new place. In doing so, they moved to Baltimore to be closer to the fire station and bought a smaller house, giving them more money to invest. So between the hefty nest egg from her family and the generous wedding gift from Danny's father—only a small portion of which went to their honeymoon vacation—they were in good financial shape. With Danny being groomed for a management position, his salary and benefits would increase in the near future. There was no reason why Julie had to keep working, but she couldn't imagine a life without the chaos and camaraderie the bar scene offered.

"You don't wanna stop working," Danny stated, no question in his tone.

Julie shook her head. "Not completely, no."

Rubbing his whisker-covered jaw, he nodded. "So we'll figure it out. While you're on maternity leave, I'll be working my way up at Red Bar. By the time you're ready to go back part time"—his eyes softened the way they did just before he told he loved her—"we'll figure it out, honey. Love you. We'll always figure shit out."

"Danny Marcus, if I wasn't already totally and completely in love with you, I'd have fallen just now."

"Julie Marcus, if you hadn't just fucked my brains out and we weren't both about to be late for work, I'd take you here and now."

Her face flushed at the image of him thrusting into her from behind, and a sigh escaped her.

"Fuck," Danny roared, and he took her there and then.

CHAPTER TWELVE

That's Gonna Leave A Bruise

"YOU ALL GOOD, honey?" Danny asked as he closed Julie's car door after she got in. He stood at the window under an umbrella.

"I'm fine, babe, I promise." She giggled. "I could have held my own umbrella." She loved when his eyes squinted like they were, as if he couldn't quite fathom what she was saying.

He shrugged. "You could've, but why?" Cutting off her snappy retort, he continued, "Don't forget to beep me when you get to work. Plug in 1-1-1 so I know you got there safe, okay?"

The day Julie had learned she was pregnant, Danny went out and purchased a pager. He said the thought of him being unreachable was unacceptable. Mobile phones didn't get signal in the bar where he worked, so pagers were the best option. After all, there were payphones on every street corner. He could return a page no matter where he was.

"I won't forget, handsome."

"Jules…"

She sighed. "Okay, I won't forget *again*, I promise."

"You get off at midnight. You beep me before you leave O'Brian's and as soon as you get home," Danny stated with no humor, just expectation, in his voice. The further into her pregnancy she got, the more Danny hovered. She had to admit, she kind of loved it.

"Yes, sir. I love you."

His voiced gentled, as did his expression. "Thank God for that." He winked. "Have a good night." He leaned into the window of her car and touched his lips to hers.

"You too. I'll meet you in our bed when you get home." Danny closed the umbrella and shook off the excess rain before tossing it over Julie and onto the passenger seat.

She rolled up her window and watched as her husband walked through the pouring rain to his car, without hurry or care. He got in, buckled up, and turned on his ignition. She then pulled out of their driveway and left for work.

Work was unusually busy for a Wednesday and ridiculously busy for a rainy one. Neither she nor Sheila could figure out why the volume of customers was so high. All they knew was they were jammed with impromptu big parties in the dining room and not enough staff to cover them, which left Sheila calling in favors to get coverage while Julie ran food orders from the kitchen to the tables in order to keep the food fresh and the customers happy.

When the kitchen closed for the night, and the two "rescue" waitresses shifted from food to cocktail service to handle what was a large drinking crowd, Julie excused herself from service. Hours of running around finally took its toll on her body, and she felt as if an extra hundred pounds had been strapped onto her shoulders, back, and feet. The baby kicked, as if telling her it was time for bed.

"I agree, little girl," she whispered, rubbing her belly. "I'm heading out," Julie called over the music. When her boss didn't respond, Julie went behind the bar, tapped Sheila's shoulder, and got her attention. "I'm going home, boss lady. It's about midnight, and I'm beat."

Sheila gave change to a patron, then turned her attention to Julie. "I'm going to announce last call. Thank goodness we close early during the week, 'cause I'm about ready for bed myself. Thank you so much for tonight, Jules. I would've been lost without you. Let me find someone to walk you out to your car."

Julie looked around at the packed establishment. "It's okay, Sheel. I'm parked pretty close to the door, and it's slammed in here. I'll be fine."

"Kay. Then go home and get some rest."

"Will do, just gotta stop off in the office and beep Danny. Then I'm out of here."

Sheila nodded before turning back to the customers. Even with three bartenders behind the bar, one of them being a "rescue" waitress that doubled as a bartender, the drinks weren't being served fast enough. *What the hell is going on tonight?*

Everyone knew that the area behind the bar was a slippery, messy place. Julie knew it better than most, since she'd suffered more bruises and sore butt cheeks than she cared to remember. That was why she and Danny had agreed that she wouldn't get behind it while she was pregnant. She hadn't thought of that agreement when she went to tell Sheila good night though. She did, however, remember it as soon as she slipped. While she didn't fall, her elbow hit the wall.

"Goddamnit," she howled. "That's gonna leave a bruise." *So stupid, Julie. What were you thinking?* She rubbed her belly and placed the call to Danny's pager. 2-2-2 was the signal that she was leaving work and heading home.

She slid on her coat, grabbed her purse, left the office, and headed into the narrow hallway toward the back door. *Wham!* The broom closet door flew open, striking Julie in the stomach hard enough to produce exploding stars in her vision and knock the wind from her lungs. Sharp pain sliced through her abdomen. She cried out before folding in half as she held her belly. When the pain subsided a bit, she looked up and stared at the two drunken people who'd practically fallen out of the closet in a drunken stupor, swinging the door open with enough force to inflict blind-ing pain.

"Aww, shit, did we do that?" the man slurred to the woman as he pointed at a crouched-over Julie.

"Naw, she prolly just listenin' to us in there. Jealous thing, ain't getting' any action in the closet." The woman leaned down next to Julie's ear, and her breath reeked from cheap beer. "You may wanna drop a few pounds there, hefty. You could get yourself a lil' some-some too."

Uncertain if anger or shock was more prevalent, Julie straightened herself the best she could—the pain made her nauseated, but her fury made her stubborn—pressed down her shirt, and cleared her throat. "I'm pregnant, you intoxi-cated slut."

"Hmm." The girl shrugged. "Then you really should work on finding yourself a man." She flipped her hair and walked away with her guy in tow.

The abdominal pain wasn't increasing and the baby was moving, so Julie decided to head home where she could think in peace and quiet.

"Fucking idiots," she said as she walked in the cold rain to her car. "Need to make sure that closet is locked. What the hell is wrong with people? I'm too tired for this shit."

Searing pain once again soared through her abdomen. This time, whether from exhaustion or shock, Julie's legs gave out from under her. She threw her arms down to break the fall, but fire shot up her right wrist before the pain once again took residence in her belly.

"You're okay, baby girl," she moaned as her left hand gripped her belly and darkness consumed her.

"THE FUCK?" DANNY'S shoulders tightened as he looked at his pager.

He hopped over the counter and ran to the payphones in the back corner of Red Bar. When he reached the phone, the pager beeped again. While the first page was from a number he didn't recognize, the second was a 9-1-1 notification. His heart seized and pounded at the same time. Dropping too many coins in the pay slot, Danny punched in the metal numbers that had appeared on the tiny screen of his pager.

"Danny?"

"Who the fuck is this?" he screamed at the female who answered.

"D-Danny, it's Sheila."

The sound of her voice sent ice through his blood.

"There was an accident. I'm with Julie…they're taking her. Y-you need to come, Danny. She needs you."

"An accident? Is she okay?" he roared. "Who's they? Who the fuck is with my wife, Sheila?" The phone quivered, the room quaked, and red film covered everything Danny saw.

He heard voices through the phone a split second before a strange man spoke into his ear. "Mr. Marcus, Ted here with the emergency team. How far along is your wife?"

"Twenty-eight weeks tomorrow," Danny answered firmly.

"We're taking her to Sinai Hospital, sir—"

Danny interrupted, "Is she okay?"

"Danny, it's Sheila again. I'm going to follow the ambulance. Please meet me there as soon as you can—"

"Leaving now." Danny slammed down the phone and ran across the hall to his manager's office. "My wife had an accident. I'm leaving."

His boss leveled him with a glare. "You're in the middle of a shift, Marcus."

Danny swallowed hard. "My wife and unborn daughter had an accident. Don't give a fuck about the shift, man. Dock me. Hell, fire me. I'm out."

And he left.

The nonexistent traffic allowed for Danny's speeding to shave nearly ten minutes off the normally half-hour drive to the hospital. Rain drops, while no longer fierce, splashed his windshield like fat tears of sadness, but just as he refused to assume the worst and let his own tears fall, the wipers cleared away the wetness, leaving fresh glass and new hope.

"JULIE MARCUS," DANNY barked at the meek-looking woman behind the counter in the emergency room.

"I'm sorry, sir, what is your name?"

Pulling in a deep breath, Danny answered. "Name's Daniel Marcus. My wife, Julie Marcus, was brought in via ambulance probably half an hour ago. I wanna see her *now*." His voice raised, making it clear his words were more of a command than a request.

"Please hold." The woman cradled the phone between her ear and shoulder, punched in a few numbers, and mumbled something into the receiver.

"Danny?"

He turned to see Sheila standing a couple of feet away by the metal waiting room chairs. She was a mess— makeup streaked down her cheeks, wet hair plastered to her head and face, and was that blood on her clothes?

"Is that blood on your clothes?" Danny gasped. "Sheila, is that Julie's blood on your fucking clothes?"

She nodded as fresh tears streamed down her face.

Acid burned in Danny's gut. He returned his attention to the woman behind the desk. "Where is my wife, god-damnit?"

The woman returned the phone to the cradle and spoke in a disturbingly soft voice. "Mr. Marcus, someone is coming out to speak with you right now. Please wait right over there." She pointed at the metal seats where Sheila still stood.

"I want to see my wife!" he shouted, startling the already leery woman, before staring at Sheila, who was wearing Julie's blood. Tears filled his eyes. *I will not assume the worst. She's going to be okay.*

He barely had the chance to walk the few feet over to his wife's employer before Julie's obstetrician briskly walked toward him.

"Mr. Marcus?"

Danny nodded. Words, just like air, forced their way out. "Dr. Burke, how is she? Can I see her? How's our baby?" The questions spewed out like lava from a volcano.

"How about if you follow me?" the doctor suggested before walking into a privacy room.

He closed the door once Danny had entered. Both remained standing as the older woman kept her eyes trained on him. Knowledge and compassion shone in her eyes—two things Danny had appreciated in the past, two things he dreaded in the present.

"By the time Julie got here, she was unconscious, blood was coming from her vagina, and her uterus was contracting due to labor. We did an ultrasound and learned that Julie had what's known as a placental abruption. It's when the placenta separates from the wall of the uterus, depriving the fetus of blood and oxygen. In Julie's case, the separation was due to abdominal trauma, and it was severe." Dr. Burke swallowed hard. "And…"

The doctor's pause felt like a dull knife being lodged into his gut.

"And…?" He refused to believe the truth until the words had been spoken.

"I'm sorry, Danny. I'm sorry, but Julie lost the baby. It died before we had a chance to intervene." The doctor's words had no time to penetrate before she unloaded even more. "Julie delivered the baby, but she was also suffering from vaginal bleeding because her uterus wouldn't clamp down, a term we call atony. She's been receiving transfusions and is being prepped for surgery now."

"Surgery?" Danny croaked as Dr. Burke opened the door to the small room.

"We need to stop the bleeding, and we will," she said, "but it may be a few hours until I see you again. We have a great team taking care of your wife. I'm going to go scrub in, and I'll see you soon."

With those words, she fled the privacy room, pushed the square button that automatically opened a door marked *Medical Personnel Only*, and disappeared through it.

"Take care of my wife," Danny screamed at the closing door. "Please, please," his voice cracked, "take care of my wife…"

"Umm, Danny?"

His name being called grabbed his attention; the woman attached to the voice captured his rage. Heat flashed through Danny's body as his hands clenched into fists. While he still saw Sheila as a woman—and therefore, he would never lay so much as a finger on her—his pain felt like a grenade and the pin had been pulled. "What in the motherfuck happened to her?"

Had Danny not been so lost in his own grief, he would have seen that Sheila was drowning in her own.

"I don't know," she said.

"That's not good enough!" he screamed. "She paged me right before midnight. She fucking paged me. She was goddamn fine then. So how's it possible that now, not two hours later, my daughter's dead?" Sheila gasped, but Danny continued to rant. "They're in there trying to stop my wife from bleeding to death. How, Sheila? Tell me how the fuck that happened?" His throat tightened when the last word passed his lips. The tears that he had held back since receiving Sheila's call finally fell. Their daughter was gone. His Julie was bleeding…"I…I can't…I can't lose her." His voice broke as the sadness left his throat and emptied his soul.

"Please, come sit down with me." Sheila gestured toward the privacy room, but Danny refused, explaining that he wanted to be in the main waiting room in case anyone needed him.

Once he'd checked in with the admissions desk, giving them Julie's insurance information and medical background, he shuffled to the waiting room, claimed a chair, and let his mind wander.

"What happened?" he asked calmly when Sheila handed him a cup of vending machine coffee and sat next to him.

The woman looked lost. "I've been trying to piece it together since we found her—"

"We?" Danny interrupted.

"Yeah. The place was slammed tonight. I can't remember it being like that on a Wednesday night, ever," she explained. "We both worked our asses off, and before you freak out on me, Danny, I know. I know she shouldn't have been working so hard, okay? But have you ever tried to tell Julie *not* to do something she wanted to do?"

Danny glared at his wife's boss and friend before admitting, "Okay, I get it. So she fell at work?"

"Not that I know of," Sheila claimed. "She said she was going to page you, then head home. That was the last I saw of her until one of my regulars came in from the parking lot, freaking out because Julie was laying, unresponsive, on the ground."

The coffee cup in Danny's grip crumpled, sending hot liquid over his fist and onto the floor. "She was outside *alone*, unconscious, on the wet ground like fucking road kill?" Rage boiled in his guts and he grinded his teeth. The deep affection Sheila felt for Julie was the only thing keeping his raw fury at bay.

"Danny, trust me—"

Nope, wrong thing to say. Boom.

"Trust you! *You?* Oh, that's rich. You run a bar, Sheila—a fucking bar filled with drunk assholes—and you let your female staff walk out to their cars at night alone?"

"Dan—"

"No," Danny snapped, "I've heard it all before. Julie's told me time and again. Your parking lot is well-lit, you have people buddy up when they can... how'd that buddy system work out for my wife tonight? How 'bout my daughter?"

Sheila sat speechless, her mouth agape.

"Know you love, Julie, and that makes us friends, but I swear on my life, if something happens to that woman, I'm coming after you, your family, your bar, and everything you hold dear. That is not a threat, *friend*. It's a promise."

He stood and stalked to the large window. Hands splayed on the cool glass, Danny leaned forward to stare into the dark sky. Movement in the reflection caught his eye, and his gaze traveled to the image of Sheila, her shoulders trembling as quiet sobs racked her body. Still rain-soaked and most likely freezing, she wrapped her arms around herself and rocked in the chair. *Shit, Julie would kill me if she knew how I treated her friend.* Thinking about Julie in the operating room hurt, but knowing he was letting her down in the waiting room felt even worse. He couldn't help her in there... he left the window and went back to the admissions window.

"Here" He placed a warm blanket around Sheila's shoulders. The surprise in her eyes made him feel worse than the gratitude from her smile. "I'm scared, Sheel. Scared to fucking death. But I know my Julie. She's stubborn as the day is long. She wanted to work, she would have. She wanted to walk to her car, she would have."

Sheila pulled the blanket tighter and wiped the tears from her cheeks.

"Not gonna apologize for acting like a dick, but what happened...Christ, there are no words. But I'm sorry for taking it out on you, Sheel. You've been nothing but kind to her, to us. I'm...sorry."

CHAPTER THIRTEEN

I'm Not Done Yet

"DR. BURKE?" DANNY left the vending machine, his coffee cup still under the drip, and hurried to the obstetrician's side. After nearly three hours of waiting, Danny's nerves were shot and his patience was worn thin. "How is she? When can I see her?"

The doctor slowly pulled the cap off her head. The eyes that had been filled with compassion hours before shone with a spark of satisfaction. "You've got yourself a fighter, Danny. It took nearly every trick in our box to get her bleeding under control. When everything else failed, we had to embolize, or in other words, block, the blood vessels that feed her uterus."

The doctor may as well have been speaking a different language.

"What are you saying? Is she okay or not?" It wasn't that Danny didn't want the details; he just needed the bottom line first.

Sheila, who hadn't left Danny's side, walked over from the vending machine and asked the question Danny was too scared to even think. "Has she regained consciousness?"

The doctor nodded. "Yes, to both of your questions. Julie regained consciousness just before the anesthesiologist put her back under for the procedure, and now that the bleeding is under control, her stats are improving."

"Thank God," Danny sighed, his knees threatening to give out. "When can I see her?"

"Give us another half hour to get her situated, and I'll have someone come and get you."

The doctor turned to leave when panic struck Danny. "Doctor Burke...does she know?"

The doctor lifted a brow as if waiting for Danny to elaborate.

"She know about the baby?" he asked.

She shook her head. "No, it wasn't something we wanted to tell her while she was unstable." Compassion was back in the woman's brown eyes. "But trust me, she knows. She may not admit it, not even to herself, but she knows."

Danny swallowed hard and nodded, unsure of how to respond. But he didn't need to, because the doctor's next words hit home.

"What you guys experienced tonight was tragic, heartbreaking...but you still have each other. Don't lose sight of that."

He barely registered the doctor leaving, hardly noticed Sheila's staring, because all he focused on was that he would never, could never, lose sight of Julie.

IT WAS COLD, unseasonably cold for mid-October. Julie could tell because people outside were bundled in coats with the collars pulled up around their ears. She watched them through the passenger window of Danny's Ranger. She, however, felt nothing. Not the goose bumps that pebbled her skin, not the fact that her usually cool fingertips were freezing, not even the way her teeth chattered as her body shook. Nothing. She was numb, empty.

"Honey?" Danny's voice held the careful tone it had had since the moment she woke up four days earlier. "How 'bout I stop at a drive-through and get you some coffee? It'll warm you up." He looked at her quickly before he cranked up the heat and focused on the road.

"I'm not cold," she whispered, her eyes glued to the window but her focus no longer on the present.

Memories of the look on her husband's face when she opened her eyes after surgery swirled in her mind. Joy, gratitude, and love—raw and real—came with his tear-filled eyes and shallow breaths.

"Welcome back," he'd said with an emotion-thickened voice. "Can't tell you how happy I am to see your eyes, honey."

She'd felt the same, relished the gentle kiss he'd placed on her mouth, but when she went to place her hand on his cheek, a plaster cast caught her attention. Flashes hit her all at once: the bar, the broom closet door, the rain...

"The baby?" she'd whimpered, inching her lips away from Danny's. Deep in her heart, she had known before opening her eyes. She remembered the sounds of doctors' voices, beeping machines, and instructions, but seeing the pain on her husband's face, the tears filling his hazel orbs, was confirmation she didn't want. "No...not our baby. Not our little girl." Wails clawed from her lungs as Danny's arms pulled her tight to his chest.

Julie fell apart that first day and had yet to locate even the first piece with which to put herself back together.

"Okay, baby, no coffee," he relented.

Other than when she disclosed the events that had occurred at O'Brian's the night of her accident—which sent Danny on a rampage of epic proportions, one so bad that he stopped screaming mid-rant and stormed from Julie's room, Danny had been soft-spoken and reluctant to upset Julie in anyway.

As their house came into view, waves of nausea hit, accompanied by the hollowness Julie had felt since she woke up in the hospital. Their baby's room...a labor of love she and Danny had worked on since the day they learned she was pregnant. A space they'd painted pink eight weeks before.

"Come on, honey, let me help you out. I'm sure your stomach is killing you."

Danny's arm threaded under her armpits as he gently assisted her down from the Ranger. Was her stomach hurting? They had performed abdominal surgery, yet she had no baby. Then again, she had no pain, just numbness.

Once she was on solid ground, Danny grabbed her bag from the back along with the assortment of get-well gifts and cards that had been sent to the hospital, while she gingerly walked to the front door. Dread crept up her spine as she entered their home and white-knuckled the banister. Pure adrenaline assisted her climb up the stairs.

She passed the first door on the left as if it were invisible, the first on the right... the same, but when she came to the second door on the left, she paused. The door was closed, but the room called to her.

"Julie...don't," Danny pled. His voice was barely a whisper from less than an inch behind her.

Her eyes rested on the door, a barrier between her and what once could have been. Her lids closed as fear wrestled with bravery. Each time Danny had left the hospital, Julie wanted to beg. Every time he returned, she wanted to ask. She did neither; now it was time to find out.

"Jules, please, honey, let's not do this today," his voice wobbled.

She inhaled and opened the door. "Danny..." In an instant, her legs no longer held her weight, and she was sobbing in her husband's arms.

In the middle of the pale pink room was a bright, white wooden rocking chair with the word Princess painted across the headrest. They had ordered it on Labor Day weekend. It was supposed to come with the rest of the furniture. Obviously it was too early...or too late.

"I'm so sorry, sweetheart," Danny murmured as he lowered them both to the carpet, she on his lap. "It came the day after your accident. It was raining, so I brought it in, closed the door, and haven't come back in since."

Guilt, more guilt, huge vats of guilt piled on Julie's shoulders as she held her empty tummy and cried. "I'm a horrible person, Danny. A terrible wife..."

"Jul, stop. None of this is your fault, I—"

"No, you don't understand. I've been so worried. I think...I think I was even a little upset with you."

"With me?" He titled his head. "Why? 'Cause I lost my shit at the hospital? Jules, honestly, I thought I handled that well, considering. I ever find the motherfuckers who did that to you, they'll wish I killed them."

Julie let out a small snort, then gripped her stomach—*ahh, pain, there it was*. Danny was such a beautiful man. He loved her to distraction, and she'd doubted him. *A horrible mother and a horrible wife*, the voice inside her head screamed.

"No, it had nothing to do with you losing your shit." She took a shallow breath, because any deeper ached her stomach, then slowly released the air. "I know that you hate when I'm upset. You like control, and this"—she touched her soft belly before motioning to the pink room—"is killing me and it's way beyond your control." Danny's brows were pinched, but he listened without saying a word, so she continued. "I was scared, and the longer I sat in that sterile place, my fear turned to anger. I thought maybe, one night after leaving me, you may have come home and gotten rid of this room."

He squinted. "Gotten rid of the room?"

"Yeah, I was convinced that I'd come home and all of this would be gone—the room painted white, the clothes packed up—and it would be one more thing I didn't say good-bye to."

The rhythm of Danny's breathing increased as his chest rose and fell against her back.

As the silence stretched on, Julie's heart ached for the pain she'd just caused her man. "Danny, I'm sorr—"

"Your turn is over for a few minutes, honey."

Shifting them so his body no longer supported hers, he sent a coldness through her that she felt clear to the marrow of her bones. But the distance lasted mere seconds before he sat facing her with his jean-clad legs encircling her and locked at the ankles. His hands held hers.

"I ever scare you? Make you think you don't have a say in our life or our relationship? Other than when I was with the fire company?" The questions came out slowly, as if they were hard to ask but he wanted only the truth.

So she gave him only that. "No, never. You have only ever made me feel secure, loved, and free. It's just, I know that you hate to see me sad, and when I cry…please, I know that tears you up."

"Yeah, honey, it does. Fucking kills me, because your happiness is important to me. No, that ain't right—it's everything to me. Always has been, always will be."

"Danny—"

"Control? Yeah, Jules, I love control, because it helps me navigate through life, but guess what? Life is beyond control. You know it; hell, I know it. The only real control I ever have is in the bedroom, and even then…come on"—he tilted his head, his hazel eyes softened pools of love—"it's based on your willingness."

"Danny—"

"No, I'm not done just yet. This room"—he pulled a hand free and gestured to the open space—"belonged to our daughter. *Our* daughter, Jules. We need to mourn the loss, honey, together. Seeing you cry tears me up inside; knowing you're hiding it destroys me. We'll get through this, Julie. Believe in us."

Tears filled her eyes and stung her nose, but words were stuck behind the lump in her throat.

"I'm done now, honey." Danny stared at her, worry etched in the lines of his forehead. "You wanna say something?"

"I'm sorry," Julie whispered, and the dam broke.

"No apologies needed, sweetness." Danny once again swept her into his arms, careful of her mended abdomen, and they rocked together on the newly carpeted nursery floor.

CHAPTER FOURTEEN

My Cousin Vinny

THE FIRST FEW weeks after Julie's accident were painful, both physically and emotionally. She felt as if comfort would forever be an arm's length away, a thing of the past and a foolish fantasy of what the future could have held. While awake, her body hurt and her muscles burned from healing, and while sleeping, nightmares robbed her of peace. Two faces—twisted and drunk on liquor and lust—mocked her and beat her, day after day, night after night. She dreamed of pain, loss, and even a few times of her baby girl waving good-bye, not such a baby at all. The more Julie dreamed, the worse the dreams got, until her dreams were nothing like the events that had taken place that rainy night, but more like every horror movie she'd ever refused to watch, ironically enough, because she feared nightmares. Julie would wake up in the dark room, pain searing her gut, sweat dripping down her spine, and a scream caught in her throat.

"I'm here, honey, you're safe," Danny would assure as his large hand stroked her pajama-covered body and pulled her close. "Shhh, you're safe."

And while she knew that she was, in fact, safe, she was forever tense, short-tempered, and tired.

———————♦———————♦———————

"I CAN'T BELIEVE you asked Dr. Burke about therapy," she fumed once Danny was seated in the Ranger with the door closed. "Don't you think that you should have discussed it with me first?"

He sighed, clearly trying his best to quell the urge to argue with her, an urge he'd mastered over the six weeks since her surgery. "I have discussed it with you. You haven't slept more than a few hours a night since the accident, you barely eat, you spend hours in the nursery, and the worst part...you do it all alone." His chest rose and fell in rapid succession. "What happened to believing in me?"

She shrugged.

"Dammit, Julie." Danny slammed his palms against the steering wheel once before reining in his temper like a fishing line. "We took vows, honey. For better or worse. You remember that? I promised to love you till I fucking die. Look at me," he demanded, waiting until she brought her eyes to his. "I'm not dead yet. And there's no fucking way I'm gonna sit back and watch you drown. We need help, honey. I'll support you, go with you, or get out of the way so you can go by yourself. But you, my beautiful wife, are done doing this alone."

A sliver of guilt broke through her shell as she looked at her husband for the first time in weeks. He was hurting too. He'd done his best to support her, love her, and give her space while he worked full time, managed the house, and held her through the night as she shivered from fear.

He couldn't possibly understand the pain and torment she felt from losing their baby, but he was doing the best he could.

"Okay," she relented. "I don't think I need any help, but I'll call the therapist Doctor Burke suggested if it will make you happy."

"Thank you, honey."

Julie shifted to face the window, missing the way Danny's mouth curled up a tiny bit. He wouldn't say out loud that the therapist wouldn't just help him, but her...them. He wasn't a dumb man. Stubborn woman needed to think she was doing him a favor, then so be it. In time, she'd figure it out.

EVER SO SLOWLY, light crept back into Julie's mercurial eyes. After her first visit with the therapist, Julie's mood had worsened. Her tears came more easily, and Danny wondered if maybe he'd pushed too hard too soon. Chester assured him that, as with soldiers returning from war, trauma was a battle fought with patience, time, and endurance, not a smile and a pat on the back. While Danny felt the loss of their baby, Julie was suffering with the guilt of not protecting what she felt was her mission, her purpose.

"Think about it, Dan," Chester gruffed into the phone while Julie was at her second appointment, "we're trained...no man left behind, yeah? We lose one of our own, and we feel it through to our gut. I know you lost your unborn child, I know you're hurtin', but she lost her life blood. She left someone behind…"

Chester's words pierced Danny, but also brought a little more clarity, as they always did. He had been the reason Danny suggested therapy in the first place.

"Let her feel the pain, son—"

"That's all she's been doing!"

"No," Chester said, "she's been feelin' nothin'… numb. The first session cracked her. Angry, tearful…she's finally feelin'. You're doin' good, boy. Hold tight, and you'll get our girl back soon. I promise, she's worth the fight."

"Fuck, Ches, you don't think I know she's worth it? I just miss her, man."

TRUE TO HIS friend's word, over the following weeks, Julie's smile returned. It may not have been as bright as before, but it was honest, and it reached her eyes.

"You're never gonna believe what movie I rented for tonight." Danny waggled his brows as he tossed the box of Goobers and the package of strawberry Twizzlers on the coffee table and headed to the kitchen to grab two bottles of beer.

"Am I supposed to sit here and guess?" Julie called from the sofa.

Her sarcastic retort made a smile pull at Danny's cheeks. *Welcome back, baby*. What he said was, "Yes, smart ass, why don't you take a guess?"

"Hmm, *Point Break*?"

"No." He placed the cold beverages on the table and served up the best glare he could. "I think seeing it twice in the theater and renting it three times so you could ogle Keanu Reeves has maxed out my lifetime desire to ever watch that movie again."

"Danny, just tell me," Julie mock-whined, giggling in a way that was musical and missed. "It's rare you have the entire day and night off, and we've been running around like crazy all day. If we don't get started soon, I can't guarantee I'll make it through the whole movie."

"No way you're falling asleep on this one, honey. Here's a hint." He cleared his throat and attempted his best Marissa Tomei accent. "'One tire spins, the other tire does nothing.'"

"Ahh!" Julie's arms flew up, narrowly missing the food and drinks. "You rented *My Cousin Vinny*? Danny, I'm so excited to see it again! We only got to see that movie twice on opening weekend. It came out right before we left on our trip."

Danny thought back to the first time they'd seen it on opening weekend. The movie came out only a few months after he lost his baby brother, left his job, and decided to work behind a bar. He'd laughed so hard the night they saw *My Cousin Vinny*, and he remembered wondering how laughter was possible even when his hurt and uncertainty felt all-consuming. The four weeks that followed were medicine to his soul and produced the tiny life he and Julie had wished for.

While he had no intentions of pushing his wife to become intimate before she was ready—which clearly she wasn't, based on the fact that the only touching she sought and accepted was being held in the dead of night when horrors pulled her from sleep and into his arms—he couldn't help but hope the movie that brought levity to him would bring laughter to her.

It did. As they recited the lines they remembered from the two times they saw the film and snorted with abandon at the silly antics of Joe Pesci and Marissa Tomei, Danny felt tension melt from Julie's body. Each tear that left her eyes may have come from laughter, but it held sadness that had been trapped for nearly two months.

At the end, when Julie kissed Danny's cheek and whispered, "Thank you," he felt the hero so many had claimed him to be.

That night, once tucked in bed, Julie tangled their fingers together as she laid her head close to his shoulder. "I love you, Danny," she whispered. "I promise, I'll get back to...*normal* soon."

His heart pounded. Her touch, as small as it was, was a magical elixir to his skin, but her words brought both comfort and discontent. "Honey, it's because I love you that your promise isn't needed. You understand? Take the time you need to feel what you need to feel." He squeezed her hand. "Not gonna lie, having your hand in mine... Christ, that small touch...heaven, Jules. But as long as you're working on coming back to not just me but you... I'll fucking wait. Just don't shut me out, darlin'."

"Okay."

The room got quiet as her breaths evened out, each exhale warming the skin of his shoulder. *She's on her way back*, he thought just before sleep claimed him.

WITH EACH PASSING week, Julie got stronger. As much as she hated to admit it, Danny had been right to suggest and all but force her to go to therapy. While she was grateful to her husband, watching him barely hide the twitch of his lips when she conceded to his fabulousness was a bit tough on her ego.

"Guilty, you've been feeling guilty…"

The resignation in her husband's voice suggested that he didn't hold her responsible for the accident that had ended the pregnancy, a point her therapist had been trying to drive home for weeks.

"Honey"—Danny lifted her chin until their eyes met—"you've been hoarding the responsibility of what happened. Got yourself a suitcase filled with blame, yeah?"

She nodded.

"Keep thinking what if you hadn't gone to work that night? What if you hadn't worked so hard or walked to the car alone?"

He's been reading my mind. How else could he know the questions that have played on a continuous loop for the past twelve weeks?

"Maybe you should place your bag next to mine," he said.

Her eyes widened. *What does he mean? He did nothing wrong.*

"You see, I gotta duffle stuffed with 'what ifs' too. What if I didn't work on the nights you worked? What if I had a mobile phone instead of a pager? Could I have gotten to you faster? What if I insisted on you quitting your job at O'Brian's the minute you hit your second trimester?" Humor lit his gaze. "Don't look at me that way, babe. I know you never would have done it, but I still battle with that regret."

She swallowed, allowing his words to wash over her, seep into her, and resonate.

"So many 'what ifs,' Jul, but none of them matter. You could have slipped and fallen on the way into the grocery store. You could've tripped down the stairs in our home. It was an accident," he said, enunciating every word.

Slowly, she repeated him, "It *was* an accident, Danny. It was."

His hazel stare burned into hers, God, his eyes saw into her soul in a way no one else's could. Unconditional love in its purest form. That was why she'd spent so much time in the past three months avoiding them. They undid her, made her want things she needed to hide from. But lately, hiding was getting harder, mostly because she was done trying. She wanted to let him in, share her burdens, and move on. Her twelve-week obstetrician follow-up appointment was the next day; she was ready to take back her life.

CHAPTER FIFTEEN

Your Mere Existence

"SO YOU'RE SAYING I'll never be able to have babies, ever?" Julie's voice broke as the question left her mouth. She felt Danny's hand grip hers, but the room shrank, closing in around her. She hadn't gotten her period since losing the baby, but at the six-week follow-up visit, the doctor had told her to be patient. In fairness, she remembered the doctor in the hospital discussing possible difficulty with future pregnancies, but she had been drugged up at the time and had refused to ask questions.

"I'm sorry." Dr. Burke's compassionate eyes moved between hers and Danny's. "According to the ultrasound we just did, you have no endometrial lining, an unfortunate outcome from the surgery and embolization you needed to stop the bleeding. None of those things could have been avoided. It was a life-or-death situation."

"Obviously there was no choice to be made." Danny's firm statement resulted in silence as Julie's eyes leaked. Danny exhaled as he ran his hand through his short dark hair."Okay."

He'll fix this. He'll make it better.

"Let me understand what you're telling us…because of what happened, we can't have children. The baby that we lost is the only one we'll ever have?" Danny asked.

"Biologically, yes," the doctor answered. "I'm so sorry. I wish I had better news for you, different answers, but I don't."

"We wish you had different answers too," he murmured.

Julie's lungs burned with the need for air. She hadn't let so much as a breath escape her body for fear of breaking down, never to be fixed again. Her gaze cut to her husband, ramrod straight in the expensive leather chair, tight jaw, wet eyes, but a supportive grasp on her hand. She kept letting him down, and he kept holding her close. They would have no children, no family.

With Danny's arm looped around her waist, they walked silently out of the building and to the Ranger. Once inside the cab, Julie pulled the cork on the emotions she'd been holding in and let loose the keening cries of a woman who'd just lost her fantasies…again.

DANNY JOINED JULIE at the first therapy session after leaving the doctor's office, which, thanks to the therapist and her magical schedule, was just hours after receiving the crippling news. In that office, they cried in each other's arms, screamed at the unfairness of life, and determined that Julie would benefit from sessions twice weekly until the initial crisis passed.

Two weeks had passed since the fateful obstetrician's appointment, and while Julie didn't revert entirely to where she had been after she lost their daughter, she regressed deeply at first.

After sixteen days, Sheila contacted Danny when she hadn't heard from Julie. Their friend was heartbroken by the news, but like the best of friends did, she came up with a plan instead of focusing on things that couldn't be changed. While Julie didn't return to work after losing the baby, she and Sheila still spoke frequently and the two couples continued to see each other socially.

With Danny's blessing, Sheila stopped by the Marcus house one day while he was at work, and she convinced Julie it was time to return to her management position. Within two weeks, Julie seemed to be crying less and smiling more. He got a kiss on the cheek before work and a hug before sleep. She seemed happier, more alive, and he was grateful.

Danny used the time while Julie was at work to allow himself to grieve. They mourned together for the first few days, but then he tucked away his sadness and focused on keeping his woman above water. However, when alone, the loss crept in and felt suffocating. Their dreams of little kids, loud dinners, big Christmases, sibling rivalries, and bear hugs felt ripped away, leaving raw skin and exposed nerves. But new dreams could be made, of that he was certain, as long as he had Julie by his side.

The problem was that it had been four and a half months since she'd let him touch her. Four and a half months since he'd given her more than a peck on the cheek or squeezed her hand. They'd spent their whole marriage sleeping skin to skin, and she now slept in long sleeves and sleep pants. While he could continue to give her space, he feared the space was creating issues that would eventually cause a rift.

Julie had always loved his dominant ways. She bloomed under his words and writhed beneath his touch. For months he'd stayed back, fearful of pushing her before she was ready, scared to lose her due to impatience.

He snickered without humor at his reflection in the men's room mirror at work. "You'll lose her 'cause you've been acting like a pussy." *New dreams will be made*. He left the restroom and headed to his post.

In the months that he'd watched his wife grieve, blocking him out, keeping pain in, it was Chester who had become his closest confidant. After work that day, Danny called Chester for advice.

"If she freely gives you control in the bedroom, she wants you to control her in the bedroom," his friend said.

"Chester, no offense, man, but she's in a bad place. She barely comes near me."

"Dan, no offense, boy, and believe me, this advice doesn't come easy bein' as I think of her as a daughter, but there comes a time when you'll need to start thinking as a couple and not just about her. The shit that went down, son—it tears couples apart. That I can promise. You'll know when it's time, and when it is, take back the control she's given you. Take it back in a way that she knows she's loved and safe, but that's it."

"What?"

Chester huffed. "She's hurtin', runnin', pushin' you away. How do you stop her from doing that while lovin' her with everything you got?"

"Ah," The proverbial light bulb pinged over Danny's head as a smile caressed his face.

"By George, I think he's got it." Chester chuckled and ended their call.

Danny began his planning.

———————————————

"A MINT CHOCOLATE chip milk shake!" Her eyes lit up as she dipped her spoon into the extra-thick novelty. "Let me guess, a vanilla one for you, huh?" He always loved watching her "drink" shakes with a spoon. "Did you do something wrong, Mr. Marcus?" Her brow arched with mock accusation as her mouth opened wide to accept another generous scoop.

"No, babe, I passed the ice cream shop on my way home from work and figured you could use a treat."

They had both worked day shift and had the night off. It was the first time in over a week their schedules allowed for that, and he planned on taking advantage of the night.

"Mmm, so good." She swiped a napkin off the kitchen table and padded on bare feet to the family room. She cozied up on the sofa with her shake and the television remote. "*Wheel of Fortune* is starting. Come sit with me."

Together, they watched the game show while calling out answers before the contestants, high-fiving when they were correct, laughing each time they guessed wrong. Danny's focus split between the show and the way Julie's tongue lapped at the quickly melting ice cream. *So sexy.* A needy rhythm throbbed in his cock each time an appreciative moan escaped her lips. *Oh, sweet Lord, let me in.*

Click.

"Danny, what…" Julie stared from the blank television screen to him. "*Jeopardy*'s on next. We love that show. Why did you turn off the TV?"

That question was the only one he needed to hear, and the answer was clear. Danny removed the empty shake cup from Julie's hand and placed it on the coffee table before turning his attention back to her.

"*Jeopardy*, huh? Okay, the answer is…*your mere existence*." Danny closed the distance between them, interlacing their fingers as he nudged his nose up her neck to her ear. "What's the question, honey?"

When goose bumps rose on her skin, excitement surged through his blood. She still wanted him; he just needed to break through the wall of fear and contentment that she'd erected over the months.

"W-what?"

"The question, babe." His tongue touched her lobe. "If the answer's *your mere existence*, what's the question?" Gently, he bit the sensitive skin and relished the tiny tremor that shook her body.

"Danny, I-I have no idea what you're doing," Julie faltered, her lids lowered, and her tongue glided across her bottom lip.

"Yeah, you do. You've just forgotten." As he whispered in her ear, his hand lowered to her denim-clad thigh. "I'm here to remind you, honey. The question—what part of you makes my life complete?"

Her body stilled beneath his touch.

"The answer—*your mere existence.*"

"Danny…" She sighed, her body all but melting with his touch.

The husband inside him exhaled with relief while his primal side roared with unrestrained triumph. "Let me give you what you need." He stood, slid his arm under her legs, and effortlessly cradled her as he walked them upstairs. "I'm your husband, babe, your man. I'll gladly watch game shows with you forever. But right now, only thing I wanna do is strip you naked and lick every inch of your gorgeous fucking body." He lowered her to her feet, flicked on the bedroom light, and stared at the woman before him. "Been so long since you felt pleasure, too damn long. You need it, and I can't wait to give it."

If her pale pink cheeks and glossy eyes weren't enough of an indicator that she was aroused, then the way her breath hitched with each word he spoke certainly was.

"Oh, God," Julie panted as her tongue caressed her bottom lip.

"Good place to start, but it'll be my name you're screaming when you're coming on my face." Danny winked as he popped the button and slid down the zipper on Julie's jeans.

Her audible swallow had him choking back a chuckle. *Fuck me.* He subtly adjusted himself. *It's been so long, I might come from my own damn dirty talk.* Danny cupped Julie's cheek, staring into her eyes for a brief second before claiming her mouth. *Coming home.* That was how it felt to press his lips to hers. Scorching, claiming desire clawed through his body, screaming for release. His hand left her cheek and moved to the back of her neck, fisting the strawberry-blonde locks as his other hand lowered them both to the bed. Without breaking their kiss, he pushed the jeans down her hips and thighs, then used his sock-covered foot to remove them completely.

He ran his palm up the length of her outer thigh. "Your skin, Christ, so soft, so smooth. Missed touching you, honey, being wrapped up in all this silk."

On his knees, he slid her legs farther apart, anticipation building with his every touch. Her shirt was a long blue number that she changed into when she got home from work. Soft and shapeless, covering her from torso to hips, it left nothing but a blue triangle of cotton panty exposed. Not the lacy thongs she used to wear, but he wasn't complaining. *Innocent...sexy.* She could try to hide it, but she'd always be the sexiest woman he'd known. Leaning forward, he touched her over her underwear. His middle finger traced the seam of her pussy, immediately earning him a throaty moan.

"That's it, honey. I can feel you getting wet for me already. Sweet little spot here on your panties."

He went to lift her shirt, and her body stiffened. Her breath paused, and her eyes tightened, but not tight enough to hold in the tear that rolled off the side of her face.

"Julie?" His low question was followed by an even lower request. "Open your eyes and talk to me." But it was more of a demand than a request. They'd come too far. No way would he allow her to bury her head back in the sands of denial.

"I can't do this." Julie opened her eyes, stared at her trembling hands, and cried. "All you talk about is giving *me* what *I* need. You keep standing by *my* side, supporting *me*. I can't give you what you need. I can't be what you deserve." She wiped at her rapidly falling tears. "I'm not the woman you fell in love with anymore, and I never will be again."

His heart splintered with each word that left her mouth.

"I'm barely a woman at all." Her half-naked body was racked with sobs as she sat up and pulled into her-self—knees up to her chest, arms wrapped tightly around her knees.

"So blind, honey. So goddamn smart, yet still so blind," Danny muttered as he stood and moved toward their dresser. He grabbed his wallet and the handheld sil-ver mirror that had belonged to her mother and returned to sit at Julie's feet. "My love, since the day I met you, you were everything I needed and more than I deserved." He stroked the soft bare skin of Julie's arm. "What do you see when you look in this?"

He showed her her reflection in the mirror and had to refrain from roaring in frustration when she quickly flinched at her image.

"I see a broken woman." The tremble in her words increased. "I see ugly, worthless, and unnecessary. I see someone who can never give you the children that we dreamed of, and it kills me."

Her truth felt like a knife slicing through his soul. But he had asked. He had brought her to the cliff and it was time to put on their parachutes and jump together, or he feared she would fall alone. He wasn't sure either of them would survive a solo fall.

Danny opened his wallet and pulled out a small pho-to. It had been taken by Chester the summer they met. "This is what I see when I look at you. The beautiful woman who stole my heart and captured my soul, who completes me in every fucking way. *Your mere existence*, Julie...your mere fucking existence..." His voice was clogged with emotion. "You're right, Jules, you aren't the woman I fell in love with, and guess what?"

Her eyes lifted to his.

"I'm not the same fucking man." Shoving his fingers back into his wallet, he pulled out the plastic hospital bracelet that Julie had worn four and a half months prior. "See that? This reminds me every fucking day that I nearly lost you. I nearly had my wife, my goddamn lifeline, ripped away from me. Think the punk kid I was when we met would've been able to handle that? Because this man"—he pressed his finger to his chest—"would have never gotten over it. I thank God every fucking day they got you to the hospital in time. Yes, honey, we lost our child. We did. And I grieve that loss, but I grieve it with you, for you, for us. Without you, there would be no fucking life, no me. You understand?"

Her eyes stayed focused on the floral comforter, but she nodded.

"Julie?" Danny put his knuckle under her chin and tilted her head back so he could see her eyes. "We got the green light months ago from the doctor"—his eyes raked over her semi-naked body—"but you needed more time and I needed you comfortable. I gave you space, babe, but I see the space was misinterpreted."

"It wasn't you, Danny," Julie protested. "I know you love me…it's just…" She stretched the long shirt farther over her knees. "I have scars, physical reminders of what I can never do, never give you."

Her scars had never crossed his mind—maybe because he hadn't seen them since the hospital, maybe because he wouldn't find them unattractive. Either way, they weren't a factor for him. He needed to prove that to her and make her see past her skin and into the woman he saw daily. Moving his hand to her exposed thigh, his thumb drew small circles over the satiny skin before it climbed up her hip, waist, and torso and peeled the shirt from her body. Reaching behind her, he unclasped her simple cotton bra, then sat back on his haunches and stared.

"You're beautiful. All woman," he growled, his dick hardening by the second. "Every single inch of you, and lucky son of a bitch that I am, it was all made for me." She was still tense but no longer crying, and Danny swiped the stray tears from her cheeks and sucked the saltiness off his thumbs. "All you, mine."

He leaned forward and brushed his lips on her neck. The sweet smell of gardenias flooded his senses as his erection pulsed. When he felt another shiver go through her body and saw goose bumps reemerge across her flesh, he knew it was time to take back his woman. Not just take her, but claim her in a way they'd never tried before.

"Do you trust me, Julie?"

SHE DID TRUST him. She'd forgotten how to trust herself for months, but never once did she doubt her trust in Danny.

"You're the one thing in this world I've never doubted," she admitted. "I think that may be part of the reason I've kept away for so long." *I can't believe I'm saying this, wearing practically nothing. I really am a disaster.*

"What do you mean, honey?" There was an inherent strength visible on Danny's handsome face. "Explain."

She gnawed at her upper lip and looked away from her husband as she tried to put into words exactly how she felt. "You're strong. You get knocked down and not only do you get back up, you get stronger. And when you love, my God, you love with your whole freaking being. I've never seen such dedication. I'm completely and totally head over heels in love with you, but I've spent months wondering if maybe you've only stayed out of loyalty. 'For better or worse,' right?" Silence fell between them as she continued to look around their bedroom, too cowardly to return her gaze to his.

"You done with that?"

Her brows snapped together. "Huh?"

"Obviously you know that's bullshit. If you didn't know before tonight, you damn well know now, yeah? Although, if we're being honest, babe, gotta admit, that's absolute bullshit."

"Dan—"

"No, honey, you've known from the start how I feel, how I felt. Never made it a secret, never kept it hidden. Never will. You were scared. You had a good reason. We lost something special, something irreplaceable. But get this straight—you will never, I repeat never, lose me." He touched his chest. "I'm yours."

"Danny—"

He interrupted her a second time. "And as for me getting knocked down and getting stronger, I'm thinking a new mirror may be needed in this house, cause you and I ain't looking at the same woman. My strength comes from you, and you're practically a gladiator." A forgiving smile played at the corners of his mouth. "Strength and beauty. Like I said, I'm one lucky son of a bitch."

"Danny?" Julie released a stuttered sigh, relieved to have the tension between them gone.

"What?"

"Make me scream your name."

FIVE WORDS, AND his dick was granite hard. If he was honest, no words were needed for her to have that effect on him. But, Christ, those five together were like porn for his fucking brain.

"You wanna scream my name, Jules?" Danny rose from the bed, opened a drawer in the dresser, and pulled out a neck tie. His pulse raced as Julie's eyes rounded and her lip tucked between her teeth. "That bottom lip, honey, can't wait to taste it."

"What…what are you planning to do with that?" She swallowed, her gaze going from the silk in his hands up to his eyes.

"I plan to make you stay while I devour you. You've been running for too long, baby. Time to stop. This will keep you steady 'till I've had my fill."

"Oh my God." The whisper barely left her lips, and Danny chuckled.

"Don't worry, Jules." He looped a firm knot around her wrists before affixing them to the headboard. He felt her head tip to the side, her eyes scanning first the silk binding, then him. She was waiting for more…maybe an explanation or direction. "You've given me your love and your heart. Now you're giving me back your body—your trust isn't lost on me, honey."

Love, desire, and hunger warred through his body, fighting each other for the chance to devour the delectable meal sprawled out before him. A flawless beauty from head to toe, including the pink scars that marked her abdomen, she was his sustenance—his water, his air, his North-fucking-Star—and he intended to prove just how vital to him she was.

And he did. Over and over again.

CHAPTER SIXTEEN

The Empty Contest

"HAPPY ANNIVERSARY, HANDSOME." Julie rested her chin on Danny's lower abs, a bemused smile gracing her swollen lips. "Did you enjoy your wake-up call?"

He could barely think, let alone formulate sentences. "Christ." Shivers bounced through his body. "Babe, twelve years married, still…you rock my world like you did that first summer." Staring down his torso at his wife, his mouth watered. Her long hair was twisted around his fist as the globes of her pert naked ass were lifted and ex-posed…so ready, willing, wanting.

She giggled. "Whatcha doing?"

Claiming control, he tugged his arm around her waist and flipped her beneath him, her gray eyes rounded but hardly focused as she stared at his naked body between her thighs.

"Oh, thought this was a full-service situation you set up here," he replied innocently. "Got my wake-up call"—his brows waggled with humor—"want my breakfast." Dropping wet kisses on her ribs, he moved south, not stopping until he reached the apex of her thighs. "Fuck, you smell incredible."

Her nails scratched at the cotton sheets the moment his tongue lapped her clit.

"Mmm, love these organic meals," he teased as his tongue made another pass at the engorged bud.

"Danny…" she gasped, equally embarrassed and aroused by the statement. But when he slid two fingers into her wet heat and found her sweet spot, her gasp turned to a moan, and all talk ended.

———————————

"TO DANNY AND Julie," Danny's father declared as he lifted a champagne-filled flute.

With Julie by his side, Danny peered at those who made up the dinner party of seven: Allan and his wife Anita, Chester, and Sheila and her husband, Chris. All people who had become integral parts of his and Julie's life.

"I knew the minute I saw you together, there would be no tearing you apart," Allan said. "Because while ever-lasting love takes years of building, reinforcing, and supporting, it doesn't have a shot in hell unless the foundation is strong. You two are made of titanium, chromium, and diamonds."

Danny reached for Julie's hand under the table, loving the way she weaved their fingers together the second his hand made purchase, as if she had been just waiting for his touch.

"You started with the strongest of the strong and have built up from there. While many couples, both young and old, have crumbled under far less than the two of you, you've only seemed to flourish. As your father"—Allan's gaze shot between them as if once again claiming Julie as his daughter—"I couldn't be more proud. Happy anniversary! May there be at least fifty more."

"Happy anniversary," was chimed in unison as the tink of crystal glasses filled the air.

For hours, the small group reminisced about the holidays they had shared over the years: the snow storms that had gotten Julie stuck at work, and both she and Sheila laughed while listening to their husbands rant over the speaker phone about why they hadn't closed the Ale House sooner and headed home, and of course the infamous Empty Contest.

"Seriously, that may have been the dumbest thing you boys ever did…EVER," Julie howled as the other two women laughed loudly.

"I beg your pardon, missy." Chester swirled the tequila in his lowball glass.

Some would fear his gravelly voice, but not Julie. She saw the sparkle in Chester's eyes and snorted.

"Lookin' around this table, there ain't no boys here," he said.

"Jules, let me handle this one, please." Sheila snorted while Julie's entire frame shook with unbridled laughter. "It is *not* men who intentionally decide to fill their tanks only to see how many miles each car can go before *empty* truly means *empty*. Those are the actions of boys. Little boys. Toddlers, in fact."

Anita piped up, "Oh, and let us not forget that if there *were* men silly enough to have come up with such a ridiculous plan, they would have checked the forecast and known that a coastal storm was coming."

185

A hiccup of giggles had the women nearly rolling from their chairs. Danny rubbed his jaw to hide his smile. Their laughter was infectious.

"All four of you idiots needed rescuing over the course of three days." Julie's stare bore into Danny.

It had been nearly three years since the Empty Contest, and still he remembered with precise clarity having to make *that* middle-of-the-night phone call to a less-than-happy wife.

"Already snug in bed when you called…" She shook her head. "Lucky I love you."

No matter how annoyed she had been that stormy night, with each retelling of the story, Danny saw the sparkle of humor and glimmer of love in her eyes and on her upturned lips. It had been there when she dropped off the gas container and shielded him with an umbrella as he replenished his tank.

"See, at least I didn't drag my wife outta work or outta bed." Chester grinned, knowing full well that Allan and Chris had faced similar unpleasant fates with their cars and their spouses. Little bastard.

"No, you dragged your poor bar manager out of her bed, you old jerk," Julie partially teased. "Tara was pissed when she called me the next day."

"Tara got real happy the next night." Chester lifted his glass and winked.

"Nice." Allan high-fived Chester, and Danny grimaced. No matter how old he got, thoughts of his father having sex still made him uneasy. "Wipe that scowl of your face, son, and let no one forget, I was the winner of the Empty Contest. Sweet Lil' Jessi Jane rode me thirty-two miles once she read empty."

Julie's body trembled with laughter while Anita rolled her eyes.

"What? I name my cars," Allan explained, "and they treat me well."

The table erupted into hysterics before Allan had finished his sentence.

"Speakin' of being treated well…" Chester's confident words were spoken slowly, grabbing Danny's attention.

Danny leaned in before making eye contact with Julie alone.

"I've spent my life servin'…first *with* America's finest, then *for* them. It's been an honor and a pleasure, but …I'm done."

"What are you saying, Ches?" There was no hiding the concern in Julie's voice, nor the strength in the way her small hand gripped Danny's under the table.

Chester chuckled. "Julie girl, alls I'm sayin' is I'm sellin' the bar and moving to Key West. Time to stop servin' drinks and start havin' some sweet lil' honeys servin' me."

With jaws collectively dropped around the table, Danny spoke first. "Wow, Ches. Holy shit, man, I never thought the day would come, but I'm happy for you. For real, congratulations." So few people worked as long and hard as Chester Murray had. The man deserved retirement while he was young enough to enjoy it.

Julie beamed. "Oh, Ches, I'm so excited for you. The women have no idea what's headed their way."

With another squeeze to his hand, Danny knew that Julie was about to share their news, so he squeezed back in approval. He swallowed back the excitement that he'd been dying to share the whole evening.

"WHEN IS THE move happening?" Julie couldn't have been happier for the man who had been like a father to her for the past fourteen years. But there was a piece, a small piece that felt selfish, that wished Chester would live a short drive away forever. Especially now.

Chester explained that he had *people* in Key West, and one of them had been looking to sell their house. Chester had purchased it a month prior but kept it on the down low until he'd found someone willing to buy Chester's Bar for a fair price. He hadn't expected the bar to sell so fast for such a profit, but it did. "I'll be leaving in about four weeks."

"Four weeks…" Allan frowned. "Anita and I'll come up here before you leave to say good-bye."

"Fuck no," Chester grumbled. "I don't do good-byes. Not ever. You two wanna come to my place and help my old ass pack, be my guest. We can all go out for dinner or drinks—hell, we can hang out at this old place called Chester's." He winked. "Hear it's under new ownership. But when you leave, it's 'see ya later.' Got it?"

Julie's heart thrummed as Chester spoke. The end of an era was approaching; big changes were on the way. Danny patted her knee, a reminder that they too had news to share, and it was time.

Julie felt a smile break across her lips. "So, Ches, do you think you could find it in your heart to make your way up north in about six months?"

"What?" the entire group asked in unison.

Excitement lit up her insides. The news was still so fresh to her and Danny. "You tell them," she implored her equally radiant husband.

Danny brought their joined hands to the table top. His fingers were warm and strong as they grasped hers. "As you know, we've been waiting for over two years to adopt a baby. For the past week, we've been in talks with the adoption agency about a seventeen-year-old girl who's only twelve weeks pregnant. Her parents aren't supportive of her keeping the baby once it's born, and the baby's father isn't in the picture. She's giving the baby up for adoption, and she chose us to be the adoptive parents."

"Oh… oh…a baby!" Anita jumped up from her chair, rushed around the table, and threw her arms around Julie.

"This calls for another round of champagne," Chester ordered to the server. "And to answer your question, Julie girl, wild cowgirls couldn't keep me away."

"My question is, why the hell did it take you two so long to share this news?" Sheila's motherly tone always tickled Julie. "Seriously, am I the only one thinking it? Or am I the only one ballsy enough to say it?"

"I'm with Sheila on this one," Allan said as his fingers drummed a quick beat on the table top. "We're having dessert already. Jeez, what were you waiting for?"

Julie turned her gaze from her father-in-law to her husband. Danny's eyes glowed with enjoyment and tenderness; she knew he felt her excitement just as deeply, just as powerfully, just as intensely as she did. "We were waiting for the sweet moment at the end of dinner to share our sweet news."

"And it doesn't get sweeter or sexier than this," Danny's gravelly voice muttered a split second before his lips claimed hers. Passion and longing met in one brief kiss—Christ, she couldn't wait to get home.

Allan cleared his throat, which cleared Julie's erotic thoughts. "Please don't forget you have house guests. Anita and I love you, but we don't want a repeat of Independence Day 1996. Some pretty explosive fireworks that night." Allan winked.

"Dad," Danny groaned while Julie felt her face heat. "We promised we'd never discuss that again."

"No, son, *you* promised we'd never talk about it again."

Laughter filled the emptying restaurant.

"Aw man, I love that story," Chris chimed in. "Nothing funnier than having your dad ask you to keep it down via Post-It note. Fan-fucking-tastic."

Julie's cheeks flamed. "No disrespect, but you guys aren't so quiet yourselves."

Instantly Allan and Anita fell silent and Danny's shoulders shook.

"It's true," Danny admitted, his lips twitching with humor. "Time we came home for Christmas—first time we met you, Anita—you guys wouldn't have a sleepover while *we kids* were staying at the house. But when I took Julie out one evening to look at the Christmas lights, you two used the alone time to your advantage. It seemed Jules and I came back a bit too soon, though you both came right on time."

Julie giggled and Danny squirmed.

"Oh… oh…" Anita gasped. "That's horrifying. You're right, we should never talk of those times again."

"Agreed," said Julie, Danny, and Allan.

———◆———◆———◆———

THE WEEKS PASSED with dizzying speed as Danny and Julie prepared for the inevitable changes coming to their lives. Chester's move had gone off without a hitch, leaving Maryland a little less…merry. That said, it seemed as if Julie spoke with him more after his relocation than she had when he lived just a few towns away.

An introduction had been arranged between Julie and Danny and Ivy, the birthmother of their future child. The meeting felt awkward, stilted, strange, but as Danny reminded her after the fact, how was something of that nature supposed to have gone? The three of them met a second time, and as Julie and Ivy chatted, a connection blossomed. Because Ivy was a minor, she was covered by her parents' health insurance, but that didn't stop Danny and Julie from offering financial support during Ivy's pregnancy. All of Ivy's maternity clothing, stretch mark prevention creams, and bi-weekly pedicures were on the Marcuses' tab, and they relished every second of it.

But that wasn't all. Julie wanted to give their future baby her full attention. Whether due to maturity, priority adjustments, or plain old guilt, she was ready to step back from her career and focus on being a stay-at-home mom.

"Honey, are you sure this is what you want?" Danny carefully removed the coffee pot from her grip, placed it on the breakfast table, and in one fluid movement, had her facing him on his pajama-clad lap.

"Yes," Julie answered softly as she stared into understanding eyes that forever stole her breath. "I'm completely certain. I want to be home with our baby. I know I felt differently last time." She cleared her throat, as well as the emotion that still came to the surface when she thought about the loss of their child. "But last time, I thought it was just the beginning. This time…it's most likely the only." Her hand met the perpetual scruff that lined Danny's jaw but never masked his face. Its feel brought instant comfort to her soul and pleasure to her body. "I want to savor every minute of the *mommy* time"—she wiggled her ass against his crotch, pulling her bottom lip between her teeth as he hardened beneath her—"and still have energy to savor you."

A shiver ran up her spine as Danny meticulously swept her long hair around his fist, exposing the sensitive flesh where her neck and shoulder met. "Honey, any child we have will be loved the world over, but you will always be *my* reason."

His large hands spread her knees as his palms worked up to her panty-covered core. The pad of his middle finger stroked tenderly over the satin panel. The contact with her clit made a soft moan escape her lips before she could think to hold it back.

"Don't you worry about energy, baby, I got enough for both of us." Husky authority laced his tone. "Only one thing you need to do."

She peered up at him through hooded lids.

"When you're home, the underwear is gone. Any opportunity I can find to sink into *my* pussy, I'm gonna take it, and you're gonna love it. Just. Skin."

The warmth of his breath mixed with the unique force of his words had goose bumps multiplying over Julie's skin before his first kiss ever made contact.

"Take 'em off now." His command made her nipples tighten, and the fire in his hazel gaze had her peeling off her panties. "Good girl, now sit back down on my lap. Gonna make you come, honey." With her back to his front, and her bare legs draped over his, he widened his feet, baring her sex to the empty room. "Mmm, can smell you, Jules," he whispered in her ear, making the fine hairs on her neck wakeup while he rubbed her clit with gentle circles. "Waiting for me to touch you, stroke you, fuck you with my fingers. Yeah?"

"Danny…" She writhed into his hand. His touch wasn't enough, and he knew it. It was his brand of foreplay, and she loathed it and loved it. "I need…more."

"More?" He flicked her earlobe with his tongue, sending chills through her body as he continued light play to the sensitive nerves above her entrance. "Got more to give, baby. Tell me what you want."

"Make me come." She panted, her nails pressed against his thighs. "Please, Danny, I need to come." Her request was barely out when his fingers plunged into her wetness. "Oh… oh… fuck, Danny." She moaned, thrusting into his touch.

"Goddamn, yes, fuck my fingers baby. Your pussy's so greedy. Fuck, Jules…"

She rocked onto his fingers as his thumb worked her clit. Sparks began to light in her belly.

"Don't stop," she mewled shamelessly, the climax building, climbing, ready to crest.

Danny leaned in and swept his tongue up the column of her neck, sending ecstasy careening through her. Breathless, she shifted on his lap, torquing her torso in an awkward position. Danny lifted his brow.

"I want to see your face, handsome," Julie answered his unasked question. In less than a second, she sat face to face, straddling the man who'd brought her unbelievable pleasure and unconditional love.

"Mmm, watching you fall apart may be my favorite pastime," Danny rasped before licking his glistening fingers. "Close second is tasting your sweet cream."

The way his tongue seductively swiped Julie's arousal from his finger mimicked the oral pleasures he often bestowed, revving her just-sated body up for another round. God, the way she wanted her man couldn't possibly be normal. She craved him.

With her legs still shaking and dangling off the sides of the kitchen chair, she lowered her small hands from his shoulders to his biceps, leaning in to press her lips to the tattoo scribed across his chest.

Julie's Main

She'd thought he was crazy when he opened his shirt on their wedding night and presented her with what many referred to as the *vow vaporizer*. People swore that inking your lover's name on your body was as good as setting your relationship up for failure. She'd frantically reminded her new husband of that very fact while openly admiring the beautiful script.

But as always, passion licked his eyes as he pulled her close and unzipped her simple wedding dress. "I'll always be yours, Jules," he said in a hoarse whisper, "no matter what."

Taut skin over hard muscle rippled under her tongue as she traced each letter of her name.

"While I'd love to play some more…" Danny groaned, reaching behind him and unhooking her ankles before standing them both up. "I need to get to work if I'm gonna meet you and Ivy at the ultrasound appointment today at five o'clock."

Desire was evident on his face and below his waist, the unmistakable evidence tenting his pajama bottoms. However, as always, he focused on the tasks that needed his attention first, knowing his needs would get tended to when time allowed.

Going to be an amazing father, she thought as she trailed him to their bedroom. "We won't start without you, babe."

She and Ivy had spoken the day before. The teen was as anxious as they were to make certain the baby was healthy, and she was grateful that Julie and Danny would be at the ultrasound appointment with her.

"Good," Danny called from the bathroom, "because I wanna be there when the tech tells us we're having a boy."

The sound of water beating on tile muted but didn't erase Danny's chuckle. They had been battling over the baby's gender since the first time they met Ivy. While Julie didn't agree with Danny's assessment, truth be told, she couldn't care less if it was a boy or girl as long as it was a Marcus.

Julie's full smile reflected in the mirror as she stripped off her T-shirt and walked naked into the shower stall.

"HONEY," DANNY MURMURED in surprise. His semi-hard cock stiffened the minute his sexy wife entered the shower. The best kind of mischief glimmered in her gray eyes.

"You said you had to get ready for work." She lowered to her knees in front of him, water spraying her firm tits and dripping to her thighs. His breath locked in his chest the second she fisted his hardness. "I certainly can't let you go to work like this. I'd feel horrible."

Her pink tongue gliding across her bottom lip had his dick throbbing with need.

"So you go ahead and wash your hair"—an impish grin curled the corners of her mouth—"and try to forget I'm even here. I'll just take care of business and leave you to finish your shower in peace."

Even the hot water didn't compare to the heat of Julie's mouth the moment she wrapped it around his cock.

"Fuck…" His groan echoed in the tiled space as Danny widened his stance to keep from falling over from pleasure.

Like a scene from his wildest fantasies, his wife was naked before him, steam surrounding her perfect body. Her strawberry hair darkened as she slicked it back from her face, showcasing her steel eyes. She stared up at him with a perfect storm of lust, satisfaction, and power. Each time her cheeks hollowed with suction, the tip of his cock touched the back of her throat.

"Christ, Julie, oh…that's it, take it down." He growled the command as release gathered in his spine.

There was no disguising Julie's mewls of pleasure, even over the pounding water and his own grunts. That, in its own right, turned him on even more. With her sitting back on her heels and her knees spread wide, just as he'd taught her, he could imagine the wetness pooling at her core and knew it was from more than just water.

"Fuck, honey, your pussy…is it dripping for me? You love sucking me off, yeah?" His dirty words were just as powerful as his tender touches, and with her mouth around him, dirty words were just about the only thing he had to offer. "Touch yourself, Jules. Let me see how you rub that pretty little clit."

His dick vibrated with her moan as Julie's long fingers rolled her swollen nub. Her nipples were drawn into hard points that had his mouth watering and his balls aching. But before he could so much as move to touch her creamy tits, her tongue glided around his cock head, touching the sensitive spot underneath. Release pushed through his body like a freight train as Julie took him deep into her throat.

"Fuck!" he shouted, and his hands twisted through her hair as he fucked her mouth, incapable of holding back. An endless orgasm rocked his body to exhaustion. His eyes fell closed, and his head hit the tiles behind him. "That was…"

Soft kisses marched from his abdomen to his lips before he could peel his eyes open.

"Delicious," Julie announced, touching her lips to his. "And exactly how you made me feel in the kitchen. Now hurry up and get done. You're going to be late for work."

The cool air of the shower door opening did nothing to squelch the heat still thrumming in his body. The woman blew his mind, ridiculous pun not intended.

"And, baby," Julie cooed over her naked shoulder, "the shampoo Mohawk went out in the 80s. May wanna wash that out before the water runs cold." She blew him a kiss and shut the door, leaving him sated, steamy, and clean. No better way to start the day.

CHAPTER SEVENTEEN

He Was Ours

"IS EVERYONE READY?" The ultrasound technician smiled as she entered the small exam room.

Danny was more than ready. Hell, he'd left work early to make certain he wasn't late for the appointment. Not that he'd been late to any of them, but because the baby wasn't biologically theirs, the need to be perfect felt tangible. Part of him knew the irrational feelings would pass once he held their baby, but for the time being, punctuality was the best he could offer.

"We're ready," Julie and Ivy responded.

"Can't wait." Danny grabbed for his wife's hand, lacing their fingers together.

After fifteen minutes of measurements and snapshots, the baby appeared perfect. As its tiny heart fluttered on screen, Danny found it difficult not to tear up just like Julie, but with a deep inhale and a throat-clearing cough, he held himself together as he held onto her.

The tech nodded, moving the curser over the screen. "Are you interested in knowing the gender of your child?"

The question was addressed to Ivy, but before the girl could answer, Danny did. "Yes, of course we want to know." His chest puffed with pride. "We're his parents."

The tech spared a quick look at an unusually quiet Ivy before pointing at the screen. "Well, Mr. and Mrs. Marcus, it looks like you've already guessed. You're having a boy. Congratulations!"

"A boy," Julie said as tears rolled down her face. "We're having a boy." Julie pivoted, craning her face up to his. "A baby boy, Danny."

"I know, Jules. Happy as hell no matter what God gave us, but it's a boy." He waggled his brows. "Since this ain't the time to tell you I was right, I'll wait 'till later." He winked before touching his lips to hers. The kiss was chaste, given the company they kept, but the promise for more lingered.

A quiet sniffle immediately shrouded the tiny room in silence.

"Ivy," Julie spoke with reverence, "thank you so much for giving us this gift. I wish I could explain what this means to us, but there are no words to describe how your act of selflessness is changing our lives." Danny's heart pounded as Julie placed her hand over the young girl's belly. "There will never be a day where this little boy goes unloved. He'll spend his entire life knowing everyone in his life wanted only the best for him, that *both* of his moms loved him with their whole hearts. And I swear to you, Ivy, Danny and I will give him the best life any child could hope for. Thank you for trusting us. We won't let you down."

Ivy's wide brown eyes shifted from Julie to Danny before she nodded. "I know you won't. You two have been incredible. Thanks for being here with me today. You helped to make things so much easier for me."

Danny's heart broke for the teenager. He would teach his son to be responsible, and honorable, and to be a stand-up man. His boy would learn that if he was man enough to get a woman pregnant, then he would be man enough to stand by her side until decisions were made. No boy of his would walk away from a woman he cared about, nor would he walk away from one he'd claimed to care about long enough to get her pregnant. "Anything you need, just call. Yeah?"

"Thanks, Danny. I'm just going to get dressed and head home." Ivy quickly averted her eyes as she swung her legs to the side of the table.

"Are you sure you don't want to go out to dinner with us?" Julie asked.

"Umm, no thanks." A stilted silence filled the room before Ivy spoke again. "I have a term paper due on Monday, and my parents said I couldn't go out for my birthday this weekend unless it's finished."

A knot formed in Danny's gut and tightened as she spoke. It wasn't what the girl was saying, but how she said it that had red flags shooting up around her.

"So, I need to get crackin'. After all, I can't miss out on my eighteenth birthday celebration. Even if this little guy makes it so I can't celebrate the way most of my friends do."

"Oh, your birthday!" Julie bounced on her toes. "We'll wait for you in the waiting room. We have a gift for you."

"You didn't have to, Julie," Ivy whispered.

Danny noticed the pale blush spread over the girl's cheeks. *What the hell?* Another bright flag sprang up in his mind. Something felt wrong.

"HEY, BABY, YOU got time for a quick lunch?"

"Danny! Of course, sweetie. Let me just tell Sheila and Chris that I'm heading out," she said.

Julie loved when her husband surprised her with lunch dates. It used to happen more frequently when he worked at the Red Bar because his shifts started later in the day and ran until the wee hours of the morning, but a couple of years prior, the hours and scenes of club life had become too much to handle. They decided together that he'd enjoy the intimacy of a pub or bar like Chester's or O'Brian's.

That said, neither Danny nor Julie thought it would be smart for them to work and live together, so he found a job managing a bar that was a cross between the two places. While it wasn't perfect by his standards, learning the business from the inside out was priceless. However, his hours mimicked Julie's, so lunch dates became scarce as dinner dates became more common.

After popping her head into the back office to announce her lunch break, and after grabbing her purse and coat from the locker, Julie practically floated through the bar to where Danny waited. She rose onto the balls of her feet and wrapped her arms around his neck. The familiar scents of pear and driftwood, a combination that had become more of an aphrodisiac than the freshest oysters and finest chocolate, hit her nose, making her insides quiver. Hunger for more than food whipped through her body as she pulled her husband close, pressing their lips together. When his strong hand wove through her hair, cupping the back of her head, she practically purred in delight, giving Danny the perfect opportunity to claim her mouth.

"Ahem, this is a public place," Chris teased from behind the bar, whipping Julie from her lust-induced haze.

"First of all"—Julie touched her kiss-swollen lips—"this is a bar. I've witnessed a whole lot more than kissing go on between these four walls. Second"—Julie glanced at the ceiling—"unless I'm mistaken, that, my friend, is mistletoe. You and Sheila are practically begging people to kiss. So as I see it, you should be thanking me for following orders…boss."

Danny's body shook with laughter as his arms wrapped around her torso. "Looks like she got you there, Chris."

"I'd have to agree." Sheila smiled as she joined her husband behind the bar. "You two go have lunch. I have to continue training my man here on management." Sheila gazed lovingly at Chris. "It's hard to go from being a silent partner to a hands-on manager, but I think he's doing just fine."

"It's all the positive reinforcement you give me." Chris winked, and Sheila blushed.

"Okay, umm, we're out of here. Stay away from the mistletoe," Julie teased before grabbing Danny's hand and leaving the bar.

Sitting in a cozy booth at their favorite café, they chatted about a new employee at Danny's job and Julie's early morning conversation with Chester.

"Oh, I meant to tell you!" Julie's insides bubbled with excitement. "I had to go to Home Depot yesterday for Sheila, and while I was there, I found the sweetest shade of pale blue paint for the baby's room. I was thinking we could go back together and check it out." Julie bit her upper lip, memories of the empty pink nursery gripping her heart. "We can buy it and wait to paint until a little closer to the due date." Julie caught the frown that marred Danny's lush lips before he had time to cover them with his palm. "Danny? What's wrong?"

His chest rose with an audible heave of air, air that he seemed to hold for longer than Julie thought possible. She watched as his chest constricted slowly, silently.

"Honey, you spoken with Ivy?"

Danny's question didn't feel like a question at all. It felt like the beginning of something unpleasant. Like the lid of a box she'd rather keep closed. But Danny's loving eyes implored her to open it. Her trust in him told her he'd be there no matter what was inside.

"Umm, kind of. Well, not really, but..." Julie replayed the past two weeks in her head. "She called the night of the ultrasound to thank us for the watch." Julie had found the waterproof watch a few weeks earlier, after Ivy had talked about going to a beach for the summer to clear her mind once the baby was born. The card attached read, *Have the Time of your Life*.

"How 'bout since?" Danny's rigid posture had her on guard.

"She's returned my calls, but I haven't spoken with her. She's busy studying for finals, and when she does call, it seems to be when I'm working. Why are you asking? What do you know?"

Danny frowned. "Is she calling you at home? Or on your cellular?"

"At home. Danny, what do you know?" Julie snapped, not noticing or caring about the prying eyes of other diners.

With brows pulled tight, Danny rubbed his hand through his hair. "Honey, I don't *know* anything. But at the ultrasound appointment, I got a strange vibe after the technician announced that Ivy was carrying a boy. Something changed, and I couldn't put my finger on it. I'm just scared, Jules. I'm worried that—"

"No," Julie interrupted. "Don't go there, babe. Please, don't go there. That's our baby, our son. Ivy is a young girl who has no plan, no support, and no clue. She'll do what's right for the baby."

Danny nodded. His Adam's apple bobbed as Julie forced air into her lungs.

"You're right," he finally said. However, there was no conviction in his face or his voice.

FOR FIVE DAYS and nights, Julie attempted to contact Ivy. She left messages on the young woman's answering machine, and when no calls were returned, Julie contacted the adoption agency.

"What's up, beautiful?"

Just the tone of Danny's gravelly voice through the phone settled the nerves that had been churning in Julie's stomach for the past ten minutes. "I just spoke with Ilene at the agency." Julie barely recognized her own brittle tone.

"Go on."

"She, umm, she's got several appointments today but will be back in her office at five and would like to speak with us. Says we can either go see her there or talk with her over the phone." Bile rose up Julie's esophagus, threatening to escape, but she swallowed it back, refusing to make a scene at work.

"Julie, listen to me," Danny spoke in a low voice. She knew he did that so she'd have no choice but to calm down and listen to what he was going to say. "I'll be with you for that five o'clock call. I'll come get you and bring you home. I do not want you driving, you understand? If you're too upset, frustrated, angry, or just don't want to be at work for any reason, call me and I'll come get you. I can think of at least ten different ways we can spend our afternoon that will leave us exhausted but have nothing to do with work."

Some flirtation was added to the command, but it wasn't the playfulness she was used to. It felt forced, contrived, and she knew her husband was as scared as she was.

"Okay, sweetie." *I can fake flirty for his sake too.* "I'll tell Ilene to call us at home at five. And Danny, only ten things? Really?" She tsked. "I'm disappointed."

His chuckle warmed what had been cold inside her since her talk with the agency worker. "I'm yours, Julie."

"I love you, Danny."

"Thank God for that." The call ended, and Julie sighed. It was bound to be a long day.

Ever since it was decided that Julie's position at O'Brian's would be filled by Chris and moving the head waitress, Renee, up to floor manager, her work had become even more entertaining. For years, Julie had known

Sheila and Chris as a strong couple, supportive of each other, and fun to be around. But with Chris working as an accountant and a volunteer firefighter, something he and Danny bonded over from the get-go, he'd never spent much time at the bar. Julie had feared how spending large quantities of time together would affect him and Sheila, but it only seemed to bring them closer together. Sheila was more relaxed, less tired, and when Chris walked into the room, her smile reached her eyes before it ever touched her lips.

"Hey, lady," Chris called from the hall that led to the office. "It's time for your break. Let Renee handle the front, and you come eat with Sheila and me."

Suspicious, Julie asked, "Did Danny call you? Maybe ask you to keep an eye on me?"

Chris's brows shot to his hairline. "I'm appalled. You act as if we never eat together, Julie."

Crossing her arms over her chest, Julie continued to stare at him.

"Okay, fine, he may have called and requested some extra eyes on you. But you know damn well that Sheel and I love you like a sister. So get your ass back here and eat with us."

Even with her gut wrapped in knots, Chris's quirky invitation was too sweet to turn down. Julie giggled. "Okay, since you asked so sweetly."

Over burgers and fries Julie opened up to her friends about what had been going on with Ivy. She explained that she hadn't shared her worries sooner because discussing it even with her closest friend made everything feel too real. She'd been avoiding the topic as much as she could while trying her best to get in touch with Ivy.

As best friends did, Sheila and Chris came up with multiple reasons why everything would be "just fine." They were so convincing that by the time Danny came to pick her up at four o'clock, Julie was certain that their worry was for naught. She spent the ride from work to their home relaying all of Sheila and Chris's perfectly rational excuses. The problem was, they didn't sound nearly as logical coming from her. *Shit.* What the hell was going to happen at five o'clock?

HAD IT NOT been so pathetic, it may have been comical the way Danny and Julie sat—huddled close, bodies touching, breaths mingling—yet not the slightest ripple of sexual current flowed between them. Two cordless phones lie inches away on the coffee table. Thank goodness neither of them could shoot laser beams from their eyes, or the phones would have disintegrated fifteen minutes earlier.

"She said she'd call at five." Julie huffed, looking once again at her watch.

Danny cracked his knuckles as the sofa cushion shook beneath him. Julie's knee had been bouncing as if she were a kid on a pogo stick since the moment they sat down, and with each passing minute, the spring increased. He rested his hand on her knee. "Honey, she's gonna call. And when she does, I don't wanna be seasick. Can you please settle?"

"Sorry, I'm just..." She shrugged, and worry etched her creamy skin. "You know."

"I do. I—" His thoughts were cut off when the phones rang loudly, sending them each scrambling for a headset.

The conversation wasn't long. In fact, it was barely a conversation at all. For the most part, Ilene spoke and Danny and Julie listened. The agency worker explained that Ivy had decided to keep her baby and wouldn't give him up no matter what. She and her parents had worked out an agreement, and they would help her once the baby arrived.

"But"—Danny's heart cracked as his wife whispered—"he's our baby."

"I'm so sorry, Julie. I really am. I know how long you both have waited for this. I can put you back on the list," Ilene offered.

Danny's gut clenched at the mere thought of that goddamn list. He squeezed his eyes closed and cupped his hand over his wife's, but he stayed quiet. If she needed to continue on this journey, he'd stand by her side, but he…he was wiped out. He opened his eyes when she squeezed his hand. Through her tear-filled eyes, he saw something he hadn't seen before. Before he could determine what it was, she spoke.

"No," she croaked. "Don't put us back on the list, Ilene."

He nodded his approval, grateful that she felt the same way and heartbroken that they would never have the family they so desired.

"We're done," she said.

The agency worker rambled on a few minutes longer, but Danny had stopped listening, his attention focused solely on the woman next him. Her eyes were stormy gray with tears already falling across her downturned features. Danny slid from the sofa to the carpeted floor and crawled between his wife's legs. The minute Julie bid farewell to

Ilene, he took the phone from her grip and, without clicking it off, pushed it aside. On his knees, Danny was only a few inches taller than her, but when he opened his arms and she leapt into his embrace, those inches felt like feet.

"He was ours." Her thin voice vibrated into his chest. "I already loved him, you know?"

God, he knew. He absolutely fucking knew. "Yeah, honey, I loved him too."

"I meant what I said to Ilene. I can't do this anymore."

Danny's heart pounded. He felt her pain on a visceral level, as if they were connected by more than just love and last name.

His gut shredded when she said, "I'm sorry I couldn't give you a family. I'm so sorry."

"Oh, Jules." Pulling her tight to his chest, he inhaled deeply. Gardenias and Julie filled his senses as he kissed her soft forehead. "Woman, you are my family. When are you going to learn? I love you, honey. I'm yours."

"And I'm yours."

CHAPTER EIGHTEEN

Then I Got A Friend

"SON." ALLAN PULLED Danny into an embrace.

Something about his father's hugs, no matter how old Danny got, was comforting. That hug was no exception. Danny and Julie had just arrived at Allan and Anita's new place, a house on a golf course they had moved into the year before. Even though they weren't celebrating Christmas in his childhood home, being with Julie and his dad in North Carolina still felt like coming home. After the devastation of the past week, he and Julie needed to be *home*.

Danny cleared his throat. "Place looks great, Dad."

Allan had already wrapped his arms around Julie before he acknowledged Danny's compliment. "Yeah, Anita and I are really happy here. Place feels fresh, yet still has the things that make it home." He angled his head toward the hallway. "You know, if you go look in the family room, you'll see the bookcases you, Neal, and I built long ago."

"Those things got trashed when...after... Neal died." The memory of seeing those bookcases cracked on the floor was branded in his brain.

Allan's eyes sparkled as he glanced between Danny and Julie. "They're a bit banged up, but they suit us fine. Just because something isn't how you want it doesn't mean it isn't perfect."

"Dad," Julie sighed, no doubt attempting to steer the conversation away from the subject of children.

But Allan continued on his path. "Loss comes in many shapes and sizes, but thank God, so does gain. You two hold on to each other and, I promise, you'll find your slice of perfection."

Julie nodded wordlessly.

"Oh, oh, you're here!" Anita exclaimed, rushing in through the side door. "I was just outside picking this from the herb garden." Her basket of fresh mint fragranced the air. "I've never had so much fun with rosemary, basil, and mint. I could just kiss the previous owners for leaving such awesomeness behind."

Allan roped his arm around his wife. "How about you just save your kisses for me?"

"Well, maybe she could spare just one for me?" a familiar voice teased as he came through the open front door.

"Chester!" Danny and Julie whipped around to face their friend. Peace like he hadn't felt in weeks settled through Danny as he watched his wife embrace his closest friend. "What the hell are you doing here, man?"

Chester ignored Danny's extended hand and pulled him in for a hug-back-slap. "It's fuckin' Christmas, that's why I'm here. And while technically I wasn't supposed to come up this year on account of the Keys dripping with gorgeous women during the season—Thanksgivin' may be our together time from now on—I'm here because you are my family." He looked between Julie and Danny. "And I needed to see that you were okay. 'Cause goddamn, you two can't catch a fuckin' break."

"Oh my God, Ches, you're a dog!" Julie laughed. "But I love you."

"Glad you're here, buddy." Danny slapped Chester's arm. "Glad we're all here."

FOUR DAYS PASSED in a flash as Julie and Anita baked cookies and the men bought the Christmas tree and strung the lights. The five of them hung ornaments, ate massive meals, and opened presents while drinking various cocktails, all holiday themed.

"One would think with three professional bartenders in the house, the drinks wouldn't be this horrible," Allan quipped after choking on a peppermint-flavored blend Danny had concocted.

Anita pouted. "Allan, they aren't *all* terrible. The one Julie made with the tiny marshmallows was pretty delicious. What was it called?"

"Santa's Balls," Julie deadpanned.

Anita hiccupped. "Potent little drink."

"Woman, I think it's time for bed." Allan winked at Chester.

Danny groaned and Julie laughed.

"Okay," Anita agreed, hiccupping again. As she stood on wobbly legs, Allan scooped his wife over his shoulder and carried her off to their first-floor bedroom.

"Don't forget you have guests," Chester called. "So keep it quiet."

Allan's profanity was muffled by Anita's gasp. Danny, Chester, and Julie howled with laughter from the sofa, by the opened gifts and the lit tree. Watching Danny maneuver behind the small bar to pour scotch for him and Chester and club soda with lime for her—she'd had enough to drink for one night—there was no mistaking the tranquility that had eased into his body since their arrival. The fact was, while neither of them had forgotten the loss they'd suffered just a few days before they left, being away from it made breathing easier.

"I don't want to go back," she blurted.

The men's discussion halted, and the weight of their stares was palpable.

"Huh?"

"What?"

Julie blinked. "I don't want to go back…"

"To where, honey?" Danny crossed the room, handed her her glass, and sat by her side. "Our house or Baltimore?"

"Yes," Julie answered simply. Her glance shifted from Danny to Chester and back. She inhaled deeply and slowly released the air to bide her time while she organized thoughts she had no idea she'd been thinking. "Our house…every time I walk through it, I see what we *almost* had but never will. Could we find another house? Sure, of course." With each word that left her mouth, Julie found strength she didn't know she had and urgency she couldn't explain. "But why? Danny, there are forty-nine other states. Frankly, after everything we've gone through, I'm ready to start fresh somewhere else. Your dad lives here.

Chester"—she looked at her friend who sat quietly in the corner—"lives down south. We're young, we have each other. Let's not go back." Her breaths were frantic as she finished her thoughts.

Her statements were met with silence. Danny appeared to focus on the circles he traced over her denim clad thigh, infusing her skin with his warmth. Slow, hypnotic motions that calmed her racing heart and loosened the knot that had formed in her belly. By the time Danny lifted his gaze to hers, maybe a minute had passed—a few seconds -a serene vibe floated through her blood. Tranquility only Danny could give her.

He cupped her cheek. "I hear what you're saying, Julie, but I need to ask, 'cause I've been where you are—I joined the Army, for Christ's sake, and problems followed me even in the jungle. So honey…you running away?"

Understanding struck hard as she shook her head. "No, I want us to find something new. Something special. A dream that's ours, that we can build together. Not running away, running toward…"

"Then I'm with you, baby." Small lines etched around Danny's eyes as his lips curled up. "Anywhere you wanna go. We'll figure it out, okay?"

"Ahem."

Julie had forgotten about Chester's presence until he cleared his throat.

"Not to interrupt this heartfelt moment, but you kids did have it in front of me so…"

Heat suffused Julie's cheeks.

"No, Julie girl," Chester said, confirming he may actually have the mind-reading skills she'd accused him of years ago, "there isn't anything for you to be ashamed of.

The two of you, Jesus, fighters the likes I've never seen before. Soldiers, warriors, survivors. In this life, I believe survivors are drawn to each other. While we don't always share our war stories, we still mend each other's wounds. You both have healed me. From the day we met." Chester's clear blue eyes focused on Julie's. "Even before we met, you offered me a life I thought long gone."

Julie's eyes watered with emotion, and Danny's arms tightened around her torso. Chester swallowed a large gulp of his drink.

"You're adults," Chester stated gruffly, the emotion from seconds before little more than a memory. "You make your own damn choices, but if you're lookin' to move, I got some suggestions."

"Let's hear 'em," Danny said.

"There's a gem of a town 'bout an hour from Philadelphia—Charistown, it's called. Peaceful place surrounded by farms and other small towns. Place thrives on local businesses. Passed through it on several occasions over the years, even stayed a time or two." Chester grinned. "Got *people* there."

Laughter bubbled from Julie's chest. "Of course you do, Ches. Where don't you have *people*? Danny, I swear, one day we're gonna find out our friend here worked as a secret agent or something."

"Anyway," Chester drew the word out, "know you two have talked about opening your own bar for years. While Charistown's farther north, if that ain't an issue, I could make some calls. I know someone who's dyin' to sell his joint and move to warmer climates."

Judging by the look on Danny's face, he felt the same tingle of skepticism that filled Julie's bones.

"Don't know, man, seems mighty convenient that every time you've needed real estate, you've had a *friend* just 'dying' to relocate," Danny probed.

"You lookin' to start over?" Chester asked.

"Yeah," Danny stated.

"You and *our* girl need a fresh start in a place you can trust?"

Julie's eyes jetted back and forth between the men. She had nothing to add to the conversation. She trusted both men and knew Danny would forever guard her with his life.

"Yeah, Ches, that'd be amazing."

"Then I got a friend who's dyin' to move. End of story."

Danny turned Julie to face him. "What do you think of Charistown, Pennsylvania, honey? I hear it's a great little town." He winked. "Nice place to start over."

"Charistown," Julie repeated. The name alone felt like a cozy blanket on a cool day. *Charistown* tumbled through her mind as thoughts of beginning anew with her husband took shape. "I love it."

Danny nodded, excitement sparkling in his hazel eyes. The understanding that he wasn't just entertaining her concerns but was once again on the same page was mind bending. When he ran his knuckles along her jaw, shivers tingled up her spine, but it was his voice that liquefied her insides. The way it had begun to change over their time together—becoming a little rougher, a little more gravelly—seeped with sexiness even when the conversation wasn't sexual.

"Tell your friend to pack fast," Danny announced. "My woman and I wanna get our shit settled in Baltimore and our asses to this special place before February one."

With her back to him, Julie heard the smile in Chester's tone when he answered, "It'd by my pleasure."

Taking Danny's outstretched hand, Julie rose from the couch and faced a still reclining Chester. "There are no words, Ches. At least none that can sum up what I'm feeling. So *thank you* will have to do."

"No words needed, Julie girl. But you both are very welcome. I'll have some details worked out for you before my flight out tomorrow. Now you two go to bed, and I'll close off all these lights. And remember...I'm right across the hall. While I may be older, I'm not deaf." His glare aimed at Danny was comical. "She's like a daughter, you punk. No need to hear the shit I heard last night. Christ, fuckin' had to bleach my brain."

Thank goodness Julie knew where the fire extinguishers were, because her face nearly burst into flames.

"Nice, Chester, real smooth," Danny teased. "Couldn't have pulled me aside for that little chat?"

Shaking his head, Chester chuckled. "That's not how we roll, boy, and you know it. Be happy I didn't leave a Post-It note on your damn door."

"Oh my God," Julie gasped.

The three laughed and hugged before turning in for the night.

CHAPTER NINETEEN

Moving Not Dying

PACKING TAPE SCREECHED as it unrolled to seal the flaps of the cardboard moving box.

"Last damn one," Danny grumbled, hefting the carton to his shoulder. "Chris, you mind getting the door for me?"

The men had spent the past few days loading up the U-Haul in preparation for Danny and Julie's move to Pennsylvania.

"I still can't believe how fast you guys pulled this together," Chris said when Danny reentered the house. Chris grabbed the last two beers from the otherwise empty refrigerator, popped them open, and handed one to Danny. "Christ, you guys go out of town a few days for Christmas, and less than five weeks later, you're packing up and moving to some bumble-fuck town? Thank God you didn't take a two-week cruise—hell, you'd've come back telling us you were moving to Ireland or some shit." There was no animosity in his friend's statement. Chris and Sheila, while sad to see their closest friends uprooting, were excited for them to experience new opportunities.

"I know, crazy how fast it all happened," Danny admitted. His gaze roamed the empty house. "But every time she steps foot in this place, every time she thinks 'bout this fucking place, it's like the light dims in her eyes. Don't know if Sheila told you, but we stopped sleeping here two weeks ago."

Chris's brows furrowed, indicating he'd had no idea.

"Thought just knowing we were leaving would make being here easier, but it didn't. Listened to Julie toss and turn each night until she'd get up and drift around from room to room," Danny said.

The memory of confronting her was etched into his brain. After night three of watching her slither out of their bed and not return until dawn, concern and curiosity had finally made him search for her. He watched her go from their daughter's room to their would-be son's, then down the stairs to the main room. He saw the tremble of her shoulders, even in a house lit only by the garden lights that filtered through the windows. Her cries were noiseless, but her pain was deafening as she faced the window and the softly lit flowers.

"Jules," he whispered as he approached, "what's going on, honey?"

"Oh." Her breath hitched. "I didn't mean to wake you."

"Babe, when you're not next to me, I'm awake. Now talk to me."

A sigh left her body, one so large he felt the relief in his own frame. "It's just...I remember when we bought this house. Our dreams were big, so filled with hope...and after all these years, we're moving, and I'm having trouble recalling memories that don't suck."

When her eyes met his, he understood exactly what she was saying. They had had many years of love and happiness under that roof, but they had lived through so much pain and heartbreak and were leaving on the tail end of devastation.

He placed his front to her back and swept her long hair over her left shoulder before pressing his lips to her right. "Baby, can give you more memories that don't suck." He couldn't hide the smile in his voice. "Well, there will be sucking, but I promise, when you think of this night…" He felt goose bumps cover her skin as his tongue slid up her neck to her ear. "This will be the final night we spend in this house, this memory the last you'll have here. Let me make it amazing."

Her moan was the only confirmation he needed before he swept her into his arms and walked to the sofa. He spread her beneath him before he took his time and made sweet love to her until the birds chirped and the newspaper thumped when it landed on their doorstep.

As promised, they never spent another night under that roof. His wife had slept peacefully tucked into his side ever since.

"Shit," Chris interrupted Danny's memory. "I had no idea it was that bad, man. I'm sorry."

"It was," Danny admitted before raising his beer to his friend. "Now it isn't."

Once finished, the men disposed of the beer bottles, slid the retractable door of the U-Haul down, and locked it before doing a final walk-through of the house and the property.

"You sure you have a pad waiting for you in Charistown?" Chris asked, even though he'd heard the plan Danny and Julie had discussed several times during the past few weeks.

Grinning, Danny allowed his buddy to worry the way he would have if the tables were reversed. "Yeah, man. We have a small apartment rented on a month-to-month basis until we can get the lay of the land. When we went up there a couple of weeks ago, we realized it'd be a mistake to buy a place without living in the area first. So we're gonna throw our shit into storage until we find the right home. There's no rush. Not running from anything, Chris, just starting over."

From the moment Danny had laid eyes on Charistown, he knew exactly what Chester had meant when he referred to it as a "gem of a town." Julie had felt it too. Tranquility floated through his veins as they drove down Main Street, and he knew without a doubt, *starting over* in that town couldn't be more right.

"Have you decided on a name for the bar yet?"

The earnest concern in Chris's question made Danny grin as he pulled the front door of the house closed for the final time. After yanking the key from the lock, dropping it into an envelope, and handing it to Chris, who would pass it off to the realtor in the morning, Danny answered the question.

"No. Haven't come up with a name…yet." The two men climbed into the U-Haul and buckled up before Danny continued. "Know this might not make a lick of sense to you, but Jules and I are at a point where we may be grateful for our blessings, but we sure as shit don't count 'em before we got 'em."

Chris's stare told Danny that his friend almost understood but hadn't quite caught it, so Danny went deeper. "We named two babies that we never held, brother. That shit ain't right. So we're just gonna wait and see which of the properties we end up with. Chester's guy was still on the fence when we were up there, so we looked at a couple other locations. Once our name is on the deed, the transaction complete...we'll name that bitch with pride and scream it out loud. Till then...we'll stay unattached to anything but each other."

"Understood." Chris nodded. And Danny knew his friend did.

When discussing whether or not moving to another state was really the right thing for them, Danny and Julie had discussed their current jobs as well as their dreams of owning a bar. That had always felt like a long-term goal, something to achieve after children and college tuition, but when the structure of their family changed, so did their goals. One evening, over too many cocktails and not enough carbs, their motto became "Go Big or Stay in Baltimore." With plenty of money in their savings account and years of business and bar experience between the two of them, they decided to follow their passion...they were going *big*.

They realized, during their visit to Charistown, that more important than finding the perfect place to lay their heads was finding the best place to pour their beers. From that minute forward, the search shifted and the real fun began. Of course, Chester had some choice words when Danny called from Pennsylvania to tell him that his *friend* was waffling on the property, but when Julie got on the phone and calmly explained that other places were equally as appealing, the older man calmed down. Danny still smiled every time he thought of the call Julie had received the following Monday from the realtor, claiming Chester's friend was not only ready to sell but his asking price had dropped. However, they hadn't been lying when they'd said they were interested in other places.

"Well, this is it." Danny parked the U-Haul in the parking lot of O'Brian's, inhaled, and turned to his friend. "I know there're no good-byes among us, but…" His throat tightened as he swallowed back emotions he'd kept at bay for weeks. "You've been a friend…a brother." He swallowed again and cleared his throat. "No words to thank you for what you've been and all you've given."

"No words needed, Dan," Chris replied. "You and Julie are two of the finest people I've ever known. Sheila and I were blessed when you entered our lives."

Danny's nostrils stung with tears. *Fuck, you're moving, not dying, Marcus. Keep your shit tight.*

"Bro, I bet Sheila twenty bucks that I wouldn't get—" her words—*all emotional*. My words—*pussied up*. So let's end this here." Wiping the wet from his eyes, Chris grinned. "You're only a few hours away, my man. That's it, no big deal. And with cell phones…holy shit, I'll probably talk to you too often."

"Yeah, that would sound stalkerish coming from a chick. Coming from a man…shit's just creepy." Danny forced a shiver and a guffaw before hopping out of the truck. Chris's laugh echoed in the afternoon air. "Let's get in there and separate the women. Can't imagine it's gonna be pretty."

"Nope, got fifty and an office blow job riding on that," Chris muttered.

"Ha, why'd she take that bet? Those two cry over Hallmark commercials."

That was one of the things Danny loved about his wife. She was stronger than any man he'd ever met, but since dealing with the loss of their baby and her infertility, she was no longer afraid of her emotions. They were her badges of survival, and only those close to her got to see them. He was proud to witness everything she had to share.

"Sheila swears she has no more tears left. All these years together, and she has no clue how well I know her. Silly woman." Chris shrugged, opened the glass door to the pub, and walked in.

Danny followed. Sure enough, the women were hugging hard behind the bar while the staff poured drinks as if the two women didn't exist.

"Oh shit," Sheila gasped, turning her head to face Julie. "They're here. I need to run to the bathroom."

"Oh, no, you don't, woman." A deep laugh rolled from Chris's chest. "Get your sweet ass over here. Hands to your sides. Don't try to get rid of the evidence."

Julie's giggles grabbed Danny's attention away from Sheila's tear-streaked face. Julie's watery eyes were filled with much more than sadness as she ran to him and wrapped her arms around his neck, touching her lips to his.

"I know you're gonna miss them, babe," she whispered. "I can see it all over your face, but it's going to be okay. We're going to be okay. I just know it."

His heart pounded. "No, honey, we're going to be amazing."

"Not to be a dick, but the lunch rush is over and, judging by the current state of my wife"—Chris winked—"looks like we have important business to tend to in the back office."

Sheila elbowed her husband in the gut, making the four of them laugh. After one last round of hugs, Danny led his woman to the U-Haul and drove to their new life in Charistown, PA.

CHAPTER TWENTY

Danny's On Main

"THE SIGN LOOKS fantastic," Julie called from across Main Street.

Her husband and Chester were directing the employees of Hang Around, the local sign company, on where exactly to hang the handcrafted, white cedar sign that was relaxed and classy rather than pretentious or tacky. After a full year of business, that same description fit Danny's on Main to a tee.

Danny's on Main. Just thinking of the name brought a smile to Julie's face.

She and Danny had been in Charistown for two weeks when they finally decided on the location. They ended up not choosing Chester's *friend's* space due to the structural damage that said friend had never disclosed but was found during inspection. Chester himself flew up for a visit that week. Within days of Chester's leaving, that pub was closed down by the health inspector and his *friend* moved to places unknown. The spot Danny and Julie chose was on the corner of Main Street. It was larger than they had originally expected, but the location couldn't be beat. With the property owner recently deceased and his family out of state and wanting to get rid of the building as soon as possible, the Marcuses could purchase the place for a steal and did so without hesitation.

Danny and Julie worked around the clock for months to make the dilapidated bar their dream bar and grill. The neighboring businesses stopped by with welcome baskets and friendly smiles, and she and Danny marveled at the good fortune that had finally come their way. The only thing they couldn't decide on was a name for their dream. He kept choosing names that were "bad-ass" (her thought), and she leaned toward "cutesie-crap" (his thought).

Then it happened. She and Danny were sanding baseboards in what would be the billiards room once the bar was completed. She stood to stretch her torso at the same time Danny was drinking from his Thermos. He peeled off his tank top, tucked it into the waist band of his jeans, and took another long pull of water. *Mmm.* His broad, sculpted chest was a thing of beauty with the way each bead of sweat clung to his skin, as if it knew how lucky if was to be up close and personal with such muscled perfection. Her eyes drifted to his ink, to one tattoo in particular, and she realized it was time to add a little color to her canvas.

Danny didn't flinch when she said she needed a break. He just told her to take all the time she needed. Turned out, she didn't need much.

Ninety minutes later, she returned to the building with a bag of takeout in her hands and tingles in her tummy. While what she'd done might have felt spontaneous, she had discussed it in the past with her husband. Would he appreciate the sweet gesture?

"I'm back and brought lunch." She heard the mischief in her own voice, so she knew Danny would question her mood.

"Hmm, if *you're* lunch, I'll definitely dig in." His brows waggled as he closed the distance between them, cupped her head, and pressed their lips together.

Sweat, soap, and Danny's distinct scent flooded her senses, melting her like always. She wanted more, and she got it when he pulled her tight against his hard body.

"Oww," she hissed, breaking the kiss and putting slight space between them. *Shit, how quickly I forgot.*

"What's wrong?" Danny's eyes scanned her body like a gentle touch, looking for a problem... an answer. "Jules, talk to me."

"Nothing's wrong, I promise." Squeezing his hand, Julie moved to place the food on the folding table before returning to face her man. The two vertical lines pressed deep between his brows screamed that he was far from reassured.

"Start talking," he rumbled. "Make me believe that you're okay."

God, that low tone turned her to mush. The dominant side of Danny Marcus had always been her weakness. Even after all their years together, that hadn't changed.

"Um," she hedged, "I've been thinking about getting a tattoo—for a while now actually."

"For real? In the past you said you liked them on me but not for you," he recounted.

"True. But as you said, that was the past, and we've started fresh." His hazel eyes twinkled as she explained. "You and I, we've been through so much. Happy, sad, joy, love, loss...all of it. And then *we* decided to start fresh."

Julie reached for Danny's hands, laced her fingers with his, and continued. "Started fresh, baby, but not started over. You and I never needed a new beginning because what we have has always been amazing. And you were right all those years ago on our wedding night. No matter what happens, you will always be mine." Julie brought Danny's hands to her waist and guided them to the hem of her T-shirt.

Understanding lit Danny's eyes as he lifted the shirt up her body, leaving nothing more than a satin bra and a gauze bandage on her torso. His mouth curled into a sexy smile as the roughened pad of his thumb stroked the skin above Julie's left ribs.

"No matter what happens, Danny, I will always be yours." She peeled off the bandage and revealed:

Danny's Main

Her husband stared wordlessly at her tattoo.

"Yes, I have a vow vaporizer too," she said. "I believe in us. Danny? Are you okay?"

Danny's laugh rang in her ears, but not as much as the words that followed. "Welcome to Danny's on Main, honey." He motioned toward the unfinished bar. "What do you think?"

Her main man, her bar, on Main Street… "I love it!"

TO CELEBRATE THE one-year anniversary of their grand opening, they purchased the beautiful sign, hired a band—regulars that had just signed with a record label—and were hosting a huge bash. Allan and Anita were flying up to celebrate Danny and Julie's wedding anniversary in July, so they weren't coming up for the bar's celebration, but Chester had refused to miss any occasion where, "beautiful women and half-priced cocktails partied together."

And party they did—until two in the morning when the drinks were empty and the music stopped. The evening was as successful as the year had been, leaving Danny and Julie smiling as they bid their customers good night.

The only thing they hadn't found success with was staff. In the twelve months since the doors opened, they had had too many people behind the bar and none of them were tending it. Late, lazy, free-loading, obnoxious, no-shows, inappropriate beyond control—that was what Julie and Danny had found, leaving the two of them working to exhaustion both behind the bar and behind the scenes.

"I finally understand why Chester kept that bitch Bunny around as long as he did." Julie yawned, sitting at her desk. "That woman may have been a walking STD, but she came to work on time and loved the hell out her job."

"She certainly loved the hell out of the customers and staff," Danny retorted. "I remember she gave good ol' Chester his fair share of lovin' too. I'm thinking that's a huge reason why he kept her around so long."

"Whatever," she admonished, staring at a spreadsheet. "The fact is, we need to do a better job of screening our hires. We're wasting a ton of time and money training people only to have them leave us high and dry. I swear to

God, I think most of them only want to work here so they can drink the booze."

SHE WASN'T WRONG. Over the next few years, many faces wore staff shirts at Danny's on Main. Some lasted six shifts, others six months, but in the end, the Marcuses never felt a connection with the bartenders. Hot men serving drinks were always appreciated by the ladies, but Julie noticed the revenue increased when women were behind the bar. Danny couldn't disagree—what man wouldn't want a sexy lady serving him drinks?

A problem occurred when one of the bartenders started crushing on him. He thought nothing of it at first. It was good for the ego to know that women still found him attractive, but the only woman who would ever have his full attention was his Julie.

"Suzette likes you," Julie stated one afternoon while the two were in the back office—working lunches, they affectionately called the time together. She was transferring their bills over to electronic bill pay while eating strawberries, and he was writing out the shift schedules and drinking a Coke.

"Honey, Suzette likes everyone. That's her job." Danny popped a grape in his mouth, savoring the sweet juice as well as the prick of enjoyment he got from his wife's possessiveness.

Shaking her head, Julie nibbled her lip. "You're wrong. She flirts with you, Danny. It's more than a friendly notion, and it's escalating. I don't like it."

Wow, is she worried? "You realize that you're it for me, right? I don't care who flirts with me. I only want you."

His dick hardened the moment his wife's firm ass found purchase on his lap. How could she doubt for even a second that his feelings for her blew his mind? When she twisted to face him, he had no doubt the vixen used the friction of her weight against his throbbing erection to gain his attention.

"I *know* you love me. That isn't the issue or the concern."

Fuck, not sure what's hotter: her confidence or the cleavage showing in her V-neck staff shirt.

"I know what you're thinking, and no, I'm not jealous," she said. "I'm annoyed. Girls like Suzette don't worry about damage. She doesn't care about boundaries, and she sure as shit won't care about causing trouble."

Bewilderment crested through him as Julie's words sank in. Never had he seen her so guarded, so ready to defend what belonged to her. While it was sexy as fuck, it wasn't something he'd ever intentionally bring out in her. "Jules—"

Her mouth met his with a kiss so claiming, so passionate, so wanton, Danny's thoughts disintegrated on his tongue.

"I'm not saying we should fire her," Julie whispered into his lips. "Just pay attention, okay?"

One more quick touch on the lips, and Julie's weight was gone. The office door clicked, leaving him alone with the taste of berry on his lips, the faint smell of gardenia, and a raging hard-on as the only evidence that she was ever there.

AS USUAL, JULIE wasn't wrong. Over the following weeks, Suzette's behavior became more brazen. Her eye contact went from confident to blatant, and her flirty comments became sexual. When she started finding reasons to touch him, Danny drew the line.

Danny arranged for the bartender to come in for a chat before her shift. He was fully prepared to work her hours behind the bar when she quit. "Suzette, how do I say this nicely? You do realize I'm a happily married man, yeah?"

What he wasn't prepared for was the answer the woman gave him.

"You think you are." Her arm slithered across the table, long talon-like nails grazing his skin. "But you're not. She's not enough for you, baby." Her saccharine voice explained, "She's good to make you dinner and wash your laundry, but I can make you happier in the bedroom. I can rock. Your. World." Suzette's tongue moved across her shellacked lips in a way that turned Danny's stomach instead of turning him on, as he assumed was her intent.

What the fuck? Chick is clearly a whack job. She isn't going to quit; I'm firing her ass. Anger boiled in his veins as Danny reminded himself to stay calm. Eyes narrowed in disgust, Danny popped up from his chair as Suzette sat back in hers, undressing him with her hooded gaze.

"Max?" Danny growled.

The new hire looked up from behind the bar.

"Over here, now." Regulating his breath was a challenge as Danny mentally shuffled through his words, pulling forth the ones that wouldn't get him slapped with a sexual harassment lawsuit.

"Boss?" While Max DeLucca had only been employed for two weeks, he'd been a lunch regular for over a month. The kid showed more respect and loyalty than all of the hires Danny and Julie had taken on in the four years since the bar opened. He stood by Danny's side, his hulking size a threat to anyone, regardless of his gentle demeanor.

"I need a witness, DeLucca. You're here, so you're it." Danny's words were aimed at Max, but his stare never left the aloof and clearly oblivious Suzette.

"Go, sir."

"Suzette, your presence is no longer needed or wanted here at Danny's on Main. You're fired."

"Fired? Stop it, baby," Suzette purred as she stood and attempted to stalk toward Danny.

"Ahh, okay." Danny grinned, arms folded over his broad chest. "So you don't do nice."

Suzette beamed. "No, I love it rough, Danny. I told you that."

Purposely obtuse? Christ, was this really happening? Judging by the look on Max's face, it certainly was.

"Rough it is," Danny conceded. "Little girl, my wife is more woman than you will ever be, and I'm the lucky son of a bitch who has the honor of being with her. You think it's okay to screw with the person who writes your paychecks? You think that person is me? Guess what—you're wrong on both accounts. You have absolutely nothing to offer us because pretty faces are a dime a dozen, and your bartending skills are subpar. So get your shit and get gone."

Had her face not made him physically ill, Danny would have enjoyed her round eyes and slacked-jaw look as Max escorted her to the door. Instead, Danny went to the office and apologized to his wife the best way he knew how—simple words followed by a mind-bending orgasm.

IT WASN'T MORE than a couple of weeks later when Danny found himself in a similar situation, although the target was different and Danny's patience was nonexistent. Max was the ideal employee. He worked his ass off, took on extra hours, and even though he was dealing with some sort of marital issues at home, he never brought them behind the bar. Women wanted him, men wanted to be him, and Danny wanted to clone him. So he did what he thought was the next best thing—he hired Wayne.

Wayne came with an impressive resume, a handsome face, and unfortunately roaming eyes and Velcrohands. Danny worked a few shifts with Wayne and found him to be slightly annoying, but the ladies liked him, so Danny worked the schedule so the two would intersect more than spend a great deal of time together. Julie didn't have much to say about the new bartender, which was abnormal but not alarming.

"Julie, cupcake, no need for you to climb that step stool when you got a man right here. I'll get that bottle down for you."

Danny's ears perked as Wayne's words traveled from the bar to the kitchen, where he and Max were doing inventory.

"What the…?" Hands balled into fists, Danny's eyes met Max's.

"Look, boss, the guy's a flirt. I've heard him call other dudes 'babe,'" Max reported. "Let it go, and let's just get this done."

Accepting Max's advice, Danny exhaled, flexed his hands, and counted forks.

"Mmm, Julie, how'm I supposed to concentrate on cleaning when every time you bend over, I get a perfect view of your sweet ass."

A red haze slid over Danny's vision as the fork in his hand bent in half.

"I'll come out with you," Max snarled. "He needs to be gone, Danny, not dead. Do you hear me? You can't protect your woman from jail."

Max's words penetrated just in time to save Wayne's life.

"Get the fuck out of here!" Danny roared as he barreled out of the kitchen and behind the bar. He grabbed the bottle of Maker's Mark from Wayne's hand and threw it to the floor. Sounds of broken glass crunching beneath his feet were lost behind the rage that fueled his movements.

Wayne's hands were held up in a surrendering pose. "I didn't mean…I wasn't trying—"

"You weren't flirting with *my* wife? You weren't staring at her ass?" Danny left no time for answers as he advanced on Wayne, leaving the man with no choice but to retreat. "Listen here, you little fucker, the only reason you're gonna walk out of this bar in one piece is because I care more about that woman you were disrespecting than I do 'bout disabling you. Get the fuck out of my sight. Catch your eyes on my woman even once as you leave, I'll tear them out of your skull. Got it?"

Wayne nodded, understanding clear on his pasty face as he grabbed his backpack from under the bar and scooted past Danny's large frame. "Max, help me out here…"

"Rats and thieves," Max rumbled, his arms crossed. "Only rats and thieves steal what belongs to someone else. Rats do it for survival…you got no excuse."

"Five, four, three—I get to one, and you'll be limping out of here," Danny snapped.

Wayne ran. The empty bar became silent.

"Thank you, Max, for having my back again," Danny said.

"Not a problem, boss." Max shrugged. "Let's just say I have some experience when it comes to cheating. I'm not a fan."

Receiving the message Max not-so-subtly put out, Danny shook the younger man's hand, "Not quite sure what I'd do without you, boy." *Christ, sounded a bit like Chester just now.*

"Happy to be here, sir."

Julie cleared her throat. "Hate to interrupt all this male bonding, but I'm standing right here in the mess that you created, Mr. Marcus, and I'm waiting for an explanation."

Judging by the playful look on his wife's face, no explanation was needed. She totally understood Danny's reaction, but she was waiting for his admission.

"Jules—"

"I could have handled it, Danny. You should have trusted me to do so, the same way I trusted you."

"I—"

"I'm gonna take my lunch break," Max broke in. "I'll be back in a half hour."

The mammoth man left the bar, but Julie's gaze never left Danny's.

"That guy was a douche bag, Jules," Danny said. "The way he flirted with you, checked you out…for the love of Christ, was that the first time that shit went down?" Even thinking it may have happened before had his blood pressure beginning to rise.

"Does it matter?"

Julie's question left him speechless.

"Seriously, Dan, the guy has only worked here for seven shifts. Does it matter if he'd flirted with me before today?"

He knew the correct answer to her question, but damn it, hearing that son of a bitch hit on his wife without cause or care to the fact that she was married pissed him off. "Yes, it matters, okay? It matters. You're mine. That punk had no right—"

"'You realize that you're it for me, right?'" Meaning danced through Julie's eyes as she repeated the words he'd spoken weeks earlier when she'd come to him with her concerns about Suzette. "'I don't care who flirts with me. I only want you.' That's what you told me and I believed you, but it doesn't feel reassuring when you watch someone trying to take away the person who holds your very existence in their hands, does it?"

Damn, the woman had a point, but he wasn't ready to concede…yet. "No, it doesn't, but Jules, that guy—"

"I know you'd never hurt me, Danny," she said. "I know you have full confidence that I'd never hurt you, but it sure as hell feels horrible having that shit in your face every day, no?"

"Now, to answer your question"—glass crunched under Julie's feet as she made her way closer to him—"no, it wasn't the first time he'd flirted with me, but it would have been the last."

The feel of her hands splayed across his chest quickened his pulse for all the right reasons.

"We both know that some flirty behavior can come with the job, but what he was doing was harassment. That is unacceptable in our *home*. While I fully intended to fire his ass before you came in all bad-ass and sexy, you sure saved me the trouble." Her eyes glittered. "How can I thank you?"

Danny looked at his wife—feisty and beautiful, sexy and smart. How the woman could take all of his anger and frustration and shape it into something entirely different with just words and her warm touch baffled him. "We've got about seventeen minutes. I'm sure I can think of something."

He led her back to their office and locked the door. A lot happened in seventeen minutes.

From that day on, when they hired staff, they found themselves looking beyond the resume, beyond the good looks, and into the eyes of the applicants. They weren't seeking workers; they were looking for team members.

Just like Max DeLucca, Kyle Marx sauntered into Danny's on Main one sunny day looking for work. One look into his stormy gaze, and Danny and Julie knew he was searching for more than a paycheck and a steady gig. They didn't know the depth of the pain he hid, but they saw enough. It took mere minutes for them to welcome him aboard.

―――――――――――――――――――

"MY HEART ACHES for both of those boys." Julie's tired voice shook as she swept broken glass into small piles for Danny to scoop up.

The scene that had gone down between Max and Kyle was one that would forever be imprinted in her mind. A confrontation that led to an explosion. Virtual strangers learning secrets about the other that even close friends wouldn't share.

Watching Max come undone as what seemed like his already fragile life blew apart was devastating. Seeing the guilt, torment, and anguish slice across Kyle's face was flat-out debilitating. Every bone in Julie's body ached to help the two men she'd grown to care about, to mend a hole that needed to heal. But Danny had held her back, both physically and emotionally. He wanted her away from accidental harm and felt no words of wisdom would be heard until the damage had time to settle.

"Jules, they'll be okay," Danny reassured. "It's gonna be tough. Hell, if I found out—from a new friend, nonetheless—that my wife was fucking someone else—hell, lots of someone elses—I'd lose my goddamn mind. But add to that that the nasty bitch allowed that shit to get filmed and uploaded to the internet?" Danny shook his head. "Doesn't matter what Max has ignored in the past. He can't ignore this." Shattered glass tumbled from the dust pan into the trash can. "Max is ashamed and angry, and he may misplace that on Kyle for a bit, but it won't stay there. Max is a good man. They both are. It'll pass, I promise."

And it did, quicker than Julie could ever have imagined. Max's wife died in a car accident the following morning, in the process of leaving her marriage behind. The minute Kyle heard the news, he got to Max's side and stayed there.

In the months and years that followed, a brotherhood formed between the two that made no sense to some, but to Danny and Julie, it felt like a blessing. Two amazing men both fighting darkness but doing it together instead of alone. That was what she and Danny had been doing for years—fighting darkness together.

She looked around the bar, their dream packed into four walls, but she heard Chester's voice and encouragement everywhere. He gave it to them, changed their lives, and she wanted to pay it forward. She went to her office and called her friend. His voice still made her smile.

CHAPTER TWENTY-ONE

We Can't Just Take Her On –
We've Gotta Take Her In

DANNY'S ON MAIN was closed on Sundays, a decision made during their second month in business.

"The bar was our dream," she'd reminded Danny as they dragged their exhausted asses into bed at three o'clock one Sunday morning. "The last thing I want is for it to turn into our nightmare. Until we find people we can trust to manage it without us, I think we need to see what day is our least profitable and not open the doors that day."

When Danny's bloodshot eyes focused on her for too long without him responding, Julie thought he'd fallen asleep with his eyes open. Not something he'd done before, but their fatigue had reached new levels. She wouldn't have been surprised.

"Woman...brilliant. Tomorrow, closed." While lacking enthusiasm, Danny's voice, hoarse from repeating orders, breaking up bar fights, and just being social, made it clear he truly did think a day off each week was a great idea.

"We can't close tomorrow, babe." Julie rubbed her hand over her husband's stubble-laden cheek. "We have staff that may or may not turn up and customers that are expecting us. But we can look at our reports, pick our day, and put up a sign with our new hours."

Within a couple weeks' time, she and Danny had determined the bar would be closed on Sundays. It gave them a full day and night to do home projects, explore the surrounding towns, or drive to Maryland to visit with Sheila and Chris. A day off gave Julie time to bake and Danny time to exercise—something he'd started doing more as he got older. Nothing sexier than Danny without his shirt, covered in sweat, and knowing that he was keeping his body healthy. *Mmm.*

JULIE SIGHED AS she fastened her seatbelt. "I love seeing Sheila and Chris. It doesn't matter if it's been a month or six months—we always pick up where we left off."

She and Danny had driven to Maryland for the day. It had been months since the four of them had been together since Danny's stayed busy and Sheila and Chris had become grandparents. Conveniently, the baby had been born on a Saturday, so Julie and Danny got to go to the hospital that Sunday with Sheila and Chris.

"Seeing that man holding a little girl..." Danny chuckled. "You believe he told me not to curse in front of the kid?"

Julie giggled. "That's sweet."

"She's a baby. What's she gonna repeat?"

Being with Sheila had been wonderful and seeing Sheila's granddaughter was lovely. But a tiny part, not so deep down inside, of Julie still grieved the loss of their family. Julie didn't begrudge her friend a family, not even a little bit, but watching Danny hold that sweet pink bundle…grandkids were another thing Julie could never give him. No children… no grandchildren. *Shake it off, Julie.*

Julie forced a laugh. "She won't repeat anything… yet. But Chris was being protective of his girl. Let him be." Julie rolled down her window as the need for fresh air overwhelmed her.

Danny's large hand covered her knee, and silent comfort filled her body. "I get it, honey. Understand exactly how he feels, wanting to protect his girl." His voice lowered. "The only thing that matters, baby."

His words, more gentle than his caress, eased the ache in her chest that she hadn't had the heart to voice. The way he knew her, saw through her, loved her was a blessing.

The way Danny could read people in general was a gift.

"WHEN'S THE LAST time you had yourself a real meal, sweetheart?" Danny stared at the skinny young woman who had entered the bar but had not taken a second step past the doorway. Sadness and loss rippled off her body in waves, too fierce for any person, let alone someone so damn young, to navigate. He'd seen that look before—every day when he'd seen his own reflection.

"Umm…" The blonde's gaze darted around the open space, looking for what he had no idea, but when her shoulders slumped, she took a second step away from the door. And then a third.

"Seriously," he coaxed, "have a seat, hun. We make a mean burger and a sweet cherry soda." He didn't leave his position behind the bar, fearing that his size may intimidate her, but he hoped the enticement of food would be enough to make her stay. Girl looked as if she'd been living off of hardly anything for weeks. She was clean and kempt but malnourished, which led Danny to believe that she could afford to eat but didn't have the desire to do so. "Hamburger?"

"I'm not all that hungry," the girl said with conviction that didn't quite reach her eyes. At that moment, Julie delivered a burger and fries to customers having lunch at a table by the window. "But I guess a cheeseburger couldn't hurt…and fries too. Please."

He wasn't sure why getting her to accept food felt like such a win, but it did. "You got it." He tapped the order into the computer system that he'd finally learned how to use, then pointed at the stools. "My name's Danny Marcus. My wife, Julie, and I own this place. Why don'tcha sit on down there, and I'll pour you a cherry cola. I don't use any of the pre-made shit." He grinned, hoping to set the poor young woman at ease. "I have my own recipe."

The girl gave a tiny smile, and just like that, her face transformed from innocent, maybe even appealing, to alluring.

Every one of Danny's protective instincts kicked in as he handed her the soda. "Here you go…"

"Ashley. My name's Ashley. And thank you. I have money to pay for the meal, so this isn't like…a handout or anything." Her brows pulled together as if she was rethinking her decision. "I don't need any handouts. In fact, I don't need anything from anyone." She made a move to grab the bag she'd placed on the bar.

"Spicy little thing, aren'tcha? Ashley, didn't your parents ever teach you there's no such thing as a free lunch?" He thought his joke was funny, but from the way her pale skin turned ashen, he'd thought wrong.

"No, our parents didn't teach us shit until it was too late." She chomped on the inside of her lip. "Sorry, that was probably too much information. No, sir, never heard that one. But I do have money for lunch."

"I'll be happy to take your money, Ashley. In fact, I can charge you double if you want." That got Ashley to smile, which made Danny chuckle.

Danny pulled up the bar phone and called the back office. "Hey, Jules, can you come up front please? Someone I want you to meet. Thanks, honey." He needed his wife by his side. Julie would take one look at the young woman and help him assess the situation. Julie was astute, smart as a whip, and just as comfortable sitting in a corner as she was front and center, which made her invaluable in just about every situation.

After a few minutes, Julie came out wearing her ever-ready smile and carrying Ashley's cheeseburger and fries. "I guess this is for you?"

"Umm, yeah. Thank you."

Danny took in the way Ashley checked out his wife. The younger woman's eyes traveled from Julie's shoulder-length sun-berry hair to her black, worn-in Converse sneakers and the fit body in between. Julie may be closer to the young woman's mother's age, but his woman was a knock-out for any age. Whatever Ashley saw, she must have approved, because her face softened and her shoulders once again relaxed.

"I'm Ashley. Thanks for bringing me my food."

"My pleasure, sweetie. I'm Julie, that guy's wife." She smiled warmly.

Danny slipped his wife the we-need-to-figure-this-shit-outlook. Julie's nod would have been too subtle for anyone else to notice, but he caught it. The questions started.

"So, Ashley, where's home?" Julie asked, sipping on a freshly poured club soda.

"Nowhere." Ashley took a bite of the burger and moaned. "This is amazing."

"Thanks, the recipe's a secret. I could tell you, but then I'd have to kill you." Danny grinned, Ashley snorted, and Julie rolled her eyes. "Where you from?"

"It doesn't matter," Ashley slowly said, enunciating each word, "because I'm never going back." Another large bite.

A chill ran up Danny's spine. *What in the hell?*

"Sweet girl," Julie spoke softly, "is there anyone you need to call? Maybe someone who needs to know where you are?"

"Yeah, there's someone. But he's dead now. So he won't be answering that call." She popped the last bite of burger in her mouth, chewed, and swallowed before reaching for her drink.

If Danny lived to be one hundred years old, the look in Ashley's eyes when she answered that question would be burned in his retinas forever. He watched his wife bite her lip, doing her best to hold back the same gasp he felt.

"Wow, that was the best burger I've ever had. For real."

"There's more where that came from. You should stick around a day or two and try the chili—Julie's recipe…it's amazing." Danny wasn't a rambler, but he didn't think this girl had anywhere to go and didn't want her to leave. He wasn't sure how to say that without sounding like some sort of sicko.

"With all due respect, I'm eighteen. I never needed a babysitter, and I don't need one now." Ashley's hazel eyes flashed with golden specks of fire.

An adult by legal standards, but still a child in so many ways. "Respect much appreciated." Danny's brow arched. "But I'm a shit-ton older than eighteen, and I know damn well when someone could use another cherry cola. So have mercy on an old man and give me your time. Yeah?"

Ashley's eyes narrowed as she glared from Danny to Julie and back, then shrugged.

"Spicy little thing we got here, Jules," he muttered as he mixed the drink.

"I SEE MYSELF in her," Julie whispered in the dark, her leg draped over Danny's, her head on his chest. "All of her pain bottled up…and those eyes…my God, it was like she was ready to explode."

"I felt it too," he admitted as he ran his fingers up the length of Julie's naked back.

Ashley had spent hours at Danny's on Main, leaving well after the dinner hour but before the heavy drinking crowd descended. She wouldn't share where she was staying the night but promised to return the following day. While neither Julie nor Danny was comfortable with Ashley's choice, they had no say in the matter. So they both hoped the young woman's promises were as good as her ability to recite the alphabet backward (very much a talent in Julie's eyes).

"She's old enough to tend bar, Danny." His soft skin felt hot under her fingertips as she drew figure eights over his bare chest.

"She is." His hand paused on her back. "But like us, loss is written over her. She's young, Jules. We can't just take her on—we've gotta take her in."

Falling more in love with someone she thought owned her was beyond her understanding, but it just happened.

Danny must have mistaken her silence for something else because he continued. "I'm not saying we invite her to live with us—I mean, we don't even know the girl. But come on, we *know* that girl. We've been that girl."

"Yes, we have." Her fingers trailed up his chest. "I was that girl until *you* found me." In the dark, her fingers found his lips and rubbed the soft skin. "And I say if she comes back tomorrow, we do what we can to keep her close. Okay?"

Her husband exhaled. "Love you, baby."

"You're an amazing man, Danny. Your heart has the capacity for so much compassion, so much love. Every day I'm grateful that we met. I love you."

"Thank God for that. Thank God."

Even though they'd made love before their conversation, his reply melted her insides, charging her sated body for another round of play. When she placed a wet kiss on his lips, he got recharged as well.

CHAPTER TWENTY-TWO

This IS Home

"MERRY CHRISTMAS, YOU guys!" Julie's greeting rang through the bar.

"Ho, Ho, Ho." Danny pulled out three small boxes and placed them on the mahogany countertop.

"Who you callin' a ho, Danny?" Ashley's eyes sparkled as a giggle pealed out of her.

"I'm thinking he was addressing you, Spicy." Kyle chuckled.

More than two years had passed since the feisty young woman entered their lives, and in that time, she'd become like a daughter to Danny and Julie. If he was being honest, even though Max and Kyle weren't as young as Ashley, he and Julie still looked at them as family...sons. Max, Kyle, and Ashley were the reason Danny's on Main had turned into the success it was. Sure, the bar had done well before they were employed, but it was doing ridiculously well now. There was a magic between the five of them that Danny didn't think could be replicated, and for that, he was grateful.

Therefore, when he and Julie had discussed Christmas bonuses, they knew money wasn't enough.

"They treat our bar as if it's their own," Julie had said over a candle-lit dinner she'd prepared one Sunday evening a few weeks earlier.

"I know. They work their asses off, above and beyond what's expected." Danny rubbed his hand over his scruff. He'd noticed a few gray hairs mixed in with all of the dark ones and wasn't sure how he felt about that. Julie had noticed too, and based on her lust-filled eyes, wet lips, and rocking blow job the night she pointed out the first few, he decided he was just fine with the grays.

"I've been tossing around an idea, so let me know what you think." Julie sipped her wine. "About two weeks ago, Kyle had to get his car from the parking lot—he'd left it there when he went home with one of the bar bunnies after work. I have no idea what he sees in those women...don't look at me that way, Dan. He could do some much better."

"But he couldn't do easier, babe, and that's what he's looking for. Get back to the topic, or we won't make the eight-thirty movie." When she rolled her eyes, Danny's pulse quickened. "So glad you just did that, honey. I've been looking for a reason to fuck you in the office when everyone's around. Pump my dick into you knowing full well that you can't make a peep. Looks like tomorrow's the day." His cock twitched in his jeans at the mere thought. "Next time, don't roll your eyes at me. It's rude."

He leaned in and touched his lips to hers. Her moan told him that her punishment would be pleasure for the both of them.

"Now, let's get back to the Christmas bonus idea," he said.

Julie licked her full bottom lip, exhaled, and continued. "Anyway, he had been a bit drunk and a lot hasty to leave after his shift, and he mistakenly left his car keys in the bar. It was freezing that night. Sleet, crazy winds, and the guy couldn't get into his car or into the bar, being that it was three thirty in the morning."

"Shit, what did he do? And why is this the first I'm hearing about it?" Danny's gut clenched at the thought of his boy stuck in the cold.

"Max came and got him, drove him to Kyle's apartment because all of his roommates were too intoxicated to answer their cell phones." Julie sipped her wine. "The whole situation got me thinking. Those three, we treat them like family, and they treat us the same. They respect our bar, treat it like home. Would it be so bad if we gave them each a set of keys in case of an emergency?"

The idea floated before it settled into his brain. "No, honey, I think that a brilliant fucking idea."

With the five of them gathered in the empty bar closed for Christmas Eve and Christmas Day, love floated through Danny's veins. In that moment, it didn't matter what was going on in the world outside; his little family stood there before him, and he felt content.

"Danny, give them their gifts." Excitement seeped from Julie's pores as Danny handed out the envelopes and the boxes.

"Oh man, this is unnecessarily generous," Max muttered when he lifted the check from the envelope.

"Shit, you two keep upping the bonuses, and I'll have my own spaceship by next year." Kyle's wink made Julie laugh, but Danny wished he could buy that boy the happiness he deserved.

"Oh...my...God. This is..." Ashley had opened the box and pulled out the key with the note card attached. Tears filled her eyes, but none of them fell as she seemed to contain them by sheer will. "I don't know what to say about this."

Danny looped his arm around his wife as they both watched Kyle and Max open their boxes and pull out their keys. Kyle's brows shot together as if he couldn't make sense of the words, *"You never knock on the door of your own home."* Kyle mouthed the words a second time before lifting his head and staring first at Julie, then at Danny.

"Is this the key to Danny's?" His voice trembled as the question left his lips.

"Our bar, not our home," Julie answered.

Kyle looked at Danny, who simply nodded.

"This is home," Ashley said, apparently speaking for the three of them by the way they all nodded. "Thank you for giving me—us—a home. This is the greatest present I've ever gotten."

What Max, Kyle, and Ashley didn't realize was their arrivals into Danny and Julie's lives were three of the greatest gifts they had ever received as well. It may not have been the loud Christmas Danny wished for once upon a time, but there in his bar stood his little family. He was a happy man.

CHAPTER TWENTY-THREE

Ashley and Ryan

JULIE AND DANNY were in the kitchen, discussing recipe changes with the cook, when on the monitor, they saw a man enter the bar and approach Ashley. They couldn't hear what was said, but they saw the way Ashley's body froze.

"Don't like that at all. I'm going out there," Danny announced.

"No, wait." Julie grabbed her husband's arm and stared at the screen. Her head tilted from side to side before her brow rose with understanding. "There's something interesting going on between those two. Something familiar. Give them a few minutes, babe."

Her tone clearly implied that her request was not a request at all, hence Danny backed away from the door. They stared at the screen, transfixed, tranquility practically hugging her husband. Ashley's voice broke the barrier of the kitchen door.

"*Hello? You still in there?*" Ashley shouted at the man. "*I asked, why the hell are you in my bar?*"

Tranquility gone. Danny snapped into action.

"Oh really, so it's *your* bar now is it, little girl?" Danny's voice held humor as he swaggered into the main bar to address Ashley, Julie right on his heels.

So that's Ryan Baker, Julie thought after being introduced to the handsome younger man. *The* Ryan Baker. Ashley's one true love. Over the years, Ashley, through tons of Julie's prompting and patience, had opened up to Julie and Danny about her past. They'd learned of her brother Leo's passing and the horrific circumstances surrounding his death. Ashley had explained her relationship, or lack thereof, with her parents, and after a while, she told them minimal details about her one true love. Looking at the gorgeous, dark-haired, tattooed, modelesque-man whose eyes barely left Ashley, Julie could understand the difficulty in moving on from him.

For the rest of the day, Ryan stuck by Ashley's side like glue, as if he was afraid if he blinked, she'd vanish and he'd be lost...again. As tightly wound as Ashley was in Ryan's presence, the spicy girl's eyes held a softness that had been missing since the day she came to Charistown.

Hmm, interesting. Maybe I can finally get her to talk to me about him. Julie saw Ashley drink another shot of tequila and head for the restroom. *Then again, maybe tomorrow would be better.*

"THEY BICKER, THEY laugh, they flirt, they fight," Danny said to his empty office as Ashley's sassy words, no doubt directed at Ryan, filtered through the bar walls. He rubbed his hand over the week's worth of scruff that lined his jaw. "Six months he's been here, and while every day is different, they're all the same. It's like that movie *Groundhog Day*. Something's gotta give eventually."

No one knew what would happen during a shift when Ashley and Ryan were together behind the bar. The only thing guaranteed was perfect service and comical entertainment.

"Those two are gonna drive me to drink." Julie shook her head as she entered the office, closed the door, and stared at Danny, who looked at her from his desk chair with a smirk.

"You own a bar, honey. Have at it. Or…" He reached for her, his eyes hungry and his brow arched with mischief. "You can take your frustrations out on me."

"Mmm, I like the sound of that." She stretched to flip the lock on the door.

"Max?" Danny spoke into the phone that connected the office to the bar. "Julie and I are taking a conference call. No interruptions for at least a half hour. Got it?" Danny's full-on smile told Julie that Max had something less than appropriate to say before the call was disconnected.

"Are you gonna share?" Julie asked about Max's comment.

"Never. Now get your sweet ass over here and let me help you with some of your frustrations."

Her man could bottle his relaxation techniques, but just like him, she didn't share.

CHAPTER TWENTY-FOUR

A Sunday Dinner

"MY GOD, THAT was amazing, Danny."

Danny peeked at his wife's face and quickly returned his eyes to the road. They had landed in Philadelphia an hour before and were on their way back to Charistown after a four-day vacation in Key West.

"It was awesome, wasn't it? All of us being together... Christ, I can't remember the last time that happened. Watching my dad, Chris, and Chester trying to one-up each other was funny as hell."

Julie snorted.

"What? What was that for?" Danny huffed, trying his best to sound annoyed even though he felt anything but.

"Really, hun? You don't think you were part of that silliness?"

Shrugging his acquiescence, memories of the weekend floated through his mind. "So how about Chester? Finally found himself a woman...I never saw that coming." Meeting his friend's girlfriend had blown Danny's mind. He wasn't surprised she was beautiful—he'd have expected nothing less—but her appropriate age and maturity...wow. Just wow.

"I'm not surprised. Not at all," Julie murmured. "Something happened to him, Danny. Something bad, tragic. He's never shared it with me, but I know it deep down in my soul. A man like Chester loves hard, and I have the feeling that he only loves hard once. Maybe he'd already found it and lost it, or maybe he never found it at all. All I know is that he's found something with Carmella. It may not be life-altering love, but it certainly has made him happier than I've ever seen him. It's like he finally found..."

"Peace. He found his peace." All of the conversations the two men had shared over the years swirled through Danny's mind. It took Chester a hell of a lot longer than it did Danny, but the older man had found his peace. Danny's cheeks lifted as the realization hit home.

"Your dad looked great...healthy," Julie remarked. "You'd never know that he'd been hospitalized just a few months ago."

Allan had gotten the flu in the fall and it landed him in the hospital for nearly a week. Danny and Julie flew down to North Carolina to be with Allan and Anita, leaving the bar in Max, Kyle, Ashley, and Ryan's capable hands. It had been a remarkable feeling when, after twenty-four hours, they realized they hadn't so much as thought of their bar or its well-being. Once they returned home, they spoke with their four bartenders, people they had taken to calling their kids, about them once again taking over so Danny and Julie could take a much needed, well-deserved vacation.

Obviously, with the two of them on their way home from the Florida Keys, the request was well received and accepted.

"What do you think about the cute duo that started coming in on Thursday nights?"

Julie's question took his mind away from Florida and delivered it to the bar.

"Lyla and Janie," Julie clarified unnecessarily.

He knew exactly who they were. He made it his business to know the regulars, and he'd made it his mission to know the people his *kids* showed interest in. Janie Silver appealed to Max in a way Danny hadn't seen in the decade Max had been working for the Marcuses, so Danny paid close attention.

He grinned. "What do I think? I think those two are gonna be around for quite some time."

"Ahh, so you noticed it too, huh?" Danny's silence got Julie speaking. "Max looks at Janie like he can't decide if he wants to devour her or run from her." She giggled. "My guess is he'll do both, though I hope not in that order. That sweet girl looks at him with stars in her eyes. I'd hate for him to ruin that. It could ruin her."

Danny couldn't disagree. As usual, his wife's assessment was spot-on. "What about the other one, Lyla?"

"Hmm, that one is tough."

He thought the same thing. From the moment he'd laid eyes on the petite brunette, he saw something he had never seen before. The woman was a complete contradiction. Her beauty was extraordinary, but often times it was masked behind sarcasm and dry wit. If one chose to only look skin deep, they might not see the kindness behind what could be considered rude.

In the few weeks that the ladies had been spending their Thursday nights at the bar, Danny had noticed Lyla's sharp sense of humor, but he also saw how quickly she could bank pain if someone else's attempt at funny crossed an invisible line she had drawn. She didn't mind receiving drinks from men but frowned upon cocktails on the house. Regardless of how she got her drinks, her tips were generous to a fault. She was fiercely protective of Janie and from the start included Ashley in their conversations, which made the protective side of Danny happy as hell.

What did he think about Lyla Dalton? Something in her blue eyes spoke to him; he just didn't understand what they were saying…yet. The woman ran deep, deeper than he could possibly imagine, but she was good people. And good people always had a place at Danny's on Main.

Danny said, "Kyle and Lyla seem to speak the same language, the way they edge around flirting with one another but take home random hookups instead. Those two are similar creatures—playing with fire. Sure as hell hope they don't burn each other."

"Kyle deserves to find a good woman. Maybe Lyla will be just what he needs. I think she and Janie are gonna fit in just fine," Julie concluded with optimism.

Danny lifted his chin. "It'll definitely be interesting."

———————————●———————————

INTERESTING WAS AN understatement. Janie Silver and Lyla Dalton were sugar and jalapeños. It didn't matter that the duo wasn't Danny's staff; they meshed with the group and quickly found their place in Danny and Julie's family. With their quirky sense of humor, willingness to listen, and the desire to help out whenever needed, Janie and Lyla seemed to give so much more than they asked for in return. But then again, wasn't that the same with all of Danny's *kids*?

When Danny found himself counting the two brunettes among his kids, he couldn't have felt more pleasure. He didn't need any more responsibility, but their eyes told him that they would accept his support, maybe flourish from it…no matter their age, they would embrace it. Chester had been there for him, and this was Danny's way to pay it forward. It just so happened that with the right people, being a mentor came with a lifetime of love as well.

"A SUNDAY DINNER, Danny," Julie practically sang as she placed her cell phone on the desk.

"Sorry, honey, what?" He had just entered the office and shut the door. Dinner hour on a Wednesday evening was packed, so the only way they'd be able to have a conversation was if the door was closed.

Excitement bloomed in her belly as she told Danny about her call. "That was Janie on the phone just now. Apparently she and Lyla have family dinners together every Sunday night. They've been doing it, just the two of them, since they were eighteen." That part of Janie's story made Julie's heart hurt. Where were their families? "Anyway, she invited us to *their* dinner. All of us, Danny—you, me, Kyle, Max, Ashley, and Ryan, having dinner on Sunday night." Her voice was practically a squeal, but her delight was impossible was to contain. "I'm baking dessert. I'm so excited."

"Sunday dinner," Danny repeated. "At Janie's place." An indefinable emotion sparked in his hazel eyes before humor crossed his face. "Why in fuck did we never think of that?"

"We're pretty amazing, babe, but we can't think of everything," Julie teased. Danny's smile was sexy. Didn't matter how many times she saw it, it still took her breath away.

"Looking forward to dinner, honey. But I came in here to tell you something less than amazing… something else I didn't think of." A grimace combined with a hint of bashfulness wasn't a look Danny Marcus wore every day —hell, Julie hadn't seen that look more than once or twice in nearly three decades.

"Dan, what's wrong?"

"I don't know how the fuck I did this, but I didn't place the vodka order last week," he confessed. "I thought I pressed 'enter' on that damn computer form, but when the shipment came this morning, no vodka. According to the receipt, I ordered everything else, but not that." He ran his hands over his scruff-covered face. "We only have eight bottles of vodka left until Friday afternoon delivery."

Julie sighed, unable to hold back her relief. "It's okay."

"It's not okay. Eight bottles may get us through tonight—maybe—but Thursday nights are our busiest night of the week. I screwed up. Damn new computer system. I liked the old system so much better."

"Danny, I love you, you know that, yes?"

Aggravated hazel eyes met hers, and he nodded.

"Then you should also know that after spending near-ly thirty years not just behind a bar but behind the scenes, I double-check all paperwork all the time. And knowing that as amazing and talented as you are with everything—except for computers"—Julie grinned guiltily—"I triple-check all the orders. I saw the mistake. The vodka was ordered, just a little late. It'll be here this afternoon."

"You're so wrong, honey," Danny murmured, shaking his head, his mouth curling up on the sides.

Julie stood up and walked into Danny's open arms. "What am I wrong about?"

"You do think of everything." He lifted her chin, tilting her head back to meet his gaze. "You're amazing." He smiled, and it was sexy as hell.

"THANK YOU FOR coming. Honestly, this was so much fun," Janie said, her turquoise eyes dancing with happiness. "Next week dinner's at Lyla's house. She has more room than I do, but she'll force you to wash the dishes."

Danny accepted her tight hug and returned it. He watched as his woman spoke to Lyla and laughed for the umpteenth time that evening, and he reveled in the sweet sound. Her laughter had been his music for more than twenty-eight years, but he noticed that with each addition to their "family," her happiness changed. Morphed. Grew into something she had always wished for—a maternal love for those she chose to care for. Those who looked at her with respect and looked to her for guidance. In return, she looked to them for trust and unconditional love.

"We can't wait. I'll bake cookies," Julie informed the women as she and Danny left Janie's apartment after everyone except for Lyla.

Their ride home was quiet. He was stuck in his own thoughts, as he assumed she was.

"Glue."

"Danny?"

"They're the glue, Jules. Those two women came to town and fastened us all together. Not saying we weren't a family before, 'cause we were." Danny stared at the road as his thoughts turned to words. "But we were pieces, and now we're not. They're the glue, honey."

CHAPTER TWENTY-FIVE

First Time For Everything

WATCHING MAX AND Janie fall in love while Ashley and Ryan fell apart was exciting, exhausting, romantic, and agonizing. One couple flourished while the other flailed. Hearts and flowers or daggers and tears, it was a coin toss. For Julie and Danny, it was a never-ending carnival—fun until it wasn't.

Then there was Kyle, Julie's special *one*. No good parent would ever admit to having a favorite child, and she certainly wouldn't, but deep down, Kyle Marx had a special place in Julie's heart. Lost since the day she met him, but he was too guarded to ask for directions. The man had been circling the drain for months, first with his alcohol consumption, which Julie feared may lead to drugs, and his excessive, but she prayed not careless, sexcapades with countless people. Nothing romantic had formed between him and Lyla, and the more Julie learned about her newest "daughter," the more she realized that Lyla and Kyle would have been as catastrophic as lovers as they were beneficial as friends. Knowing that Kyle had Lyla to turn to comforted Julie, but according to Lyla, he never fully opened up.

"Come on, we're going to be late," Julie called from the kitchen of their one-story ranch-style home. She popped the lid on the container of lemon-iced shortbread cookies—Max's favorite—turned off the kitchen lights, and strolled to the front door.

"Sorry, honey." Danny's hand slid around her waist and pulled her side to his firm chest. His soft whiskers touched her forehead barely a second before his lips. "I needed to set the DVR to record the post-game show." A second and more sensual kiss landed on her neck. "Never know what time we'll be home from dinner, and I always seem to want you more than football by the time we get back."

His lush lips and sexy words raised goose bumps on her flesh and sent tingles down her spine. "You know I'm a sure thing, right?" she teased as they walked from the house to the car. "You don't need to sweet-talk me to get in my pants."

Danny opened her car door and waited for her to slide in and buckle up before he leaned down and whispered in her ear, "Been sweet-talking you for nearly thirty years, Jules." His warm breath tickled her neck, making her nipples pucker beneath her wool sweater. "Does it turn you on?"

Julie nodded, her heart thudding.

"Then I *need* to do it." His hazel eyes smoldered. "Let me rephrase—I fucking love doing it."

Sweet pain hit her earlobe a fraction of a second before a soft lick. *Thank goodness for modern technology. Looks like Danny won't be watching the post-game show until much, much later.* But before then, they had dinner. The word barely registered in Julie's mind before the car roared to life with Danny behind the wheel. *Wait, how did he get there so fast?*

Sunday dinner was at Max and Janie's house, formerly just Max's place.

"Seeing Max with Janie…" She sighed, and Danny laughed.

"I hear you, honey. I never thought it would happen, but couldn't be happier that it did." Danny's left hand moved to the top of the steering wheel while his right made purchase on Julie's thigh.

She placed her cool palm over his warm one, enjoying the feel of his heat penetrating her jeans. "I just wish Ashley and Ryan would stop fighting the inevitable." It was only a matter of time before those two ended up together. Julie just feared the longer it took, the deeper the damage they inflicted on each other would be, and they had already suffered too much. No reason to add more.

"You can't rush these things, Jul. They may need more time."

"More time?" Her near snort would have been amusing had the topic been, well, amusing. "Dan, I think seven years is time enough. Even those who have broken mirrors run out of bad luck after seven years, right?"

A barely there chuckle left Danny's throat as they pulled into Max and Janie's driveway. "That's what I've heard, honey."

The night was lovely, as usual. Dinner was delicious, the company entertaining, and the Eagles were winning during the first half of the football game. It was a cozy Sunday night, aside from the weird vibes bouncing between Ashley and Ryan.

But Kyle's health and overall appearance put Julie on edge. More and more often, Kyle was coming into work hung-over and leaving his shift drunk, but that night, he looked saturated in more than booze; he looked strung-out.

Julie wasn't certain if she felt better or worse when Danny pulled her aside to get her assessment on Kyle. "He's getting worse, yeah?"

"Danny, my heart hurts just looking at him."

"Shit, I kept praying the boy would pull it together." Danny ran his fingers over his short salt-and-pepper hair. "Fuck, can't talk to him when he's like this. It'll go in one ear and out the other. I'll call him tomorrow, stop by his place if I need to. We need to get him sorted."

"We will," she said.

During the football game halftime, Julie, Lyla, and Janie went to the kitchen to grab drink refills. The sound of the television got louder. Quickly returning to the family room with her eyes glued to the large screen, Julie heard a forecast that would forever change her life and the lives of those around her.

Tropical Storm Leo is gaining strength in the Atlantic as we speak. We are expecting it to morph into a hurricane by Tuesday possibly hitting landfall as early as Wednesday night. Get ready, people. This is going to be a big one.

Many things happened in the seconds during and after the meteorologist spoke, yet for Julie, the world slowed to an impossible pace. Frame by frame, she watched as devastation hit, and the actual storm was still more than twenty-four hours away.

THEIR CAR WAS quiet on the way home from dinner. Danny white-knuckled the steering wheel, and Julie replayed what had happened in slow motion. Ashley had left the house almost immediately following the forecast, Ryan on her heels. The rest of the group tidied up what was left from dessert and left Max and Janie's house, barely a word spoken between them.

"Leo! Of all the fucking names in the world, the one hurricane to hit Charistown in decades had to be Leo? What are the goddamn chances?"

Just hearing the name hiss from Danny's mouth was like a physical blow to Julie's gut.

Leo had been Ashley's brother and Ryan's best friend. He died in a horrific car wreck during a hurricane when she was a senior in high school. His death brought about the end of Ryan and Ashley's relationship.

"How much more can she take, Danny? How much more should she have to?"

The muscles in her husband's jaw bunched. "She's a strong ass woman. She'll take what she's given and not just survive but thrive. Reminds me of you, Julie. She always has."

His silken words touched her in a way she couldn't express. It wasn't sexy or slick but loving and truthful, words she felt straight down to the marrow of her bones.

"You told her tonight before she left that she wasn't alone," Danny reminded. "And she's not. She has a family now, and this time, she has Ryan. Promise you, babe, he won't let her down, not ever again. Of that, I'm fucking certain."

"I believe that too." And she did.

As soon as their car pulled into the garage, the couple started preparing the list of things they needed to purchase from the hardware store to safeguard the bar against hurricane damage and the super market in case they were without power for a day or two. The next couple of days were sure to be long, exhausting, and hopefully full of unnecessary concern.

THE LATEST FORECAST said the hurricane would hit Charistown in less than twelve hours. While under normal circumstances, Danny wouldn't put much faith in the weather predictions, the sky had already begun to darken and the winds to whip. He watched out the window as his store-owning neighbors and Charistown residents scurried around, preparing for the rare storm. Danny pulled his cell phone from his pocket, dialed the number, and lifted it to his ear.

"Fuck," he mumbled when Kyle's voice mail picked up once again.

Even with the chaos of the past two days, Danny had been trying, unsuccessfully, to get in touch with his boy. He and Julie had stopped by Kyle's apartment, only to be met with an unanswered door. He had even called the police station to make certain Kyle hadn't been arrested while Julie contacted the hospital. All searches came up empty. With the storm coming, they needed to batten down the hatches before they could continue their search for Kyle.

Ryan, Max, and Max's best friend since childhood, Sebastian Gage, all came to Danny's on Main to assist with the storm preparation. The windows got taped, awnings stowed, booths covered in plastic, tables and chairs hugged tightly together in the center of the bar. Danny had had emergency generators installed several years prior, after they lost electricity for twenty-four hours due to an electrical storm. The food in the freezers would be fine if the power went out this time around.

"Go home, boys. Thanks for helping me handle stuff around here." Danny looked at the men he respected, cared about, and loved. He felt a great sense of accomplishment in having found so many good men to call friends— family. As the group filed out, Danny called, "Ryan, you don't want her to be alone too long in this weather."

No other words were said because none were needed. Ryan nodded and left the bar with Max. Danny called Kyle again before removing the cash from the register and waiting for Julie to arrive so they could sort through their office before going home. No reason to be open in a ghost town.

* * *

"WOMAN, HOW MANY candles did you buy?" He couldn't hide the humor in his voice even if he'd tried. The woman must have pulled forty jarred candles out of the shopping bags he'd helped her unload from the car.

"Dan, you're lucky I could even find these." She held up the white wax-filled jar. "The whole town has been emptied of batteries, but I got my hands on an eight-pack. Even that was tough. I thought some woman was going to

LISA N. PAUL

throw a punch in order to take it from me." She shook her head in the way she did when people's actions confounded her. "Anyway, being the wife of a former firefighter, I knew better than to buy candle sticks—last thing I want to do is burn our house down if the power goes out—so I bought these candle jars instead. Figured if it came down to it, we could light them and place them away from the curtains and furniture. At least we'll have some light."

The way his wife's mind worked forever amazed him. Some people multitasked; Julie multithought.

"I love you, honey," he said, setting the jar on the table.

He cupped her head in his hands and crushed their mouths together. Her taste on his tongue as he slid it against hers, deepening the kiss, made him need more and want it all. His free hand moved to her breast, kneading it through the thermal shirt, finding her pebbled nipple and plucking it. He swallowed her moan while slowly grinding his hips against her. He loved the way her body melded into his, the ultimate trust she'd given him since the day they started their love affair.

"I want you now." His command was uncompromising yet gentle. Heat roared through his body as every primal nerve awakened to play. Walking her backward from the dining room to the couch, he saw hunger enflame her sparkling gray eyes. "That bottom lip, baby, mmm, I need that fucking lip." He took it, sucked it into his mouth, savored its smoothness, and pictured it around his throbbing cock.

"Danny, oh, touch me."

Her throaty request had him stripping off her clothes before another word was spoken. His dick pulsed in his unbuttoned jeans."Ahh, no panties. You were planning to get fucked by me, weren't you?" His fingers brushed her naked sex, already glistening with arousal and waiting for his touch.

"A girl can hope, can't she?" Julie panted, her eyes closing when Danny pressed his fingers into her wet channel. "Ohhh, yesss."

The no-underwear rule had stayed in effect even when they'd lost the opportunity for adoption. If they were home, Julie was to be pantyless. At the bar, if she chose to wear undergarments, Danny had the right to tear them off. Either way, easy access was the name of the game. She tended to wear panties at work—felt cleaner that way, she claimed. So she kept spare pairs in her locked drawer in case they fooled around, which wasn't all the time.

"I need your skin, baby." Her eyes narrowed, her voice a husky murmur as she slid Danny's shirt up his torso and over his head.

The cool air did nothing to quench the fire burning in his gut. Twisting his wrist so his palm faced the ceiling, Danny rubbed his woman's pleasure spot and marveled at the delicious sounds that came from her throat. When his thumb circled her clit, Julie's body tightened around him.

"That's it, your pussy loves what I'm doing, doesn't it? Wants more. Ride my fingers, baby, gonna give you what you need to come hard. I want it, Julie, give all you got."

As if his words summoned her climax, she released. Trembling, moaning, panting, giving him all of her—raw. He loved seeing her that way, loved fucking her that way. His pants were at his ankles, his cock in his hand before her orgasm fully left her body.

"Danny, yes, I want it," she cried, her eyes round as she watched him stroke himself. "Fuck me, please."

Poised at her entrance, he rubbed the tip in her juices and swallowed back a groan that would have sounded more animal than human. He entered her slowly, teasingly, uncertain who the joke was on: her or him.

"Fuck me," she repeated.

And he slammed home. Seated balls deep in her tight pussy, her warmth consumed him. He slowly pulled back.

"No," she pled, locking her ankles around his waist in an attempt to keep him close.

"Shh, I'm fucking you. Now lay back and enjoy the ride."

The sides of Julie's mouth ticked up because she knew she'd love what he dished out. She always did. Slow pumps led to deep thrusts as Danny's hands slid over Julie's silky skin. Every inch of her body was perfection, and every piece of her body was his. His skin prickled when she ran her cool fingers down the length of him, touching his muscles, gripping his ass. Her long legs wrapped around his torso allowed him in deeply, but he wanted more.

"Stand up, honey. I wanna sink into you from behind."

His conscience kicked in a bit when he saw how jellified her leg muscles were, but he held on tight, slipped through her folds, and fucked into her like a man who'd gone without for years instead of days. His orgasm began to build in his spine, a fireball picking up speed, not yet ready to burst. Until... Julie's hand slipped through her thighs and touched his balls. A light stroke, right behind his sack.

"Fuck, Julie…fuck."

She continued her massage as his release rushed through his body, out of control. Out of his mind pleasure. His legs buckled, bringing him to the floor. Thank Christ he had the wherewithal to break the fall and bring Julie down on him instead of under him.

"Fuck…holy shit. Where'd you learn to do that?" he heaved through broken breaths.

She winked. "You have your guy talk; we have our girl chats. I learn a shit-ton from our girls."

Danny's body still shook with pleasure as he brought his wife's lips to his. "Keep up the good work, woman."

THE WINDOWS RATTLED with the force of the wind and the driving rain as Danny and Julie snuggled on a pallet by the lit fireplace. The power hadn't gone out, but after witnessing an old maple tree crack in half and a dozen or so branches whipping around the yard, they thought it best to make a fire, fill the cooler with ice and beverages, and stay away from the windows. Their cell phones were charging, and Julie had found an old corded phone in the attic that she plugged in just in case the power went out.

"This is shaping up to be some storm." Danny shook his head at the Weather Channel. "I can't believe they actually predicted this shit right."

"First time for everything," Julie answered, lost in thoughts of Ashley and Ryan.

"What's going on in your mind, honey?" Danny muted the television and faced her.

"I'm worried about Ashley and Ryan. I called her about an hour ago and Ryan wasn't home yet. That poor girl told me she was okay, but come on, Dan. You think she's okay?"

"What I think is that she needs to get through this. Did you ask her to come and stay with us?"

Julie smiled. Her husband knew her well. "Of course I did. When she declined, I offered to go to her. She declined that too. So what are we supposed to do?" When Danny's arms opened wide, she curled into his embrace.

"We let her deal for now, and we check in on her in a couple of hours. She isn't alone in this, but she is an adult. So if it's time she needs, we have to give it to her. I will, however, call Ryan and make sure he's okay. Tell him to get his ass home."

Once Danny confirmed that Ryan was only minutes from his place and Ashley, Julie relaxed a bit and tried to enjoy the romantic ambiance with her man—until Danny's cell phone rang.

Julie was pouring them each a drink when Danny's voice hardened. "What?" Her eyes went to his face, his skin ashen even by the firelight. "Was anybody hurt?"

Julie's stomach dropped when she heard that question. "Danny?" His gaze found hers, but it gave nothing away. In that nothing, he told her so much. "Danny…"

He nodded. "Let me repeat what you're saying, Officer. One of the old trees across the street from the bar snapped in half, crashed into a utility pole, and sent it and its live wires into our bar."

Every word that left Danny's mouth was a lashing to bruised and battered skin.

"Put him on speaker…Danny, please."

By the steely look in his eyes, she knew he wanted to shield her from the horror that was filling his ears, but he pressed the button.

The officer's voice filled the room. "The liquor acted as an accelerant."

"We're on our way," Danny gritted out.

"Mr. Marcus, I'm asking you not to come down here—"

"You don't call a man and tell him his property, his livelihood, is on fire, then tell him to sit back and let it burn. I was a fucking firefighter, for Christ's sake."

Their bar is on fire? Julie's lungs froze as Danny's statement hung thick in the air.

"I know I'm asking a lot, Mr. Marcus, but with the storm at full force, we're asking all residents to stay off the streets and in their homes."

"That is our home," Julie's voice cracked.

The officer continued as if he hadn't heard Julie's comment, and maybe he hadn't, but Danny had. Tear-filled hazel eyes met hers as he pulled her to his chest and hugged her tightly.

"You're a respected member in this community, Mr. Marcus. I'm sorry about your business, but not nearly as sorry as I'd be if something were to happen to you. Please stay put until the storm passes. We'll contact you the minute we have the situation under control."

Once the officer had Danny's verbal agreement, the call was disconnected, the power flickered twice before leaving the house in candlelit darkness and Julie and Danny on their knees, waiting for word of what would become of their fresh start.

"I NEED TO call the kids," he rasped after speaking with the officer again and crying with his wife. "Don't want any of them to hear it on the news."

"Danny, the whole town is without power." Julie sniffled, her tear tracks glistening in the firelight. "Where would they hear it?"

He swallowed the grapefruit-sized lump in his throat. If any of them found out about the bar from anyone but him, they'd be devastated, and that would destroy him. So despite Julie's logic, Danny picked up the phone. "Max."

"Danny?" Max's voice was firm. "Everything okay?"

"No, son, everything is far from okay. We lost the bar tonight…"

"What the hell are you talking about?"

"Few hours ago, Julie and I got a call that the place was on fire. They just followed up. What wasn't eaten by flames was ruined by hose and hurricane damage. Place is totaled, boy." Danny did his best to hide his anguish, but his best wasn't good enough.

Max's sob traveled through the line. "Why'd you wait so long to call me, Dan?" Max cleared his throat. "We would've come to you, sat with you, and waited until you got the news."

Even through devastation, they all looked out for each other.

"That's why we didn't call you, son. We need you and Janie safe at home. We needed all of you where you belong. We're gonna figure this out, Max, I swear we will.

Just hold your woman tonight, hug her for us, and tomorrow we'll talk."

"Okay, Dan. You do the same. Give our love to Julie. We're in this with you, no matter what. Whatever you need, man."

After they disconnected, Danny called the rest of the group. There was still no answer from Kyle, and Danny refused to leave a message with that kind of information, so he requested a call back and hung up. Talking to Ryan was difficult, because not only did the kid have to process the loss himself, he needed to share the news with Ashley. That wouldn't be an easy task.

During each phone call, Julie sobbed, but as he spoke to their kids, he became stronger. Their reactions were all similar: shock, sadness, and complete support. Not one of them wavered or folded. They all promised to support Danny and Julie, and he truly believed they would.

"It's gonna be okay, Jules. I swear it." He knew that deep in his soul. "The bar is insured, no one got hurt. It's just stuff, honey. That's all. Just things."

Sniffling, she nodded. "You're not wrong. I think the tears are more from shock." She wiped at her face, but the tears continued to fall. "We've had enough bad in our lives. I thought we were done. This was a reminder not to get too complacent, huh?"

Danny's eyes narrowed. "No, baby, maybe it's a sign that things needed to change." Once the thought left his mouth, he found himself believing it. Was he currently happy? Certainly not. His business was destroyed, the building ruined, fifteen years of memorabilia gone, but his wife was snuggled into his side, his family was healthy, and they would be able to rebuild if that was what they chose to do.

It could have been worse. They'd both lived through worse. And survived it. They'd survive this as well.

CHAPTER TWENTY-SIX

Silver Lining

TWENTY-FOUR HOURS AFTER Hurricane Leo left Charistown, Danny and Julie walked around what was left of Danny's on Main.

"This is painful," Julie said, holding up the mangled picture frame that used to hang near the kitchen door. The image inside was water-logged under the cracked glass. "I'll never forget the day Kevin Bacon walked through those doors. The best burger in Charistown, he said." Tears stung Julie's eyes as she stared at the ruined image. She swore if she looked hard enough, she could still see Kevin, one arm around Danny and the other holding a burger. She blinked, and only a shredded mess remained.

"It was a great day, honey." Danny gently removed the broken frame from her hand and tossed it in the trashcan. "We'll have more great days. Besides, I heard Bacon is a vegan now. Ironic, huh?"

She giggled at her husband and continued the walk-through.

Danny's father called to check in, heartsick that he couldn't fly up to help with the wreckage. With snow in the forecast, it was better for Allan's arthritis if he stayed south until spring.

"Love you, Dad," Julie shouted as Danny said his good-byes and disconnected the call.

"We're here," came a voice from the front of the bar.

Max, Janie, Lyla, Ashley, and Ryan walked through the hole that had once been the entranceway. Judging by the looks on their faces—grimaces on the men and tear-filled eyes on the women—the destruction hit them almost as badly as it did her and Danny. If she could have shielded them from seeing it, she would have, but there was no hiding what had become of Danny's on Main.

The smell of pine, along with Danny's strong arms and strong chest, surrounded her.

"I got you," he whispered.

Like a freight train, Ashley threw herself against them, sobbing quietly as they enveloped her in their embrace. Before long, they were all hugging and crying, laughing and sighing. Never had anything felt more right.

"Where in the hell is Kyle?"

The question came from Ryan, but Julie and Danny had been worried about him for days. They'd been calling and texting with no response. The fire at Danny's was all over the local news, so for him not to check in meant something had to be wrong. Really flipping wrong. As if on cue, Danny's cell phone rang. Like a trained reaction, Julie's stomach clenched. Once she heard it was Kyle's brother, Nixon, on the phone, her lungs seized up as well.

"What happened?" they all asked in various ways when Danny hung up.

Twice in as many days, she saw *that* look in her husband's eyes. *No, no, no, nothing can happen to Kyle.* Bile rushed up her esophagus. *I can't handle that. Please, let him be okay.* Danny's fingers threaded through hers and tightened, grabbing her attention and pulling her eyes to his before he spoke.

He explained that Kyle had been in a car accident the night before, during the hurricane. He was drunk and wrapped himself around a pole. While Danny listed the things broken and bruised, the surgeries Kyle'd gone through and what more he'd face, she was just thankful he was alive.

Before they left for the hospital, Julie looked from Ashley to Ryan. There was something different between them, in the way his arm draped over her shoulder, the protective way he held her close. In the midst of anguish and pain, a ray of sunlight bloomed. She cleared her throat in a purposeful fashion.

"Jules," Danny grumbled, a smirk creeping across his handsome face, "you can't possibly be thinking about our bet now, while all hell is breaking loose in our lives?"

She grinned, wiping away the last stray tear from her cheek. "Danny Marcus, you, my sweet husband, have always preached about finding the silver lining when the skies are at their darkest, and here it is, buddy. Now pay up. The rest of you too. Don't think you can get away with stiffing the boss lady."

When Ashley looked concerned and Ryan upset, Danny explained that everyone else had made a bet. Julie had said Ryan and Ashley would get back together during the storm if the power went out, and everyone bet against her.

"Pedicures on me, spicy girl." Julie smiled before leaving the mess behind.

CHAPTER TWENTY-SEVEN

Welcome Home

WEEKS PASSED AND the group was busy, not just with spending time at Danny's going through debris and saving anything salvageable but doing the same with Kyle. Danny and Julie took turns bringing Kyle and Nixon home-cooked meals and fresh laundry. When Nixon went to work, between the eight of them, they made certain Kyle was never alone.

As a group, a family, they worked together to restore health, happiness and normalcy into each other's lives. Of course there were disagreements and disapproval, but as Danny sat in bed with his wife and thought about Christmas, he realized that each year, he assumed life couldn't get better. Yet the following year, it always did. Even with losing the bar and the unspeakable fear of losing Kyle, Danny still saw the year for what it was—better than the previous one. Julie's head lay on his chest, her soft hair wrapped around his knuckles.

"Christmas is almost here," he said.

"Yep. I'm thinking we should have it at our house this year. I'd like to do something special for the kids."

The woman had read his mind. "What were you thinking, beautiful?" His fingers massaged her neck.

"I'm thinking if you keep doing that, you'll be having this conversation with a sleeping, drooling wife," she teased.

A chuckle left his body, but he didn't stop his massage. "Seriously, babe. I have an idea, but it's big...huge. I'm not sure what you'll think about it."

She pulled the sheet around her breasts and sat up straight. "Dan, you've got me so curious now. When have I ever not liked one of your ideas?"

"Umm, you do remember the Empty Contest, right?"

Her giggle made him laugh. "Let's not discuss that ridiculous contest, Mr. Marcus. Tell me what you're thinking."

He'd been tossing the idea around for a couple of weeks, working on the logistics of it. But he couldn't make it work, not even in his mind, without Julie's input. He needed her even in his imaginary *whatifs*. "How would you feel about inviting them to be partners in the bar? All of them. We obviously don't need their money to rebuild, but Danny's on Main has been a family-run business since the day Max showed up. Since they are our kids, I was wondering how you'd feel about making it family *owned* and operated?"

The way her eyes glowed in the soft light from the nightstand lamp was striking, but not nearly as magnificent as her smile. "It's an amazing idea. I love it."

"You do?"

"I do! And I love you."

"Thank God for that."

ON CHRISTMAS EVE, with everyone except Kyle, who was still hospitalized, sitting around the tree, bellies full, and drinks in hand, Julie and Danny gave out small wrapped boxes. Julie began to explain how much each of them meant to her and Danny, but her throat tightened with emotion.

Danny took the reins and finished her thoughts. "Julie and I are going to start rebuilding Danny's on Main, but well... we'd like it if you all were part of the process."

Butterflies flapped in her stomach as each couple and Lyla unwrapped their gifts. In each box was a white tag attached to a long, ornate, iron key.

In your home, you are always loved. Welcome home. Danny's on Main ~

"Look at me," Danny said, his tone not offering an argument. "This is a no-pressure deal. If you want it, we want you. If you don't, we still want you in the same way you've been with us up to this point. If you want in, but money's tight, we'll come up with something. The only thing we're asking for is honesty. So no answers tonight or tomorrow. Think about it and get back to us. But know we love you all like family, and the new Danny's will be about our family."

The noise was deafening as everyone spoke at once. Squeals of excitement and grunts of appreciation carried through the room.

"Think it's safe to say they like their gifts." Danny chuckled.

"Yeah, well, you've always been a very generous giver," Julie said.

"I got something large to give you the minute they all leave." His brows lifted with his sexual innuendo, making her face flush and her body heat.

"Okay," she called to the group, "the later it gets, the worse the roads get with drunk drivers and such. So you should all get going."

Danny's chuckle turned to a laugh.

"Why don't you just admit you want us to leave so you guys can fool around?" Max challenged.

Danny picked up the challenge and ran with it, leaving Julie's mouth gaping. "We want you to leave so I can make my woman come till she can't see straight. That what you wanna hear, DeLucca?"

"Yep." Max popped the *p* and ducked when Janie punched his arm.

"Yeah, so that isn't at all awkward for my date here," Lyla deadpanned as she pushed her *date*, Rick, out the front door, then spoke over her shoulder. "Lord, I was hoping he'd think I was a sweet, virginal kind of girl." She giggled and hugged Danny.

"The dude has met you, right?" Ryan jabbed. "Hell, the shit that came out of your mouth tonight alone would cause lesser men to rock in a corner."

"Whatever." Lyla waved off the comment. "He'll be gone by the end of the night anyway. It's just fun." Lyla hugged Julie and left.

Ashley giggled. "Love that woman. And we're out of here too. Night, guys."

"Merry Christmas, everyone," Julie shouted and closed the front door behind them just before Danny lifted her over his shoulder and carried her to their bedroom.

CHAPTER TWENTY-EIGHT

The Woman Still Blushes

MONTHS PASSED, AND construction progressed on the bar. With everyone, including Kyle, on board as partners, Danny's on Main was shaping up to be better than ever. Maybe Danny had been correct. Maybe the bar's destruction was indeed a way of making something great into something fantastic.

Seeing the happiness on Ashley and Ryan's faces and the sparkly magic on her left ring finger made Julie giddy with excitement. His proposal on Christmas morning had been a surprise to Ashley but not to Julie or Danny. Receiving the call from a tearful and blissed out Ashley was a Christmas gift Julie would never forget. The two of them weren't looking to set a wedding date yet, but they were elated to finally be official.

As for Kyle, while his body was mending, he was emotionally stagnant. It didn't seem to matter what she, Danny, or anyone else did or said. No one could get through to him…until Cate Lockton, the mysterious woman who saved him the night of his car accident, showed up when Danny's on Main reopened its doors. Kyle referred to the woman as an angel, and Julie and Danny—while watching Kyle transition from lost to found, broken to breathing, pieces to whole—had to agree.

Danny grinned over lunch one afternoon. "The woman belongs here. I say this with nothing but respect, but she's got that look, Jules. You know, the one that we all started with, the one that screams, 'Love me or leave me, but if you love me, please don't leave me.'"

"I know the look." Julie arched her brow. "And in case you missed it, Kyle isn't going anywhere. That boy is holding on to her for dear life."

She was proud. Kyle had found love. She saw it in every move he made, and he was going the distance to make sure his woman knew he was all in. Knowing Cate, it may not be easy for him, but Julie believed his strength and stubborn nature would finally work to his benefit.

Cate and her business partner, Elliot, owned a party-planning business, and they were hired to organize a grand reopening bash for Danny's on Main. Live entertainment, catered food—the whole nine yards—all to thank the crowd who had supported the bar and come back the minute the doors reopened.

Two weeks after reopening, Julie and Danny had a working lunch in one of the two new back offices. She looked at the computer screen, then at Danny, who sat off to her left. "Here I thought it would take months for word to spread and our customers to return, but looking at these numbers, after two weeks, our Thursday nights are nearly back to where they were before."

"Of course they are." Confidence oozed from the grin that overtook Danny's mouth. "Baby, when are you gonna believe that we're destined for greatness?"

"Maybe you should show me some of your great-ness." Her bottom lip met her teeth, and Danny's eyes flared.

"No, Jules, I think you're gonna show me a little of your greatness. I'll lock the door; you get on your knees."

No wonder every time I walk into an office supply store, I get aroused. Then she got on her knees and only thought about the delicious task in front of her.

DANNY FELT A certain kind of peace watching how each of the *kids* found happiness with their significant others. Kyle was still struggling with Cate, but he had no doubt that in the end, Kyle would get his girl. Which left Lyla.

Lyla, after more than a year, still managed to con-found him. Sometimes Danny thought he saw light strug-gling to escape the cracks in her veneer, but for the most part, the woman was locked up tight. Free to laugh, open to play, but sealed up when it came to her past or her emo-tions. She hooked up with random men, had her fun, and moved on. She never dated, and she treated the guys like…like Kyle had treated women before Cate. And like with Kyle, Lyla's actions worried Danny.

He watched as something formed between Lyla and Max's friend Gage. They had a barely there connection with super-charged sexual tension. Lyla actively ignored it, and Gage seemed to purposely retreat from her.

Having known Gage as long as he had known Max, Danny knew Gage was a good, honest man with a penchant for fast cars, fast women, and few words. He owned the local racetrack and the best garage in three towns, and since women found the giant of a man irresistible, there wasn't much Gage wanted that he couldn't have. Except for Lyla.

Danny wasn't sure why the two hadn't hooked up, but in a way, he was relieved. Something about those two together felt different, special, and Danny didn't want them to find each other before they were ready.

"Knock knock."

"Max." Danny smiled. With Max a partner but no longer a bartender, Danny didn't see him every day. "Come on in, son. Why are you standing in the hall?"

"I may not work here anymore, Dan, but I know damn well what goes on in this office." Max chuckled. "Why do you think we all voted to have a second office added during the rebuild?"

Danny threw his head back and laughed from deep in his gut.

"Hey, Max. What's so funny?" Julie asked from behind him, a bag of takeout tucked under her arm.

Danny eyed his wife, forty-seven years old and absolutely fucking gorgeous. "Max here says that he and the others believe you and I do things in this office other than work."

Julie's gray eyes widened while a pale blush rose in her cheeks. *Twenty-eight years and the woman still blushes. Always been a lucky son of a bitch.*

"Hmm, can't imagine what would give them that impression." Her humor-filled answer had both men chuckling as she shimmied past Max and placed the food on her desk. Danny noticed she was careful not to let her rosy cheeks show until the color was back to its natural hue.

"You know what? Whatever you guys are doing is clearly the secret to success, because while my parents are still married, and I believe happily so, I've never seen them look at each other the way you two do on a daily basis," Max said.

"I like to think we're pretty damn amazing. So thank you for noticing. But I'm guessing you didn't come down here just to talk about how Julie and I make our marriage work. What's going on, son? Take a seat and fill us in."

MAX STRADDLED A chair and looked from Danny to Julie. "I'm going to ask Janie to marry me."

Julie gasped. Her heart actually sighed.

"No...I'm going to tell her she has no choice but to marry me because I can't imagine being without her," Max said. "I want to start a family with that woman, have children... a forever. Christ, I've lived and loved long enough to know that every minute we aren't married is a minute wasted."

His impassioned speech left his emerald eyes sparkling and Julie's heart beating a fierce tattoo. *family.* She wanted that for him, for them. Oh, how she wanted that.

"Max, sweetie, that's wonderful." Julie lunged forward and wrapped her arms around his wavy form. Her tears made it hard to see clearly.

"Good man," Danny rasped. "Although I'd definitely give her a choice. Women don't take too kindly to that kind of pressure."

CHAPTER TWENTY-NINE
The Perfect Day For A Party

IT WAS THE perfect day for a party. A bright azure sky promised lovely, warm spring weather, the caterer was in route, the band that Ryan had secured was doing their sound check, and Cate and Elliot were working their asses off to make everything look easy. Julie had refused to let desserts be brought in by caterers, so she had been baking for three days. She created hundreds of cookies, pastries, and a huge cake, all made with her hands and waiting to be enjoyed.

It was also the night Max was going to propose to Janie. After Julie and Danny approved, he'd spoken with Lyla, Kyle, Ryan, Ashley, and Elliot about sharing the spotlight, and everyone loved the idea. Ryan and Max had coordinated with the band leader, and the proposal was set to go.

Julie knew it was coming. Knew when it was happening. Had seen the ring. But when she watched Max go down on bended knee and saw Janie's eyes widen first with surprise, then acceptance, Julie's knees buckled. Thank God for Danny. As always, he was there, holding her tight to his chest. The steady beat of his heart calmed the erratic thud of hers.

"That was…something else," he muttered into her ear, his breath sending chills up her neck.

"Yeah." Something in her gut felt off. She couldn't have been happier for the couple—for all of the couples. But inside, she felt smaller, as if she'd been shrinking for the past few weeks, and she wasn't sure why.

Inhaling deeply, her gaze landed on Janie and Max, dancing in each other's arms as an aura of happiness glowed around them like a bubble. Releasing her breath, Julie also let go of the niggling unease that had been growing in her gut since Max had visited them in the office those weeks ago…at least, she tried to.

CHEST PUFFED AND proud, Danny watched from the sidelines as Max and Janie were bombarded with well wishes and congratulations. But when his chance came to hug and kiss the bride- and groom-to-be, he gushed like any father would. The night was successful on all fronts, both business and personal, and he had his wife to thank. *Where'd she go?*

He stalked to the back bar to find Ashley tending instead of the new bartender, Ando. "Where the hell is Ando?" A cursory glance showed that Kyle wasn't around either. *Hmm, maybe smoking in the alley?*

"Dan, have you seen Lyla?" The concerned look on Gage's face sent ice through Danny's veins.

"Let's find her."

"Not me!" Kyle's scream echoed through the metal door that led to the alley. "Ando, help Lyla. Now…"

Adrenaline surged through Danny's body, pulling him toward the furious, fear-filled voice.

CRASH! The metal door slammed into the cinderblock wall, and a roar—Danny later learned that came from Gage—filled the air.

Danny looked from the man in Kyle's grip to a semiconscious, bleeding Lyla on the dirty ground, and the situation clicked together. The punk had put his filthy hands on Lyla. He'd abused her, touched her who knew where, and tossed her down like garbage. He *wanted* to kill the bastard in Kyle's hands, but he knew by the way Gage's fists were clenched and his body coiled that Gage *would* actually do it. Gage's nostrils flared as his booted foot took its first step.

"Sebastian, stop!" Danny couldn't let a man who cared that deeply for Lyla do something that would take him away from her. "Think," Danny whispered, "this how you want this to go down? Physically she's gonna be okay, son. Don't you want to be here to get her through the rest? You see what I see when you look at her, I know you do. Let us take care of that motherfucker, and you worry about her. Yeah?"

A nod. That was it. Then Gage knelt by Lyla's side, and those hands that had been ready to kill gently tended to the broken woman on the ground.

FOR DAYS FOLLOWING Lyla's attack, Julie and Danny did their best to care for her. For the first twenty-four hours, Julie stayed at Lyla's house under the threat that if Lyla didn't allow it, they would call Janie and inform her of the incident. Lyla didn't want her friends bothered on their engagement night, so Julie stayed and Lyla moped.

After the initial twenty-four, the family did what it always did—swooped in and took over, leaving love and kindness in its wake.

For Janie's sake, Lyla smiled brightly, turned on the charm, and laughed her way through days and weeks. But as they always said about Lyla Dalton, the woman couldn't lie for shit. Even as her face was delighted, her eyes stayed dim. Unlike when Kyle was going through his rough patch and acting out, Lyla did the opposite. She kept everything in. There was no behavior to correct, no issues to discuss; she was just flat and gray behind the happy mask.

In some ways, Julie began to feel a connection to Lyla when it came to hiding behind a mask of gray. She was hiding too. In doing so, she was creating distance be-tween herself and her husband, distance she didn't want, but needed in order to figure out what was going on in her head. Danny had enough to worry about—the last thing she wanted was to add to his burden with an unidentifiable problem. She'd figure it out, solve it, and move forward without anyone being the wiser. Yep, that was what she'd do.

CHAPTER THIRTY

Remove The Space

SOMETHING WAS GOING on with his wife. He'd noticed it for weeks and done his goddamned best to let her figure it out on her own. *But enough is enough.* He wrapped a towel around his freshly showered waist. *I'm gonna get to the bottom of this today.*

The rich smells of coffee and bacon led him to the kitchen, where Julie's firm yoga-pant-encased ass had his mouth watering more than the breakfast foods. Sweeping her hair to her left shoulder, Danny nibbled on her neck. "Mmm, better than bacon any day of the week."

When her hips tilted back and rubbed against his rapidly growing erection, she looked over her shoulder and purred, "Mmm, better than sausage any day ever."

"Fuck..."

Before either the play or the breakfast could go any further, the phone rang.

"Don't get it," Danny gruffed.

"Dan, it's seven thirty on a Saturday morning. If someone is calling this early, I answer the phone."

She wasn't wrong. While everyone knew they were early risers, everyone, even his dad and Chester, also knew not to call someone's house before nine in the morning. If the phone was ringing, no matter how badly he wanted to slide into his wife, the phone needed to be answered.

"Hi, sweetie. Is everything okay with you and Max?"

Danny poured them each coffee and filled their plates with food.

"Okay," Julie drew out the word. "No, it's totally fine. Of course we'll be here."

The lilt in her tone grabbed Danny's attention. Was something wrong with Janie? Max?

"You got it, Janie. We'll see you then. No, don't bring food, honey. We'll order in. Bye." Julie placed the phone on its cradle, grabbed the butter from the refrigerator, and sat in her chair at the kitchen table.

"Are you fucking kidding me?" Danny blurted. "Woman, you actually gonna make me ask you what that was all about?"

"What what was all about?"

Her innocent reaction amused him. "Nice try, honey, but spill. Seriously."

"She apologized for the early call, but was worried that if they waited too long to call, we'd be busy. They want to see us for lunch today."

Danny rose from his chair and paced. "She say if anything was wrong?"

He searched his wife's eyes for answers, but he only saw confidence when she answered that Janie sounded fine, happy even. It would be hours until he saw them with his own eyes, and worry churned in his gut as he paced the main room, breakfast all but forgotten.

"I wonder what's so important that Max and Janie are coming over here to speak with us instead of just waiting till tomorrow at Sunday dinner," Danny questioned for the third time since receiving Janie's phone call just minutes before. Julie opened her mouth to speculate, but Danny's follow-up question was quicker. "Jules, they're okay, yeah?"

His normally gruff voice sounded uncertain. He was worried about his family. Nothing bad was ever allowed to happen to them. Not ever. Obviously his dad, Anita, and even Chester were advancing in age, and while it pained him to know a day would come when they would no longer be around, that was something he and Julie would have to deal with. But when it came to the kids—*their kids*—bad things were unacceptable. End of story.

"Yes, honey," Julie reassured him again. "After all, she just got engaged to the man of her dreams."

She crossed the length of the room, not stopping until her breasts rubbed against his chest. Her hands climbed his torso, fingers splayed so every muscle could be felt under her loving touch. He smiled as they continued their ascent, not slowing until her soft palms glided over his salt-and-pepper whiskers. She locked her hands around his neck, sifting her fingers through his hair. The touch sent shivers up his spine.

"And I know how that feels." Tilting her head back, she looked him straight in the eyes. "Not even my dreams could have compared to the reality you've given me."

Danny exhaled, holding her chin between his forefinger and thumb. "Woman, you've made it so damn easy to love you all these years." The crinkles framing his eyes deepened as his trademark smirk made an appearance. "I'm so fucking grateful. Jules, you have been honest, supportive, and loyal since day one, and that makes me the luckiest son of a bitch around." His brows waggled with sexual suggestions. "I don't give a shit what those kids think they have goin' on between the sheets—no one, I repeat, no one, can hold a candle to us."

"Danny." Breathless and trembling, Julie exhaled, her desire an electric current just waiting to connect with the right target.

"Not kidding. Closing in on thirty years, baby, and I still see you at work and think of new ways to fuck you till you scream my name. It'll never get old with you, honey. Never."

Her soft lips opened a mere second before his mouth ravaged hers. Taking what he needed, he gave what she wanted and unleashed the hunger that only she had ever brought out in him.

She hummed as he pressed her flush against the wall. Arms above her head, a whimper escaped her when he wedged his thigh between her legs and captured her wrists in one of his large hands. God, he loved her. She owned him. She thought it was the opposite, even after all their years together, but the fact was, she owned him.

"Love it when your nipples rub against me," he growled, dragging her cotton T-shirt up her torso and over her lace-covered breasts. "Fuck, Jules." Effortlessly, he unhooked her bra and dropped it. "These tits…"

He sucked her full breast into the warmth of his mouth. With each swipe of his tongue on her sensitive peak, more gooseflesh blanketed her body. *So responsive.* Twenty-eight years together, twenty-seven of them married, and such a simple move still caused such an enormous reaction.

Cool air prickled her wet skin, making her nipple pucker beautifully, the moment he released it from his mouth. His adoration lasted only a second before his tongue swept over the other sweet, neglected breast. Lick after lick, sharp tugs, and warm suckles had her writhing in his arms within seconds. His free hand began its descent down her naked torso as a small smile touched the corners of her mouth. Their game was about to begin, and she loved to play.

He slipped his hand into her yoga pants, and all play ceased. "What do we have here, my love?" Slate eyes stared at him with what could have been insecurity or a challenge. It was the moment he'd been waiting for, so he treaded lightly. "Panties?"

"Actually, babe, it's a thong. You know the difference, one covers my ass and one...goes up it," Julie teased.

She's being playful...

"I figured with Janie and Max coming over—"

Danny ran his fingers along the waistband of the pale blue thong. *But she's guarded. What the hell?* "You were already dressed when they called to say they were stopping by."

Her breath faltered when his gaze dropped to the offending cloth.

"Try again, honey," he said. "And remember, even though Saturday nights at the bar are long and busy as hell, I can find plenty of time to drag you away to the office, noticed or not. I don't care what our partners think is happening back there as long as they don't see what's *mine*."

He felt her shiver and relished that he still had that effect on her. She knew damn well what he was capable of doing to her behind closed doors, but there were times when his sweet woman topped from the bottom. He knew when she was doing it, and he knew when she needed it. At those times, he let her have control. If it would get her to open up, he'd let her have control now. But only so far, for so long.

"I...I—"

The tear of satin replaced Julie's lack of words.

Danny tucked the torn panties into the pocket of his jeans. His stare was as bold as his voice was whisky rough. "You haven't been yourself for a couple of weeks, Jules. I tried to heed the advice I've heard you give the kids, and even though it's been fucking brutal, I've done my best to give you some thinking space." He slipped his hand down the front of Julie's yoga pants and leaned forward, his lips touching the shell of her ear. "We don't do well with space, baby. Do we?"

Julie shook her head, her eyes sliding closed. His fingers parted her smooth, slick folds and entered her body.

"So wet for me." Touching her made him throb, but he refused to allow amazing chemistry to deter him from what was going on in his wife's mind. She was the most important thing in the world. Sex would come after he found out what was bothering her. His thumb gently rubbed circles over her swollen clit, and he swallowed her soft moan as she grinded herself against his hand. "Already so greedy, honey?" His movements stopped, leaving her balance unsteady. She wore a look that jostled between frenzy and frustration, pleasure and pain.

"I need more, Danny," she whimpered.

"So do I, Jules. Tell me what's bothering you." His thumb swept over the sensitized bundle of nerves just as his teeth nipped her earlobe. "Tell me, and I'll make this better." His deep rumble, along with another graze to her clit, had her nipples drawn tight and arousal pooling around his fingers. "I'll make everything better, baby, always. It's time to remove the space, Julie."

"I love you, Danny. I'm yours."

"Thank God for that." His usual response to her declaration should've felt tired, worn out, but every time he said those four words, her eyes glowed, "Now, remove the space."

"I wish I could have given you more."

His breath hitched at her words, his own stuck in his throat.

"When I couldn't, I should've been selfless enough to walk away," she said. "Now Max and Janie are starting their life. They want children, a family, and I fear that they'll go through what we did. I want more for them. I want them to have it all."

Time stopped. Her face paled as Danny removed his hand from her core and placed inches between them. Space. Until recently, he had never allowed it been between them, but in that moment, with his world spinning off its axis, an emotional chasm, coupled with the physical distance, felt unbearable. Heartbeats and shallow breaths continued to fill the room as tears leaked from Julie's eyes. After a moment, she lifted her gaze to his.

"Broken," he rumbled with a hoarse voice.

"What?"

"Had you ever left me, if you ever do, I'd be broken. I wish for Max and Janie—hell, for all of them—a marriage exactly like ours. We've lived hard, baby, but loved even harder, and there is nothing, not one fucking thing, that I'd do over if given the chance. We're *here* now because we were *there* then. We have seven amazing children when we may have only had one. Wouldn't change a fucking thing, baby. Not one thing. Question is, would you?" In his heart he knew her answer—he'd never doubted it over the years—but seeing the pain in her eyes made him need the words.

"No, Danny. Not one minute. That's why I feel self-ish. Because even if you wanted me to, I could have never let you go."

INSTANTLY THE DISTANCE between them was erased. He cradled her in his arms and walked her through their ranch house to the master suite.

"I think it's time we revisit the past, you and I. Because it seems like maybe you've forgotten some things along the way." He dropped soft kisses along the top of her hairline. "I intend to remind you exactly how things between us went. But first, you need to get naked." He sat her on the mattress, and slid her pants around her thighs.

"I'm pretty much there, Danny. It's you who is over-dressed for this occasion." Gone was the wall that she'd erected between them, evaporated like sugar over warm pastry.

His large hand held her face gently. "Then get me na-ked, honey. Need to feel you on my skin."

Blood coursed through her veins like a river that had broken through a dam. While it hadn't been long since she'd felt his touch, it had been weeks since her soul was bared. His metal belt buckle clanked, bringing her lust-frazzled mind back to the task at hand. Jeans unbuttoned, fly unzipped, pants and boxer-briefs lowered, all done between shallow breaths and racing heartbeats but with steady hands. Julie looked up at hungry eyes that consumed her and every move she made.

His voice was low, seductive. "Take off your pants, spread your legs, and touch yourself. I wanna see how wet your pussy gets while your lips are wrapped around my cock."

"Oh, my…" Heat pooled at her naked core, making her brazen. Two of her fingers inched down her torso, between her folds, and dipped into her most intimate place.

"Open your eyes and show me," Danny commanded.

She hadn't realized her eyes had fallen closed.

He bent forward and pulled her hand to his mouth. One finger at a time touched his tongue. "Mmm, so goddamn sweet."

She became more aroused with each heated suck. She tugged his jeans the rest of the way down and latched onto his cock like a starved woman. His groan became her music, his thrusts her rhythm.

"Fuck me," he roared, pulling out of her mouth. "Plans changed, baby."

She watched in awe as he shucked his pants from his feet, whisked her onto his lap, and lay flat on his back.

"A taste wasn't enough, honey. I need that sweet pussy in my mouth just as much as you want my dick down your throat."

His words made her tremble as she scooted up his torso.

"Mmm, that's right, straddle my face. I wanna inhale you."

The moment his hot tongue touched her clit, her knees slid out from under her, planting her most intimate place against what she'd consider his most lethal. With him not only offering wonderful service but also a delectable meal, Julie wrapped her hand around his hard cock and pumped until his moan vibrated into her clit. Oh, sixty-nines were so good.

Her mouth watered as she massaged the length of him with her tongue, delighting in his every groan. When his thick fingers slid into her pussy, she grinded against his face with reckless abandon, loving the way his scruff added to the friction and brought her higher. She wanted to bring him with her, wanted him to explode when she did. Opening her throat, she sucked him down until her lips touched his pelvis.

"Jesus Christ, Jules, fuck."

She increased her suction as she slowly released him almost completely before deep-throating him again.

"No, baby, you first," he pleaded before pulling her clit into his mouth and sucking with perfect pressure while thrusting his fingers into her pussy. "Mmm, tastes like candy."

When his fingers hit her g-spot while his tongue was still wrapped around her clit, white spots filled her vision. Her body crested into bliss she'd never tire of experiencing. With his gentle fingers giving her more pleasure, she licked salty liquid off the tip of his cock and hummed while doing it.

"So good," his whispered voice came from behind her.

She could do better. She could give him what he'd just given her—brilliance. Pulling him in with practiced rhythm, she hollowed her cheeks and once again deep-throated him. She lightly caressed his balls, nearly smiling when he grabbed onto her ass cheeks and his hips thrust up, fucking her mouth.

Repeating the motion, Danny groaned, then panted. "Jules, fuck…fuck, Julie. I'm gonna come, baby."

And when he did, she greedily swallowed what he gave her.

"THAT WAS…WOW." Danny could barely speak as he tangled his fingers through his wife's hair. How was it possible for sex to still feel new after almost thirty years? Hell, they hadn't even had intercourse, and he was sated. He didn't want to question it; he just knew that he was a lucky man. Soft fingertips drew familiar patterns on his chest. He loved those damn figure eights.

"It really was…wow." Julie's head rested on her hand, her elbow propped up on the bed, and her eyes found his. "I'm sorry, Danny. I shouldn't have kept my feelings from you. You'd think I'd have learned by now, and truth-fully, I have. I guess just seeing them all starting their lives and knowing how many things can go wrong for them made me nervous." Her eyes darted to the side, then back to him, a misty sheen over the gray. "I may not be their mom, but I love them. I want to protect them."

Danny looked at his wife, his life partner, the love of his life, and tucked some strawberry-blonde hair behind her ear. "I was going to wait until our anniversary in July to give you your present, but I think today is the perfect time."

Sitting up, he planted his feet on the floor and left his bed and his woman behind as he walked from their bedroom to the basement door, completely naked. Downstairs, he went to the corner where he'd been hiding his project, a labor of love he'd been working on for months. With contributions from Max, Janie, Ashley, Ryan, Kyle, Cate, and Lyla, Danny had finished the piece mere days before. Little had he known he'd be giving it to his bride early.

Hefting the five-foot-by-three-foot paper-wrapped, framed canvas over his shoulder, Danny made his way back upstairs and into the master bedroom, where Julie awaited him, wrapped in the bed sheet.

"Dan, what is that?"

Slowly, he unwrapped the art and turned to watch Julie's eyes eat up the painting.

"Oh...Danny, my God. What...how...you made that, didn't you?"

The way her lip trembled and her wide eyes filled with tears was all the reaction he could have ever asked for, but when his Julie nearly floated from the bed, reaching for the gift he'd created for her—his breath caught in his chest.

The textured painting was more than just a large tree. It was *them*. Their names and wedding date appeared carved in the thick, strong trunk. A tiny butterfly with bright pink wings floated next to their names. Danny knew the instant Julie's eyes landed on the butterfly that the meaning of its presence was not lost on her. Roots twining beautifully into the ground were made up of Julie's parents' names, as well as Danny's mom, dad, and Anita.

Two roots grew together, twisting until they met with Danny's, and they had Jeff and Neal's names inscribed in them. Toward the top of the trunk, just before the branches sprouted, Chester Murray's name and an intricate rabbit appeared branded in the wood. Watching Julie's face brighten when she realized that the rabbit stood for a certain redheaded manager made Danny chuckle. But the fact was, Bunny had been there at the beginning of *them* and therefore couldn't be forgotten. Danny watched Julie's eyes roam farther up the tree.

Each leaf was painted on a separate piece of canvas and affixed to the large panel, giving the tree a layered, lively look. Hundreds of leaves in various shades of greens, each hand-cut (by Lyla or Cate) and hand-painted, though only a few had special designs. The kids had printed out pictures of what they wanted on their leaf so Danny could draw and paint them.

"Sheila and Chris are on here. Danny..." Her arm extended to the canvas, fingers about to make contact, but she abruptly pulled away.

"It's okay, honey. You can touch it. The paint's been sealed."

Her long fingers once again reached out to the miniature O'Brian's sign that hung on the leaf with Sheila and Chris's name.

Just as in life, their kids' leaves were paired off. Max's had a tiny racecar and a checkered flag while Janie's had an apple. Ashley's leaf had a slanted crown sitting on a rainbow, and Ryan's had a guitar. Kyle's showed a broken brick wall with half of a face behind it. The eyes were smiling. Cate's leaf had a hand holding a brick with a heart on it. Quite telling, no? While Lyla's leaf, with a quill and a bottle of ink, was next to the rest of the kids, the one directly linked to hers was blank. Danny had high hopes it wouldn't remain that way for long. Many leaves were painted and attached to the tree, beautiful and waiting for the time when their family expanded further.

"Danny, this is the most incredible thing I've ever seen." Her voice was thick with emotion and truth. "When did you do this? What made you think of it?"

"A wise woman once told me that a family didn't have to come with blood, it only had to come with love." Julie's eyes widened, but Danny didn't give her time to respond. "We've been building our family since the day we met. I thought it was time you saw, actually saw, what we've created together." Danny pointed at the family tree. "There is nothing but love there, baby, because you made it that way. It's always been about you. I love you, Julie Marcus."

"Thank God for that," she replied.

EPILOGUE

FRESHLY SHOWERED, JULIE slid on a clean pair of yoga pants, sans panties, and a lacy pink bra.

"You're just begging to get fucked again, aren't you?" Danny groaned as he ogled her reflection in the mirror.

They had made love—and yes, fucked—after the incredible sixty-nine experience just a few hours prior. The man had the turn-around time of a teenager and the stamina of a stud.

"Wouldn't be opposed to it, handsome. But Max and Janie will be here any minute, and that might make for a weird conversation," she teased.

Danny touched his lips to hers before retreating into the closet to get dressed while she applied makeup. It was Saturday, after all, and once Max and Janie left, she and Danny would be headed to the bar for the rest of the evening. They didn't need to be there—Ashley and Ryan had it covered—but they were still getting used to letting go.

Ding-dong

"I'll get it," Julie called into the closet on her way to the front door. Before she could turn the handle, Danny was by her side.

"Hey," Max said.

Janie smiled. "We're here. Can we come in?".

ACKNOWLEDGMENTS

PHEW – THIS BOOK…this book was one that was never supposed to be written. It wasn't in my timeline, it wasn't part of my plan, but as I started writing *Cheers in Charistown* (the next story, a novella, in the Charistown series), Danny and Julie started talking to me and refused to stop until it was their words I was writing on paper. They *needed* me to tell their story and once they started talking, telling me about their beginning, their love, loss, heartbreak and strength, I had no choice but to keep on writing until nothing was left but peaceful silence. I'm grateful they finally opened up because unbeknownst to me, it was their love that truly shaped this series for me.

That said, this book could have never been written without the help of several special people. While I'm just a storyteller, a person who dreams up tales and creates worlds in which my characters struggle, flail, and hopefully succeed, our world is filled with incredible people who spend their days, years even lives helping others find freedom, safety, health and happiness.

Combat veteran David Clark was an amazing resource to me while I was writing Danny's early days as a soldier. Mr. Clark let me pick his brain, pester him with questions and bother him endlessly with trivial silliness until I shaped Danny into the soldier and man I needed him to be. Thank you, David.

Tommy Barresi was not only my perfect physical vision of Danny Marcus but, he was kind enough to give me his time and access into his mind when I was searching for key elements into the thoughts of a dominant but gentle man. Thank you, Tommy, for allowing a virtual stranger into your personal space.

Captain Jerrad Ihlenfeld and his lovely wife **Devlynn** were both kind enough to answer questions about firefighting and fire safety. Their knowledge and time (on a weekend no less) was more helpful than they could ever know. Thank you, Jerrad and Devlynn.

Dr. Thomas S. Dardarian was a kind and patient man. The poor man was basically thrown to me by one of my high school friends (thank you, Arpi) and he spent an entire afternoon fielding questions and explaining situations for me. When I came up with medical problems, he would kindly tell me, "No, that wouldn't happen in real life," and then he would give me a better option. The man seemed to be more of a saint than a doctor. Thank you, Thomas.

Donna Salzano, my travel agent extraordinaire. I found Donna through a close friend and asked if she would mind helping plan a vacation for Danny and Julie. This beautiful woman didn't just plan a getaway, she mapped out a step-by-step tour that even the most seasoned globe-trotter would be jealous of. Donna, I'm so sorry I couldn't use more of your work in my story, but D and J needed to get back so that their life could fall apart. I truly do adore you!

Trudy Stiles my co-worker and friend gave me quite a bit of time when I decided to have Danny and Julie adopt. She offered me invaluable information that I would have *never* found on my own and she gave it with love and sincerity. While D and J's adoptive journey was much shorter than I had originally intended, my knowledge of the situation allowed for the feelings to come to the surface while writing those scenes. So thank you, Trudy, I owe you.

As always, the process of writing a story and turning it into a book is a lengthy one. It's something I never take for granted and something that will never become less special no matter how many times I do it. I will, however, be a little quicker with the "thank you" part this time.

Thank you to ~

S.K Hartley – for my gorgeous cover design. I look forward to working with you again ;)

Cassie Cox – my editor. You my friend, have been great. Thanks for dealing with the craziness that is me. There are no words…hahaha, just kidding, I have tens of thousands of them!!

Julie Titus – best formatter ever! Five books! FIVE!!! Can you believe it? You rock, lady. Thank you for just being you. I couldn't ask for more.

The ladies in FTN – you make me laugh out loud every single day. It's true. Sooo, thanks for that. I love you hard.

My Beta team – ladies, I'm so grateful to you. For real, your opinions, bad or good, help me become a better writer. Thank you for being by my side.

Peeps – You get sweeter every flipping day! <<< See what I did there?... Sweet...cause you're Peeps...heehee.

Joanne Schwehm – Our laugh sessions help me in two ways, first, they get rid of tension and second they strengthen my ab muscles. I've never cried more than I have since meeting you...wait...that sounds horrible. Oh well, you know what I mean. I love you. Thank you for being exactly who you are.

Ilsa Madden-Mills – Hearing you say, "Good Morning," in your sweet southern voice makes me smile. Hearing you say something wildly inappropriate makes me howl with laughter. You are a gift in my life. Thank you for finding your way to me.

You – the **Readers**, **Bloggers,** and random people who are looking at this page – Thank you for continuing to read my stories. Your support overwhelms me. Every email, Facebook message, and review I get tells me that my words have been read. There is no better compliment to a writer than that. So thank you.

To my Husband and Sons – Your continued support is a blessing. I love you with my whole heart.

XO,

Lisa N Paul.

ABOUT THE AUTHOR

LISA N. PAUL is a wife, mother, daughter, sister, friend, reader, writer, blogger, and self-proclaimed comedian—just not always in that order. Ever since she was a little girl, she has devoured books. Falling in love with the Sweet Valley High series at a young age drew Lisa to series books and inspired her to write her own. *Thursday Nights*, *Storm Front* and *Breaking to Breath* are the first three books in her Charistown series. *Blocked* is a stand-alone novel.

When not writing, Lisa can be found eating French fries and Godiva raspberry truffles, or hanging out with her husband and two sons.

Visit her website at *http://www.lisanpaul.com*

Other Titles by Lisa N. Paul

THE CHARISTOWN SERIES

Thursday Nights (Book One)
Storm Front (Book Two)
Breaking to Breathe (Book Three)
Danny's Main (Book Four)
Cheers in Charistown – COMING SOON

STANDALONE

Blocked

www.ingramcontent.com/pod-product-compliance
Lightning Source LLC
Chambersburg PA
CBHW020403260626
47156CB00007B/2218